Savage Pride is a work of fiction. Names, characters, places, and incidents are the products of the author's imagination or are used fictitiously. Any resemblance to actual events, locales, or persons, living or dead, is entirely coincidental.

Copyright © 2021 Jill Ramsower

All rights reserved. In accordance with the U.S. Copyright Act of 1976, the scanning, uploading, and electronic sharing of any part of this book without the permission of the publisher is unlawful piracy and theft of the author's intellectual property. Thank you for your support of the author's rights.

Print Edition ISBN: 9781734417272

Cover Model: Lewis Jamison
Photographer: Chris Davis
Edited by Editing4Indies

❦ Created with Vellum

Books by Jill Ramsower

The Savage Pride Duet
Savage Pride
Silent Prejudice

The Five Families Series
Forever Lies
Never Truth
Blood Always
Where Loyalties Lie
Impossible Odds
Absolute Silence
Perfect Enemies

The Fae Games Series
Shadow Play
Twilight Siege
Shades of Betrayal
Born of Nothing
Midnight's End

This one's to Sarah because Austen will always be better than Brontë.

CHAPTER 1

I AM MY FATHER'S DAUGHTER. FROM HIS MATCHING SET OF dimples to his wry sense of humor, I am more like my father than any of my three sisters. Should scientists attempt to genetically engineer a female version of him, I'm not sure they could do a better job than my own DNA, except for my blue eyes and one other critical component —my lack of patience. My father was gifted an eternal wellspring of patience that gives him the ability to shrug off annoying roadblocks to his day and find amusement in otherwise infuriating circumstances. Today is not the first day I find myself questioning why I couldn't have acquired a fraction of his even-tempered tolerance.

"I *told* you, I don't know why I'm not on the approved visitor's list. My name is Luisa Banetti. My parents run the Hardwick house and live in a cottage on the property. Just *call* them and ask." I stare expectantly at the new security guard stationed out front of the Tuxedo Park gated entry.

We'd spent the past ten minutes talking in circles about the absence of my name on his guest registry. Tuxedo Park is one of the most exclusive communities in New York. An hour from Manhattan, the priceless estates are nestled in the thickly wooded hillsides around Tuxedo Lake—a serene oasis fervently protected by its wealthy residents. Unlike many security guards, those stationed at Tuxedo Park are paid enough to care who enters and who doesn't. For most of my life, a man by the name of Cleatus welcomed guests during the daytime hours with a smile and a helpful nature. Of course, he'd known me since I was in diapers, so there was never any issue when I came for a visit. However, Cleatus retired six months ago, and now I'm stuck arguing with Sergeant Protocol, who can't seem to grasp concepts outside of a pure black and white palette.

"I called the cottage, ma'am. No one answered." His eyes trail yet again to the black SUV stuck waiting behind my Uber. "I'm going to need you to move so you aren't blocking the entrance while we sort this out."

"This is ridiculous," I grumble under my breath, jabbing my phone to complete the payment for my ride. Using more strength than necessary, I fling open the passenger door and ask my driver to open the trunk.

"What are you doing?" the guard asks warily.

"I'm getting my bag and waiting here with you. If you won't let me in, then you're stuck with me until my family can come pick me up." I haul my scarred black suitcase from the trunk with a grunt when the car door shutting behind us announces that we've drawn yet another party into our little contest of wills. Making a scene wasn't my intent, but it's looking more inevitable by the second.

"Do we have a problem here?" The masculine voice at my back sends a shiver of familiarity down my spine.

Zeno De Rossi.

We don't speak often, but I'd know that commanding tone anywhere.

Of all the possible people who could have pulled up behind me, it had to be Zeno. He'll probably pretend he doesn't know me just to make my life more difficult. My eyes take a long, heavy blink before I turn to face my childhood neighbor.

"Hello, Z," I say with forced calm.

"Luisa," he responds curtly, his deep blue eyes locked on mine.

The guard looks back and forth between us. "Uh, Mr. De Rossi. I'm so sorry for the delay. Miss Banetti here isn't on the registry, and we were trying to get things sorted."

Zeno ignores him, choosing to stare me down instead. "I wasn't informed you were coming."

"I wasn't aware my family had to inform you of my visits." Is he honestly going to keep me from going home? He may have pushed me away through the years, but refusing me entry to the Park would bring him to an all-time low. Incredulity primes my tongue with fighting words.

"Considering the circumstances, the information would have been appreciated." He finally severs our connection with his brusque retort and turns his attention to the

Guardian of the Gate. "Luisa is a member of the estate. You can put her on the list of universally approved." He stalks back to his car without another word.

Thanks, Z. It was good to see you, too.

Zeno De Rossi was one of my childhood best friends, but you'd never guess it now. That bridge burned long ago. I suppose he must be visiting his parents as well. Both of us live in the city, but we only see each other a couple of times a year if we happen to be at Hardwick at the same time. Hopefully, that will be the one and only run-in I have with him during my visit. He tends to make me grumpy, and I'd just assume not.

"I appreciate your patience," the guard says, suddenly all smiles. "Let me help you get your bag back in the car."

"Yeah, thanks," I mutter. Opening the passenger door of my Uber, I peer questioningly at my driver. "I'm so sorry about all this. You okay to drive me to my house?"

"Absolutely. After all the fuss, I gotta see what's in here."

I slide into the passenger seat with a weary chuckle. "Happy to oblige."

The gate in front of us coasts open, permitting us entry.

"I had no clue this place existed. If you live here, why on earth don't you have your own driver or like, a car that drives itself?"

I choke on a laugh. "I wish. My parents manage an estate. We're just the help."

"Still, I bet you see some crazy shit in here."

"I guess that depends on what you consider crazy. If you mean obscene displays of wealth, then yeah, all the time." People here may be as varied as those in the city, but they keep it under wraps better. The freak flag isn't so much flown as kept rolled up in the closet only to be displayed at extravagant private functions.

I direct him to my parents' home and give him an extra tip after the long trip from the train station and the delay at the gate. The kid drives off, clearly taking the long way around the lake. I can't blame him—the scenery is gorgeous, and most people will never be granted access or have reason to enter.

My favorite thing about the area is the explosion of color from the fall leaves. The warm hues are the perfect complement to the chilly, serene landscape. For now, summer is just spreading its wings. Everything is green as far as the eye can see, which isn't all that far since the forest of trees is full of new leaves. The lake isn't even visible from my parents' house, but I know exactly where it is. I know the wooded pathways of the Hardwick estate so well that I could walk them blindfolded. Even now, the shaded trails call to me, urging me to explore. And I will, but first, I need to get my suitcase inside.

After lugging my heavy bag to the front steps, I'm surprised no one has raced out front to greet me. I can only assume they're all out, which is unexpected. At the very least, one of my younger sisters should have been home. They all knew I was coming. Luckily, the front door is unlocked. Mom never sees any point in locking the house when so many other more valuable homes are nearby to lure potential criminals. She isn't totally wrong, but personally, I still believe in the benefit of a good deadbolt.

In this instance, however, I'm glad for her lack of security measures. I let myself inside and take in a deep breath—the smell of aged wood that goes hand in hand with old homes and the cherry tang of my father's cigars. The scent lingers in the upholstery, despite my mother insisting he only smokes on the back porch. Every time I step inside, no matter how many years I've lived away, I regain a sense of my childhood. I cannot exist under this roof without resurrecting dormant emotions and memories. Hugs from my father. Secrets whispered between sisters. School and friends. Arguments with my mother. Her signature brand of chaos can be found in a heap of dishes piled in the sink as well as the living room window framed on either side with two totally different drapes. She'd decided to make new curtains several years ago, then moved on to another project midway through when the winds of her creative mood shifted. She has yet to complete the project, like so many others. No corner of the house remains untouched by her flighty whims.

I love my mother, but she's exhausting—maddening, even—yet visits are worth it to see my dad and sisters. Especially the eldest, Gia. We are only eighteen months apart in age and have always been as close as any two sisters. She's the biggest reason I come back as often as I do. If I could get her to move to the city with me, I would. Her repeated rejection of my offers never keeps me from trying to convince her of the merits of city life. I have no doubt this visit will be no different than the others. I'll urge her to come to the city with me, and she'll find a reason to refuse.

Gia just turned twenty-nine. She's the oldest of us girls,

and I can't understand why she won't leave. I get that she's family-oriented, but she has her own life to live. I moved out the second I graduated. Of course, Mom doesn't bother her the way she annoys me. Apparently, Gia got that sneaky strain of patience from my father, along with the uncanny ability to be blind to people's faults—that's her own special gift without a known origin, and it's frustrating as hell. I adore my sister, but she is the worst person in the world to vent to. She'll insist there's been a misunderstanding and assume all parties are acting with the best intentions when I really want someone to empathize about a messy situation. My next-door neighbor did not *accidentally* sleep with my boyfriend, and even if she did, I don't want to hear it.

I digress.

Returning home always involves baggage, and I don't mean of the Samsonite variety.

I shake off the swell of unwanted emotions and take my suitcase to the room Gia and I shared throughout our childhood. We still share the same double bed when I visit, even now as adults, and I wouldn't have it any other way. I slept so many years snuggled up with my big sister that her slumbering form next to me provides instant comfort. A boyfriend or cherished pet could never compare. Gia's love and acceptance are absolute.

Happiness draws my lips back into a broad smile at the same time the front door flings open downstairs.

"Lulu? You here?" Daddy's coarse voice resonates through the house.

My smile stretches farther to a vibrant grin. I abandon

my suitcase and zip down the stairs straight into my father's open arms. "Hey, Daddy!" I move from him to my mom, then each sister in turn so as not to elicit any sore feelings by showing favoritism. The entire family has come home to greet me.

Mom begins to chatter before I even finish my hugs. "We heard you'd arrived, but where's all your stuff? I figured you'd come loaded with boxes since your new place isn't ready for another week. You are staying here for the whole week, right?"

"I decided to put my things in a storage unit rather than lug it all here. There's not that much, but it would have been a pain." After living in a tiny studio apartment with another girl for the past four years, I've saved enough to sublet my own room in a two-bedroom place. The new room isn't available yet, but my old lease expired, so I took the opportunity to visit my family … for a whole week. It's longer than my usual stay, which is a mixed blessing. A week is *a lot* of family time.

"Those things are so damn expensive. You shouldn't have wasted your money. We could have had your uncle help you bring it from the city."

"It wasn't too bad. And now, I can sit back and enjoy seeing you all." *Without worrying my stuff will find its way into one of your closets.* Mom has a communal closet philosophy with her daughters. Not a big deal, except that she doesn't take care of other people's belongings any better than she does her own. My budget is tight enough. I don't need her accidentally ruining things that took me weeks to save up for.

"Well," one of my younger sisters Livia starts in, "you couldn't have picked a better time to visit. Although, we won't have as much time for fun stuff, it'll be totally worth it. Mr. De Rossi died, and now *everyone* is coming to town for the funeral. They've already started arriving—so many hot guys—capos and everything. Even Gia could land some deep pockets if she'd do her hair and try a little."

"Liv, have some respect," Gia chides softly. "This is a time of mourning, not a singles mixer."

She rolls her eyes. "Whatever, more for me then."

Marca, the youngest, snickers while I gape in confusion.

"Silvano De Rossi? He died? When? Why didn't you tell me?" My gaze flitters from one person to the next in search of answers. I hadn't been close to the man, but I'd known him all my life. He was a sort of king in my world—both the estate owner and the underboss of the Giordano crime family, of which my father was a member. He'd always been such a guaranteed fixture in my life that it was incomprehensible for him to be gone.

My mother starts to speak, but Dad cuts her off.

"It was sudden. He died not even two days ago. We've been so busy with preparations that we haven't had much time to think of calling." His already sad eyes are rife with loss. I'd been so overwhelmed with my own excitement at seeing him that I'd missed the sorrow so clearly lining his face. A dull ache radiates through my chest.

"I'm so sorry, Daddy." I wrap my arms around him again, this time with the tenderness of sympathy. I may not have been close to Silvano, but he and Dad had known each other for over thirty years. They'd been trusted friends, despite the disparity in their ranks. My father had never been elevated beyond the level of a soldier. Silvano had trusted Dad with the security of his family and the operations of his home—responsibilities that spoke volumes of his respect for my father. A promotion to capo would have been even better, but Dad always seemed satisfied with his station.

"It was unexpected, that's all." The pain lacing his words undermines their brave façade.

"How did it happen? I didn't think he was all that old."

"Just sixty-six. Heart attack."

"It's a shame," Mom adds with exaggerated sincerity. "But it also means a world of work for us. That's why no one was at the house when you got here. Zeno has invited everyone his dad ever knew for the funeral the day after tomorrow. We have to prepare for that and the wake, plus the big house will be totally full for the next few days."

Dad says something about needing to get back over there, but I hardly hear him.

Considering the circumstances. Zeno's words come back to me, and I cringe. Silvano was Zeno's father—a father he idolized. I thought he'd just been rude like so many times before, but now, a sliver of guilt wedges uncomfortably between my shoulder blades that I hadn't been a touch more compassionate.

I'm not even entirely sure why. He is no one to me. Not anymore.

We'd been good friends as children, then ... we suddenly weren't. No explanation. No inciting incident. One warm April day, Zeno stopped talking to me. A few years later, he moved to the city while I was finishing high school, and we rarely saw one another since. If our paths did cross, he was curt and aloof, keeping our brief interactions as sterile as possible.

He's grown into an attractive, successful man, quickly making a name for himself in the Giordano family. According to my father, who keeps me somewhat informed on family affairs, Zeno is poised to take over his father's role as underboss. But that isn't what ties my tongue at the prospect of seeing him again this week. More than anything, he stirs up a distressing sense of confusion inside me. For ages, I wondered what I'd done wrong. I'd shed tear after tear with each of his rebuffs in the early days. As I grew to accept the loss of our friendship, my suffering was limited to a melancholy remorse each time our paths crossed. Maturity assured me that his issues had nothing to do with me, but without an explanation, the jagged wound he'd inflicted never seemed to fully heal.

"And to top it off," my mother's voice draws me from my turbulent thoughts, "the girl we'd hired to help Cecelia in the kitchen quit a couple of weeks ago. I was kind of hoping you wouldn't mind giving us a hand, just for these few days."

So that's why I hadn't been informed of Silvano's death. Despite Dad's repeated attempts to keep my mother from gossiping, she always blabs. The death had definitely been major enough for her to at least shoot me a text. She hadn't said anything because she didn't want to scare me off with the imminent possibility of being put to work. She knew this was one of the few breaks I had from work and school, but she didn't care. She would prefer I lighten her load than allow me the chance to change my plans.

I sigh heavily.

Not only had I hoped to relax but working at the house might mean running into Zeno for a second time. Not that it's my problem—he's the one with issues. I simply prefer to avoid his brooding negativity on my vacation if possible. However, if I don't join my family and help at the main house, I'll hardly see them at all, and that was the whole point of visiting. If alone time had been my goal, I could have crashed at a friend's apartment for the week.

My eyes drift to Gia, who gazes back at me warmly. Any complaints I might have staged melt away at the reminder of her gentle grace and the sight of my father's apologetic smile.

"All right, let's head on over. You can update me on what still needs to be done on the way."

Dad drops a tender kiss on my forehead, chasing away my irritation. "Having you here means the world to me," he whispers.

I am never happier than when I am the center of my father's world, which is often the case as he makes no effort to hide his favoritism. He has my heart, just as I have his, and despite my mother's manipulations and Zeno's looming presence, I will always stand at my father's side if he needs me. After all, it's only a few days. How bad could it be?

CHAPTER 2

My parents use a golf cart to shuttle them back and forth between Hardwick and their cottage. Fitting all six of us is a tight squeeze, so Gia and I offer to walk to the main house. We prefer to catch up privately, anyway. Mom and the younger girls quickly dismiss joining us because of the rising heat. I can't totally fault them. It's not even a quarter of a mile between the main house and our cottage, but it can feel like longer when the sun amplifies the humidity. They slide into their seats and wave as the cart lurches forward.

"This may not be your ideal vacay, but I'm glad you'll be around to keep me company." Gia bumps my shoulder as we walk through the tall grass.

"I'm happy to help. Mom just makes me twitchy."

"Mom? There isn't someone else that made you hesitant

to join us at the main house?" Even an older sister as angelic as Gia finds joy in goading a younger sibling.

"You're right. Livia is more obnoxious than ever."

Gia snorts. "You know that's not who I meant."

I shoot her a look from the side of my eye. "If it's Zeno you're referring to, I'd have to care in order for him to rile me up. He hasn't been a part of my world in a very, very long time."

"I suppose. Some people stay with us no matter how long it's been since we were close." Her words resonate with me in a way I don't care to analyze.

"You sound awfully sage for someone who's hardly stepped foot from her Hardwick bubble."

She shrugs. "You don't have to live in the city to learn to read people."

"You're right, of course, except that there are a lot more *learning* opportunities when there are more people. You would have loved my world literature professor last semester. Maybe you two would have hit it off, but I guess we'll never know."

"Is that the same guy you told me had a stain on every shirt he owned?"

A laugh tumbles past my lips from deep in my belly. "Yeah, but that's why he needs someone like you. Someone who loves to take care of people."

Gia shakes her head, but the corners of her lips hook upward. "One more year?"

"Yeah, I've got just enough money saved up for tuition and expenses so that I can limit how many hours I have to work. I'm so ready to get my degree and move on."

"It's been, what? Five years?"

"Almost six," I grumble. "But I've done it all mostly on my own."

"Who cares if you had to spread it out so that you had time to work—that makes it all the more impressive. You're so determined!"

"I am now, but that wasn't the case early on. If I'd gone straight to college when I graduated high school, I could have been finished by now. Better late than never, right?"

"Absolutely."

Two birds lift off from the grassy covering ahead of us, drawing my eyes skyward. The sun is pushing higher in a clear sky that promises to be a perfect summer day.

"What else has been going on around here that I might have missed?" I talk to my sister regularly on the phone, but she is always more tight-lipped than when we talk in person. She's one of those maddening internal processors who doesn't think to pass on information. It's not that she necessarily makes it a habit not to gossip, but it simply doesn't occur to her. I have to draw the information out if I ever want to learn anything. As I said, it's maddening.

"Nothing, really. Like Mom said, Anna, the kitchen girl, quit. Well, she didn't quit so much as disappear. She was with us for nearly six months when … poof. Gone. She just never showed up for work one day. People do that all the time, but I didn't expect it from her."

"How strange!" I think back to whether I'd met the girl and draw a blank. I rarely see the other staff when I visit and have only been home once during the past six months. I may not have met her, but a sudden departure doesn't necessarily surprise me. Mom supervises the in-house workers, so I could understand if the girl had gotten so fed up that she walked away. If I worked for my mom, I would probably do the same.

I refrain from sharing that thought with Gia. She'd just point out that Mom does the best she can. In my opinion, that's a convenient excuse for bad behavior. It's right up there with "boys will be boys." Bullshit. People will behave as poorly as they are allowed to behave. Mom could stop putting my parents in debt with her ridiculous spending, but she doesn't seem to care. She only thinks of herself. Sometimes, I wonder if living among the rich has given her a false sense of entitlement—as though she has a right to own all the pretty things she sees. I can't explain the source of her issues, but it's been an incessant drain on our family. Even more of a mystery is why my father doesn't stop her. As far as I can tell, he gave up trying with her long ago. Their entire relationship confounds me, though, so I don't try to understand because I'll only end up more confused.

As we near the house, its stone exterior comes into view, surging up over the treetops. A clearing encircles the house with perfectly manicured green grass like a blank wall highlighting the masterpiece of architectural design at its center. I would venture to guess not a penny was spared on its construction. I was told growing up that the home was originally built by a steel magnate akin to Rockefeller or Carnegie. I couldn't even fathom what something like Hardwick would have cost back then.

In my opinion, Silvano De Rossi's dedication to maintaining the integrity of the original design spoke volumes about his person. It would have been cheaper and easier to remodel with modern touches, but he kept the historical accuracy of the home intact. He didn't feel a need to put his own mark on the place. Instead, he chose to honor its original magnificence.

"I wonder what will happen to the house now that Silvano is gone," I muse aloud.

"Zeno already talked with Mom and Dad. He said that he was moving in and would retain their services. I suppose that means not much will change."

Hopefully, that's the case. Zeno is such a mystery that I would never presume to know his intentions. But saying as much serves no purpose, so I merely nod.

The approach of a vehicle into the circle drive snags our attention. When it parks near the front door, I see that Carter Bishop, owner of the neighboring estate, is behind the wheel. He exits the driver's side and immediately turns toward us, meeting us halfway to his car.

"Gia, how are you?" His kind eyes linger on my sister. I don't know him well since he moved in after I left home, but my family is longtime friends with his live-in staff, the Larsons, who worked for the previous owner as well. Our cottages are both near the property line, making them our closest neighbors. Gia has mentioned Carter's name only briefly in passing, but judging by the pink glow of her cheeks, her interest in him is more substantial than I'd been led to believe.

"I'm doing well, thank you," she offers, her gaze flitting to his, then down to her hands. "Carter … Mr. Bishop … this is Luisa, my sister. I can't recall if you two have met."

It's easy to offer him a warm smile as I grasp his outstretched hand. He has an openness to him that is disarming. "I believe we have, but it's been a while."

"Yes," he agrees. "And please call me Carter. It's great to have you here. I mean, not the circumstances, of course, but I'm sure Gia appreciates having you visit." His nervous bumbling is endearing, if not a touch surprising, considering his age and station in life. I've found most middle-aged, affluent men are usually dripping with unearned confidence.

I think I like Carter Bishop.

"The timing was a bit coincidental—I already had my trip planned—but I'm glad I could be here to help. There's a lot to be done."

"I assumed as much." His face sobers. "That's why I wanted to check in with Z and Elena. I want to offer any help I can provide."

I haven't had a chance to think about Elena, Silvano's widow. My heart sinks at how bereft she must be. No matter how poorly my friendship soured with Z, I will always have fond thoughts for his mother. She's a beautiful person, and I hate that she's grieving.

A car door shuts, and I peer over Carter's shoulder to where an elegant woman now stands haughtily next to the car. It's hard to say if she's in her thirties or forties. I've found the wealthy have access to some rather impressive age-defying treatments, so it can be hard to tell, especially at a distance. Her blond hair frames her face in professionally coifed waves that rest a few inches below her shoulders. She's wearing a powder-blue skirt suit perfectly tailored to her thin frame and an expression of unquestionable superiority.

"Carter, dear. I'm sure the staff are busy today, and the De Rossis will need our company far more than these two need our interference with their day." Her voice is more mature than I would have thought, making me lean toward a guess of mid-forties.

He flashes a thin smile. "I'd better get going. I'm sure Z will refuse any help, but please let me know if I can do anything."

"Of course." Gia grins. "I'll make sure to reach out if we need anything."

We both watch silently as Carter joins the woman at the front door. They disappear into the house when greeted by someone inside.

I turn narrowed eyes on my sister once we are alone. "Gia Antonia Banetti, what in the blazes was that?"

Her eyes widen innocently when she looks my way. "What do you mean? That was Carter Bishop, the neighbor."

"I know who he is. Since when does he make you blush like a schoolgirl seeing her favorite boy band?" This is the first time in my adult life that I can recall my sister ever showing genuine romantic interest in anyone. She's not the dating app type and doesn't run into many eligible men at Hardwick, so her options are limited. I'm absolutely ecstatic to discover she has a thing for the handsome man next door.

Her cheeks flush a deeper shade of crimson. "Don't be silly. I was just surprised to see him."

Uh-huh. Right. I slowly shake my head so she knows I'm not buying it, but I don't force her to tell me more. We'll have plenty of time to ease into the subject during the week once she's warmed up to the idea.

"Who was that with him? Did he get remarried?"

"No, that's his sister, Cora. She moved in about a year ago to help with the kids."

Carter was widowed a few months before moving to his Tuxedo Park estate. He's been living there for years now without remarrying, and if memory serves, his two kids are approaching their teens. It makes sense that he might bring in someone, family or otherwise, to help with their undoubtedly busy schedules.

Now that I know his relation to the woman, I note the similarities in their appearance. Carter has the same blond hair with a natural curl that Cora likely hides by straightening and curling to form more controlled, silky waves. They are both relatively petite and not as fair-complexioned as some blonds. As for their natures, I got the sense no two people could be more different. He was attentive and thoughtful while the grass frosted over and died wherever she stepped.

"Poor kids," I murmur. If she's their caregiver, I don't envy them.

"Don't say that." Gia smacks my shoulder. "I'm sure she was just having a rough morning." Her voice lacked the strength of confidence.

"How come you haven't mentioned her before?"

My sweet, considerate, selfless sister raises a brow. "I

figure, if I don't have anything nice to say, I shouldn't say anything at all."

I double over in a fit of laughter while Gia fights off a grin. Cora must be a piece of work if she can't even gain favor with Gia. A person has to try hard to fall from her good graces.

"Like I said, poor kids."

Melancholy eclipses her mirth when she nods. "Let's head to the kitchen. I'm sure Mom's wondering where we are."

We bypass the front door and walk around to the servant's entrance at the back of the house. While the building was maintained true to its original character, certain modern amenities such as kitchen appliances and other upgrades were discreetly added to the home in a way that didn't upset the old-world charm. We find the cook, Cecelia, stationed at a twelve-burner Wolfe stovetop overseeing three steaming pots while Mom kneads a massive ball of dough.

"I started to think you two had gotten lost. Your sisters have both been sent out on errands, and I could really use your help upstairs. All twelve bedrooms will be occupied tonight. I've got Laney working on that, but she's been slower than molasses lately. If she's left to do it all on her own, she won't finish until midnight."

Laney is the dedicated housekeeper who lives in a small suite on the third floor and works with Gia. She's in her mid-forties and has worked for the family for more than a decade. It always strikes me as a little odd that she doesn't have her own family and still lives at Hardwick, but Gia is in nearly the same situation, so who am I to judge? Laney seems to like her job and living arrangements, and her opinion is the only one that matters. She reports to my mother, who managed to score a job overseeing the household staff not long after Dad was offered the job as groundskeeper and head of security. Mom's job is a bit ironic since she can't maintain her own home worth a flip, but she somehow manages to perform adequately enough that she has yet to be fired, and by some stroke of luck, her staff turnover rate has been surprisingly low.

Only a few De Rossis live at Hardwick full-time, so a large staff isn't needed. Mom fills in when the family hosts a party or houses guests, but this funeral is an entirely different matter. People will be gathering from all over the country to honor the late Mr. De Rossi, who was intricately involved in politics and who knows what else.

"We'll go ask Laney what rooms still need to be prepared," Gia assures her.

I follow my sister from the kitchen to the walk-in linen closet, where we luck out and find Laney collecting supplies for her next room.

"Hey, Laney." Gia smiles warmly. "Mom sent us to help. Where should we start?"

The thin woman's shoulders slump with relief. "Thank God. I wasn't sure how I was going to get everything done. Most of the bedrooms haven't been used in over a year, so Mrs. De Rossi wants all new sheets put on the beds. I'm also giving the bathrooms a scrub. I'd been working room-by-room doing both, but if you two could get the beds taken care of, I'll finish up the bathrooms."

"Absolutely. What rooms have been done already?"

"It's early, so I've only gotten to the first two on the far east end of the hall. I had enough fresh sheets clean for half the rooms but have stripped the other half already to get those sheets in the wash. Here." She snatches two piles of white linens from the shelf and hands them to Gia, then places a bucket of cleaning supplies in mine. "The next two rooms are queen bedrooms. And do a sweep for any extra touches that may be needed—a quick vacuum of the drapes or the removal of any cobwebs. We don't do a thorough clean of those areas except maybe once a year, so there's no telling what we'll find. But don't tackle too much because we only have so much time." She suddenly stops and takes a shuddering breath. "Heavens, I can't believe this is happening. It was so sudden. He was there one minute and gone the next." When her eyes find us again, they're red and glassy.

Gia places a hand on Laney's shoulder. "It's a hard time for everyone. Try not to overtax yourself, and don't worry about the bedrooms. We have them covered."

Laney nods and picks up her bucket. "Holler if you need me." She gives us a sad smile before disappearing down the hall.

A somberness settles over us that is amplified by the quiet stateliness of the old home. The rich mahogany wood and Persian rugs are a testament to time. Owners will come and go, but Hardwick will long remain. The empty silence in its hallways is a stark reminder of our temporary nature.

"Well"—I shake off the despondency—"let's get started

upstairs." *Where the windows will let in some sunlight and cheer.* While I feel bad for the De Rossi family, I prefer not to embrace their sorrow. Maybe it's shallow of me, but I don't like to be sad. For someone like Gia, who is a natural empath, it can be hard to avoid feeling the full extent of another's grief, but I'm not so unfortunate. And as such, it has always been my role to lift her spirits as well.

I flash her an encouraging smile and signal for her to lead the way. We used to play hide-and-seek with Zeno and his brother, Nevio, at Hardwick when we were kids, so I know the house well. Not much has changed within these stately walls, even though it's been years since I've stepped foot inside. Any uncertainty I feel is a matter of me being an outsider rather than an issue of familiarity with the floor plan. If we should run across the new master of the house, he will most certainly deem my presence an intrusion. He made that clear years ago.

As luck would have it, we make it to our destination without encountering a soul. Our first bedroom contains a hand-carved poster bed and other furnishings either original to the house or expert reproductions. There's even an ornate vanity decorated with a set of colored glass perfume bottles. The attached antique mirror is mottled with webbing and flecks of gold—clearly kept for its aesthetic rather than function. The drapes are a heavy tapestry material held back by two giant tassels and match the blue and gold rug beneath the bed. The room is exquisite, if not a tad stuffy from being closed off for so long. If it wasn't for the modern alarm clock on the nightstand, I could swear that I had stumbled onto the set of *Downton Abbey* or some BBC murder mystery show.

"Something is comforting about a house that's been around for so long, as though it's impervious to the changing world around it. Maybe that's why De Rossi moved here from the city—to find a sanctuary for his family," I muse.

"I'm pretty sure it has more to do with the other high-profile residents in the area, but that could have played a part." He had frequently schmoozed with his fellow landowners over the years. I wasn't sure what he did in his role as Giordano underboss, but he was friends with people in high places.

I grab a corner of the comforter and peel it back, mirroring Gia's movements on the opposite side of the bed. "Whatever the reason, I'm glad the family is staying. I'm not sure what would happen to Mom and Dad if they had to leave. I doubt they could afford to be unemployed for long."

Gia is suspiciously quiet after my comment.

I narrow my eyes and study her. "What aren't you saying?"

"Nothing, exactly. I've just had an odd feeling lately. Mom bought several things a while back like a Louis Vuitton bag—things she has no business buying. Then all of a sudden, the items started disappearing. I'm guessing she's selling them, but I'm not sure why, and I'm afraid to ask."

"That sounds about right," I grumble.

We put fresh sheets on the bed, replace the comforter

and pillows, then survey the room for any other areas that need attention. Once satisfied with the room, we step across the hall to a more feminine bedroom overlooking the lake behind the house. After briefly losing myself in the view, I join Gia at the bed. We begin our process over again, but this time, when we unfold the new sheet, it's obvious Laney has accidentally given us a king-sized set.

"You run down and grab some queen sheets while I touch up the room," Gia instructed. "The inside of these sconces look like they haven't been dusted in ages." She scowls at the decorative glass fixtures on either side of the arching headboard.

"Okay, I'll be right back." I slip from the room and make my way down the long corridor to the grand stairwell in the center of the house. I take my time now that I'm alone, perusing each piece of artwork and refreshing my memory on the many wonders of the house. I have so many cherished memories of this place from my early years, though each leaves a bittersweet aftertaste when I think of how it all ended. I don't dwell on those memories. In fact, I try not to think of them at all. Some things are better left in the past.

I feel like a ghost passing silently down the halls of Hardwick. I conveniently chose to wear sneakers for my trip out of the city, which is a relief. Anything but rubber soles or the softest of Italian leather would resound throughout the marble entry. I am nearly silent in my descent of the stairs. On the ground level, I curve back behind the stairwell and toward the kitchen on the ground floor. I quickly grab two more stacks of sheets in the linen closet, both set on a shelf labeled queen. When I retrace my route back toward the stairs and the front of the house, the sound of voices carries down the hallway and slows my steps.

Not just any voices. Zeno's baritone rumble.

Soundlessly, I inch forward until I am beneath the stairs, only a dozen feet or so from where Zeno is sending off Carter and Cora at the front door. My heart flutters up into my throat at the knowledge he wouldn't want me here. That I am essentially spying on him.

"Not an intrusion at all. I always appreciate a visit from you both." He speaks with more warmth than I am used to hearing from him, which denotes a genuine affection—something I wasn't sure he was capable of at this stage in his life.

"I hope you know that we're always here for you, Z. Reach out anytime." Cora's saccharine voice claws at my ears until my molars ache. Not an hour before, she had no patience for Gia and me but is now bending over backward for her fellow neighbor.

"I appreciate that, Cora. I'm confident my staff has everything under control."

"Yes," Carter agrees. "I saw Gia on our way in with her sister who lives in the city. They're a lovely family. Always willing to step up and lend a hand."

Zeno clears his throat, and I strain to catch every word of what he might say about my family. About me. I am shamelessly eavesdropping, but I don't care. Now that they are talking about us, I have to know what he'll say.

"Gia is certainly one of a kind. It's a shame everyone isn't as genuine and honorable."

Carter chuckles awkwardly. "Well, I can't say that I know Luisa well, but in the few minutes we spoke, she seemed genuine enough."

"And that's the problem," Cora interjects. "You're too easily taken in by a pretty face."

Zeno clears his throat to speak, and my heart rate kicks up at the prospect of him defending me. "I will say that she is less abrasive than some of the other members of her family. But they do their jobs well, and that's all that matters."

Less abrasive. That's the best he can say about me? My family has practically been a part of his for decades, yet he talks about us as if we were a necessary evil. His grief doesn't give him the right to be hateful.

Heat scorches up my neck and licks across my cheeks.

My family may not be perfect, but his arrogance knows no bounds. At least my family doesn't treat others like dirt simply because they have more or less money than us.

What an arrogant ... self-centered ... ugh! Asshole.

My anger and frustration muddle the words in my head. I have to take several deep breaths in order to compose myself.

"Yes, well, perhaps we'll have everyone over for dinner sometime this week." The door creaks open as Carter continues. "I can imagine the circumstances have been difficult for the entire household."

"You're a good man, Bishop," Zeno says warmly.

"Too good, if you ask me," Cora adds wryly. Though it's

meant to tease, there is conviction behind the statement. She thinks her brother could use a touch of her callous nature.

Carter clears his throat. "That's a conversation for another day." The sound of hands clasping reaches my ears. "I'll check in with you tomorrow, Z. And don't forget about my offer. I'm happy to help in any way."

"You have my word. You both take care, and I'll see you at the funeral, if not before."

The Bishops say their parting goodbyes, and the door clicks shut.

I should stay hidden. I should allow Zeno to return to whatever cave he's been hiding in and ignore him, but I can't. I'm too riled up to offer him leniency, even when his father has just died. It's his own damn fault. He's the one who packed the heavy baggage I'm lugging around. He's the one who hurt me, and his comments have triggered my anger so thoroughly that it cannot be repressed.

I tug tightly on the reins of my emotions as I stroll forward into the entry. I don't want him to figure out that I was listening, but I need to strike back. I need to hold my ground and take a stand so he won't think he can push me around while I'm here.

For the briefest second, Zeno's back is to me, his hand still clasping the doorknob. My eyes gobble the opportunity to sweep his tall, suited form from top to bottom, only snapping back up to his face when he slowly swivels in my direction.

He is carved stone. Impervious. Untouchable. Breathtaking.

Power wafts off him like mist drifting from the lake. I would be mesmerized by his ominous stature if the air about him wasn't lightly tainted with disdain. Violent blue eyes slice through me with silent accusation.

"What are you doing here?" All traces of the warmth with which he addressed the Bishops have disappeared. His voice is jagged ice scraping against my skin.

"Helping my sister get the house ready." I hold my chin high and hit him with a blast of confidence. I won't let him think he can scare me off.

"You didn't mention you would be at the house."

"Is that a problem?" I challenge.

His eyes flinch the tiniest bit. Almost imperceptibly. "No. There's no problem." As if reconsidering, his jaw clenches. "How long will you be staying with your parents?"

"A week."

He nods as if this news is acceptable, but his nostrils flare and lips thin as though he's conflicted. "Are you helping for the weekend, or will you be at Hardwick the entire week?"

Jesus Christ. He sure does know how to make a girl feel like a pariah.

"I'm not here to harass you, Zeno. I hadn't even heard about your father until I got home. I know my presence bothers you, but my mother asked for my help, and I'm sure you can find a way to ignore me. You've become so good at it through the years. Now, if you'll excuse me. I've got work to do." As soon as I'm done, I turn for the stairs, not giving him time for a response. I'm not interested in whatever demeaning, insensitive garbage he might want to throw at me.

Our exchange goes as poorly as every other encounter we've had in the past ten years. And as always, I deflate upon his departure. My shoulders slump, and my mood darkens. I am equal parts violence and sorrow. If I could hammer him with my fists and force him to remember how we used to be friends, I would. But Zeno De Rossi is not a man to be swayed. He is determined to hate me, and I am not a woman who will beg for acceptance.

CHAPTER 3

Zeno, Age 13
Luisa and Nevio, Age 10

"I THINK WE SHOULD GO TO THE CLIMBING TREE BY THE LAKE. Or we could play hide-and-seek." I look at Zeno and Nevio expectantly, hoping they'll like one of my suggestions. Summer is drawing to a close, and it's harder to find activities we all agree upon.

"You need more people for hide-and-seek. Where's Gia?" Zeno asks.

I pull off a blade of green grass from the lawn beneath me. "She's painting her nails," I grumble. The colors are cool. I like polish as much as the next girl. But I can't stand how long they take to dry. I don't have the patience. Even when I do wait long *enough, I inevitably chip them ten minutes later. There's no point. I'd rather skip the wait and play outside.*

"We could go down to the lake," Nevio suggests.

Z tosses a small rock at the trees. "Nah, let's go for a bike ride."

I jump to my feet. "Okay! You guys wait for me, though." *I turn to race back to my house, knowing it will take me longer to get my bike than them. I only take a few strides before Zeno calls out.*

"Isa, make sure you wear your helmet."

I screech to a halt and spin around. "What? Why? You never wear one."

"Don't care. You ride with me, you wear a helmet."

"If I have to wear one, Nevio does too." *I'm not going down on this ship alone.*

"No way!" *Nevio groans.*

Z smirks. "Fair enough. Now go get your bike. We'll swing by and grab you on our way out."

I leap into action, giggling at the incredulous bellow Nevio releases behind me. Back at the house, I roll my bike out of the shed and clip on my bright red helmet. I check my tires for air, then pedal down our long driveway. The boys are waiting for me beneath a shade tree, Zeno propped against his black mountain bike, and Nevio sitting on his blue BMX style bike wearing a gray helmet and a scowl.

"Let's go up to the clubhouse, then we can coast back downhill on the way home." *Zeno throws a long, lean leg over his bike and leads the way. As the eldest, he almost always runs the show when he's around. There are only three years between the two brothers,* but it seems like more. Sometimes, Nevio challenges Z, but he rarely wins. Z is way bigger and a little scary sometimes. Nevio is scrappy, but he gets so angry that it hurts his chances. When they fight one another, which happens, Z always comes out on top.

I'm happy to do whatever they decide, so long as I'm not bored and alone.

The clubhouse is about half a mile from Hardwick and is a gathering facility for the community. There is a boat launch for those without water access, picnic tables, and a pier that people use for fishing. Most of the ride there is shaded by a canopy of trees, so even the uphill climb isn't too terrible. When we arrive, we have the place to ourselves. It's probably too hot out for anyone else, but that works for us.

Z hops the curb and leads us over the grass and around the clubhouse toward the lake on the other side. As we approach the shoreline, the terrain becomes increasingly rocky, especially in the six feet or so of the bank where the water regularly rises and recedes, depending on the weather. I'm not crazy about riding over rocks, but I refuse to show weakness in front of the boys. They already treat me differently because I'm a girl—case in point, my helmet. Whining about the rocks would only make things worse.

I power on along the shore behind the others until my front wheel rolls over an extra-large rock, sliding sideways and toppling me over onto the unforgiving ground. I try to catch myself but am mostly unsuccessful and land on my side with the bike draped over me. I hiss as I scoot away from the offending bike and take in my scraped hands and leg. My hip took the brunt of the fall. Fortunately, my jean shorts kept the skin there safe. The side of my knee wasn't so lucky.

The two brothers throw their bikes down and come running over.

Zeno takes my hand in his and examines my wounds. "Are you okay? Is anything broken?"

"I don't think so." I wince at the stinging now pulsing from multiple places on my body. "It just burns a bit." Tears begin to form in my eyes, but I desperately blink them back. I'm not even sure why I'm crying. I'm not hurt that bad, but the scare has triggered my tears.

Nevio stands my bike upright and assesses the front wheel. "I don't think it's bent. Sometimes a fall like that makes the steering all wonky."

Z doesn't acknowledge his brother. Instead, he looks up in search of something, then scoops me into his arms. I cling to his neck, taken by surprise when he lifts me off the ground. I'm a scrawny thing, but carrying me can't be easy. He's stronger than I thought.

Even though I really appreciate him taking care of me, I don't want him to think I'm a baby. "I can walk, Z. You don't have to carry me."

"No, Isa," he murmurs. "I got you."

I believe him. Z would never drop me.

He sets me down on the bench of a nearby picnic table, then squats to look at my knee, slowly lifting my foot to straighten the joint. "How does that feel?"

"Okay."

"How about you try to stand."

I nod and do as he says, putting weight on my hip. "I think it's okay, just a little sore." I sit back down and wipe the moisture from my cheek.

Z reaches up and gently raps his knuckles on my helmet. "Aren't you glad I had you wear that thing now?" he teases.

I chuckle and roll my eyes. "I guess."

He joins me on the bench, and we watch Nevio skip rocks for a few minutes. Once I'm feeling better, I suggest we join his brother, and the rest of our afternoon unfolds as it would any other day. When I go to sleep that night, curled up next to my sister, I recall the feel of Zeno's strong arms supporting me. I'm not sure why it comes to mind, except that it felt so good. I almost wish he were here now so that I could hear the thundering of his reassuring heartbeat.

I fall asleep with that thought in mind, comforted by the fact that I have such an amazing friend.

CHAPTER 4

I take each step upstairs with calm control. Zeno already stormed away—no one is watching me—but I refuse to look like I'm scurrying away with my tail tucked between my legs. I use the time to recenter myself and remember why I'm here. Zeno may be a dick, but that's irrelevant to me. *He* is irrelevant. I get a week to spend with my favorite people on the planet, and I will not let him ruin that.

When I locate Gia, she's moved to the bedroom next door to where I left her and already has the old sheets piled by the door.

"Housekeeping," I say in a sing-song voice, holding up the fresh sheets.

"I was starting to think you'd gotten lost."

"Nah, only delayed a minute. Come on, let's finish the bed next door." I lead the way back to the unfinished room, and we fall into easy teamwork.

"You know," Gia muses after a bit. "I could get used to working with you. With Anna gone, we'll need to take on someone new. You and I could get an apartment together nearby."

"As tempting as it is to be closer to you, school and Mom make that impossible."

"I figured, but I had to mention it. We could even hold off until after you graduate. I could do the extra work until then."

"Oh, no." I grin. "If one of us is making a move, it's *you*. I'm going to have my own bedroom now. We could share, like the old days."

Gia won't meet my gaze. "I know how excited you are to have your own space. And besides, I hate to leave when Marca is still here," she says softly. "Liv and Marca need me now more than ever. They need a good influence in their lives." She's not wrong, but I hate that the burden falls on her. I'm not bothered enough to volunteer myself, but I understand.

"Livy may be a lost cause, as much as I hate to say it. I couldn't believe how insensitive she was about Mr. De Rossi's death right in front of Dad. All she's interested in is getting her hooks in a man with money."

"Trust me, I know," Gia grumbled.

"As much as we want to help guide Marca, she's an adult now, too. She may not even stay with Mom and Dad much longer. You sure the girls are the only reason you want to stick around?" I watch my sister closely.

A delicate flush creeps up her neck.

"Tell me something is going on between you and Carter," I urge.

"There isn't, I promise."

"But you'd like there to be?"

"Isa, he's a wealthy widower, twelve years older than me, with two kids and a real estate empire. And I'm ... *me*."

"And?" I gape.

Her answering smile is so sorrowful that my chest clenches. "It's just not meant to be."

She continues with her task, effectively ending the conversation, but my thoughts continue down a dark path. I hate that she doesn't see her own value. Aside from her loving temperament, she looks like an angel on earth. While my hair is a sandy color, she's the only one of us girls who managed to snag Dad's blond hair. Gia's long waves are spun silk, and her warm brown eyes shine with love and acceptance. She's a few woodland creatures shy of being a living, breathing Disney princess. It baffles me that she doesn't see the immense worth of all her amazing qualities. I would find a way to show her how the world truly sees her if I could, but my attempts would be meaningless unless she's willing to believe in herself.

What irony. The humility that makes her so loved by everyone she meets is the very reason she can't comprehend their adoration. Then again, maybe it's best to leave things alone. I love her exactly the way she is, and if Carter or any other man isn't willing to swoop in and claim her, she's better off without them. The only person worthy of Gia's perfection is a man who appreciates his good fortune in earning her affection.

We spend the rest of the day in lighter spirits, finishing our work minutes before guests begin to arrive for dinner. Gia stays with Mom to help Cecelia with the meal while I walk back home with Livia and Marca. Dad is already at the cottage enjoying a cigar on the back porch when we arrive. I pause to say hello while my two sisters bolt inside and up to their room.

"I'm going to get stuck making dinner, aren't I?" I ask Dad wryly with my eyes trailing after the girls.

"That's the first time Livia's put in a full day's work in ages. You'd have a better chance conjuring dinner from thin air than getting her to help." His rounded lips draw deeply on his cigar, making the embers on the end spark with life.

"She's twenty-three! What's her problem?"

"I prefer not to ask that question. It only brings on a headache."

I roll my eyes and head into the house. Dad hasn't forced Livia or Marca to do much of anything—ever—so I don't know why I expect him to now. I guess I'm no better because I can't summon the energy for an argument about his need to be firm with them. Instead, I check the fridge and find enough ingredients to throw together a simple meal.

The girls come down to eat, and as usual, Livia does most of the talking. Marca's eyes light up when she watches her older sister, and it worries me. Marca is intelligent. She's quiet and more rational than Livia, but her desire to gain her big sister's approval has more sway over her than it should. Especially when Livy is such a hot mess. Throughout dinner, I try to engage with Marca but find Livia often interjects her opinions. Separating the two would be a difficult feat—more of a challenge than I am up for at present. With food in my belly and a long day on my feet, exhaustion fills my limbs with lead. I pile the dishes in the sink to be dealt with later and join my dad in the living room.

He pats the sofa next to him. "Come sit with me, Lulu."

My chest warms in anticipation of snuggling with my dad. I miss having quiet time with him, just the two of us. Sinking into the old sofa, I sit with my knees up and lean into his side with his arm curled around me.

"Tell me about school. You've been able to keep your grades up while you work?"

"It's a lot of reading and essays, but I manage."

"You love to read, so hopefully, it's not too much of a burden."

I laugh. "Yeah. It would be more enjoyable if I wasn't graded on that reading, but overall, I like my classes."

Daddy grins down at me with adoration in his sad eyes. His eyelids sag above his eyes in a way that makes him look weary, regardless of whatever he's actually feeling.

"I love hearing that. I only wish I could have helped you more so you didn't have to juggle work and school."

His words remind me of Gia's concerns about Mom and possible financial troubles. It's not a subject I normally discuss with my dad, but G has me a little worried.

"Daddy? Is there anything going on with Mom that we should know about?"

His brows furrow. "What do you mean?"

I shrug. "Gia mentioned she thought Mom might be selling stuff—that maybe finances were tight. I thought I'd check and make sure everything was okay."

"There is absolutely nothing for you to worry about. And besides, you should know by now that your mother's life choices are not your problem." His words are reassuring, but the remorse in his coffee-colored eyes breaks my heart. It's not the first time the emotion has aged his features.

I try to smile, but the result is brittle and frail.

"Hey," he says with renewed energy. "I forgot to mention earlier than Z asked about you today."

Dad's attempt at a subject change successfully wipes my mind of all previous conversations. Shock and curiosity are now my only companions.

"When?"

"This afternoon. He asked how school was going and what your plans were after you graduate."

He what? After we'd already talked and he'd acted like he couldn't wait to get rid of me, he'd gone out of his way to ask my father about school and my plans? I can't make a lick of sense out of it.

"I'm sure he was only being polite. He couldn't care less about my plans, trust me."

"Don't go judging him right now. He's been devastated

at losing his father—you know how much he adored Silvano. And besides, just because he's not charismatic like his brother doesn't mean he doesn't care. Sometimes that's easy to misinterpret."

Dad always assumed Z stopped hanging out with me because he was older than me, and that was the nature of maturing. I know there was more to it, but it's not worth arguing over. "Where is Nevio, anyway? I figured he'd have come home as soon as he got the news of his father's passing."

"I think he's supposed to get in tomorrow for the wake. There's no telling with him."

That's something to look forward to. I haven't seen Nevio in ages, and he is always loads of fun. Maybe not so much now, considering the circumstances, but it will still be good to catch up.

Dad tilts his head closer. "You three used to be thick as thieves."

"That was a lifetime ago."

"True." He sighs. "There was a time when Silvano and I used to wonder if something might develop between you and Zeno, considering the way you looked up to him."

The laugh that slips past my lips is tinged with bitterness. "Z doesn't want anything to do with me."

Dad frowns, but his eyes spark like the ends of his cigars. "I'd say that's his loss, then. But I'm not sure anyone is truly deserving of you."

I'm about to brush off his compliment when I realize he's having the same conversation with me that I had with Gia earlier today. And he's right.

"Thanks, Daddy." I rest my head on his chest and try to sear the moment into my memory banks. Mr. De Rossi's passing was an unfortunate reminder that loss is often unexpected, and every hug from my dad is worth cherishing.

CHAPTER 5

THE NEXT MORNING, I SLIP FROM THE HOUSE EARLY TO catch up with my childhood friend, Grace Larson. Knowing I'll have to help my family all day, I made sure to set up a visit with her before going to bed. Aside from Gia, Grace is my closest friend back home. She and G are in similar situations in that they both still live with their parents, but Grace is not so content with the arrangement. Gia stays because she feels compelled to, while Grace stays because she believes she has no other options.

Back in her teens, Grace was diagnosed with polycystic ovary syndrome or PCOS. It wreaked havoc on her hormones and caused her to struggle with her weight. She's worked hard to balance her hormones and do what she can, but it hasn't been easy. Grace is funny, clever, genuine, and one of the best people I know, but her size and health have affected her confidence. Plus, her family has even less money than mine. Dad may be a glorified grounds keeper, but he's also technically a member of the Mafia, which brings in extra funds. Mr. Larson is a modest man with no criminal ties. Curvy and penniless, Grace has convinced herself that no man could possibly want her. It's heartbreaking.

On the bright side, she's improved her mindset over the years, focusing on finding happiness rather than obsessing over what she lacks. The last time we spoke, she told me about her aspiration to move to the city. Living among a variety of people from all walks of life would help her immensely. I hope she'll make the move. Plus, that would be one more friend close by.

When I approach her house, she's waiting for me on their porch swing.

"Oh, Isa, I've missed you!" She jumps up and meets me in a tight embrace.

"I've missed you, too, Gracie. FaceTime just isn't the same as a real visit." The radiant grin on her face warms my heart.

"No, it's not. You look as fabulous as ever, of course! How have you been?"

"I've been really great! Finally moving to a better apartment and almost done with school. This was supposed to be a happy visit until I got here and found out about Silvano. I feel terrible for Elena and everyone."

"Oh, I know! Such a shame. Hey, you want to walk a bit while it's not too hot yet?"

"Absolutely. We could head down to the water. I haven't had a chance to make it down there yet." I hook my arm in hers, and we move in step toward the trees separating the lake and the house.

"Sorry to hear you ended up getting put to work."

"Gia and I got to spend the day together yesterday, I had dinner with my dad last night, and now I'm getting to spend time with you—I'd say that's not so bad!"

She squeezes my arm in hers, and we grin at one another as though we're still teenagers. I've made some good friends in the city, but something is special about a childhood friend who's been there through braces and breakups from day one.

"Mr. Bishop told us to make sure we helped you all out if you need anything. Not that he has to tell us to do that, but he wanted to make sure we knew he wouldn't need us at the house if something came up over at Hardwick."

"I got to talk with him briefly yesterday. He seems very thoughtful." I pay extra attention to how Grace responds. I'm curious about her opinion now that I'm seeing our neighbor in a new light.

"He's exceptionally kind. His sister can be nasty, and I'm not sure why he tolerates her, but he's great in every other way." It seems Cora Bishop is universally disliked.

"Does Gia ever go over to the house?" I ask nonchalantly.

Grace slows and studies me from the corner of her eye. "I'm not sure what you mean. She sometimes drops cookies by for the kids. But I don't see her over often."

"I was just curious."

"Well, I'll say this. I *have* noticed when she and Mr. Bishop are together, they gravitate toward one another. His kids absolutely adore her. Do you think something is going on with them?" Her eyes brighten with romantic hopefulness.

"There's nothing official between them, but I think Gia wishes there were."

"Why doesn't she make a move? She's absolutely stunning, and he definitely likes her."

I breathe deeply through my nose and resume our walk. "She's convinced he's out of her league."

Grace snorts, and we both start giggling.

"I'm sorry, but that's the most absurd thing I've ever heard. She's so gorgeous with her golden hair and warm brown eyes. Her figure is to die for, and she's so incredibly sweet. Why on *earth* wouldn't he want her?"

"I agree. But *some* people don't see themselves clearly." I peer at her meaningfully. "*Some* people think that simply because they don't have a lot of money or fit into a certain size of jeans that they aren't good enough." A single brow arches high on my forehead.

Grace shoots me a dry stare. "I get where you're going with that, but *I* am no Gia."

"You two aren't the same person, but that doesn't mean you don't have just as many admirable qualities." I raise my hands in surrender before I ruffle her feathers beyond repair. "I'll stop there. Just food for thought."

"I'll keep that in mind," she says with a smirk.

We walk for several seconds in silence before I launch us into a new topic of conversation. One I'm hesitant to share but know of no one else who would fully comprehend my jumbled feelings on the matter.

"I ran into Z yesterday."

All of us kids used to play together when we were young, though I was closer to the boys than Gia or Grace. She wasn't as affected by Zeno's transformation, but she consoled me through bouts of tears and knows what I went through. She knows about our years of awkward encounters and my endless frustrations, and unlike Gia, Grace will offer to help me spike his coffee with a laxative rather than lecture me about being understanding.

"And?" she prods.

"He would have incinerated me from existence if he could have. I just don't get it. He looks at me like I killed his dog and hung its severed head on my wall, and every time we're together, he finds a way to point out my family is nothing but staff. At this point, it's hard for me to deny his arrogance. All I can figure is that he's worried someone might think he has a relationship with *the help*."

"What an ass."

"No kidding. If he's worried about me crushing on him, he's got another thing coming. I wouldn't date him if he was the last man on earth. Not after the way he's behaved over the years."

We emerge at the waterfront and slow our pace to admire the sweeping view.

"Fortunately, you don't have to put up with him for long. Once you're back in the city, you can do whatever you want." Her voice was edged with nervous excitement.

"Are you still considering moving?"

She bites her full bottom lip and nods. "I've crunched all the numbers, and it may take me a bit longer to finish saving the money, but I think I can do it. The biggest hurdle is the initial cost of getting over there and finding a job, but I'm almost ready. If I'd been better about saving over the years, I would already be hunting for apartments. Oh, well."

I clap my hands and jump with excitement surging up inside me like little champagne bubbles. "Oh, Gracie. I'm so excited for you! Anything you need, just let me know. I'll help you move or whatever you need."

"Don't get too excited yet. It'll still be a while, but it's in the works." The tightness in her smile and the glimmer of nerves in her eyes speak to how desperately she wants this new adventure and how anxious she is about making it happen. Grace and I are both twenty-seven years old. If I were her, I'd be itching to get out of my parents' house as well.

I take her hand in mine and squeeze. "You'll make it happen, Grace. I know you will."

"Thanks, honey. Your support means the world to me."

"Of course, I support you! Now, we better head back to the house. I'll need to head to Hardwick soon." I roll my eyes and sigh dramatically.

Grace giggles. "You better keep me posted on how that goes. I want to hear *all* about it."

When we get back to her parents' house, the sun has risen up over the trees, and her dad is standing out front talking with Carter and Zeno beside a fancy four-wheel-drive golf cart. All three men are casually dressed, which would otherwise be unremarkable had I seen Zeno in anything other than a suit since we were children. He looks like a corporate Grecian god when suited in sleek Armani, but formfitting jeans sculpted to his corded thighs are equally as mesmerizing, maybe even more so because of the rarity of its occurrence. A good three-piece suit may be the equivalent of sexy lingerie for men, but the gentle drape of a soft cotton shirt molded over muscle should never be discounted. The sight of a casual Zeno De Rossi threatens to scramble my brain.

It's fortunate I have absolutely no interest in him because the sight of so much masculine perfection might stir up a girl's hormones. Not me. Only righteous indignation here. Woman scorned and something about wrath. Yeah. That's it.

"What did your dad just say?" I whisper to Grace.

She eyes me curiously as we approach the men. "He said he wondered where we'd gotten off to. You okay?"

"Yeah. Shh." I grin and swath myself in feminine grace. "Hello, gentlemen. Is there something we can help you with?"

Mr. Larson waves his hand. "Not at all. Mr. De Rossi here was going to borrow some chairs and tables for the wake tonight, but they're in storage. I'm about to have a look at what condition they're in."

"It appears the rental company we contacted double-booked," Zeno explains. "Now, we're shy some seating."

"It won't be a problem, Z," Carter assures him. "We'll

get the chairs all cleaned up and brought over. You don't need to worry about a thing."

"Absolutely," Mr. Larson agrees. "I've got it covered. You can head on back. I'm sure you have plenty of other arrangements to be made." Then the older man turns back to me. "I hear you're helping out as well, Luisa. I'll bet that's a big relief for your mom."

"It is, and she's probably wondering where I'm at, so I better get to the house." I give a parting smile and start to turn.

"No reason to walk. Mr. De Rossi is headed that way. Surely, he wouldn't mind giving you a ride."

Zeno's gaze collides with mine.

My heart stumbles, skipping over beats and rushing blood to my face. It takes every ounce of my composure to formulate a coherent response. "Thank you, but the walk will do me good." My eyes stay locked with Zeno's, neither of us willing to withdraw.

"The temperature is already rising," Z points out in a low rumble. "If you're out for long, you'll burn."

"I appreciate your concern, but I'd say the heat is far *less abrasive* than a jostling ride in a cart. But thank you for the offer." With my parting jab at his own heartless words, I sever our connection and turn to Grace. "I'll see you later."

His hostile stare burns at my back as I walk into the knee-high grass.

I can't believe what I've done—thrown his words back at him like an armed grenade. He'll know now that I overheard him, assuming he cares enough to remember what he said. Would that bother him? I haven't the slightest clue where Zeno is concerned. All I know is that I stood up for myself, and the resulting high has me convinced I could conquer the world.

CHAPTER 6

WHILE OUR PARENTS ARE AT THE VIEWING, US GIRLS GO home to quickly clean up and change. There's not time for much, but I'm able to rinse off, fix my hair in some semblance of an updo, and add a thick layer of smoky eye shadow to make my blue eyes pop. After I dab on an extra coat of mascara, I slip on one of Gia's dresses and a pair of heels since I didn't bring anything appropriate to wear. We're close enough in size that it works.

Several guests are milling about when we return to the De Rossi house. Gia and I go directly to the kitchen to check on Cecelia and the food preparation, not that there is any concern. Mrs. De Rossi wanted us to participate as guests and not employees, so everything was kept simple—finger foods and self-service for the most part. We'll keep an eye on the food and bring out more when needed while still getting to visit with other guests. My parents, in particular, will appreciate the chance to catch up with people they haven't seen in years. According to my mother, Mrs. De Rossi had initially suggested bringing in caterers, but Gia and Cecelia jumped in and refused before Mom could get out her acceptance. Hosting Silvano's closest friends and family was their way of paying respects, as they explained it, which sounds just like Gia. I have no complaints. I'd prefer to have responsibilities because they give me an excuse to escape any small talk.

Once everything is set out and ready on the plaza outside, I wander back inside as Nevio De Rossi slips through the front door. While Zeno is rigid strength with sandy hair and shards of blue ice for eyes, Nevio is relaxed charisma shining from beneath espresso eyes and a single perfect dimple. He's rarely at his parents' house, so I've only run into him a couple of times through the years. He hasn't changed much from his youth, as far as I can tell. Nevio was the idea man. He came up with games for us to play and told stories better than anyone I've ever met. Even after Z stopped hanging out with us, Nevio and I were close. At least, as close as we could be, considering we went to different schools even before he left for boarding school our junior year. He and I are the same age while Zeno is three years older, but personality played a key role in our continued friendship rather than age. Being friends with Nevio was as easy as breathing.

The second our eyes meet, he flashes that trademark

dimpled grin. "Look who's here." He holds out his arms to draw me in for a hug, which I readily accept.

"I'm so sorry about the circumstances, but it's lovely to see you."

He pulls back and studies my face as though I'm a ghost come back to life. "I can't believe it's you. And you're every bit as beautiful as the last time I saw you, which was entirely too long ago."

The girlish giggle that tumbles from my lips is foreign to me, but that's what Nevio does to people. Women, especially. They flock to him by the dozens, or at least, they did in high school. I never could keep up with his latest interest. Knowing that side of him as well as I did kept me from developing any foolhardy attachments to him.

I wonder if he's settled down now that we're older. He's not wearing a ring. Not that I'm interested—just … curious.

"Did you make it to the viewing?" I ask.

"No, I came straight here. I'm not sure why people want to look at the dead body of a loved one. Seems morose to me. I choose to remember Dad without the smell of embalming fluids."

"Ah, well, I guess I can understand that. Your family is all still over at the funeral home, though."

"Perfect, I can get settled without any hassles. Zeno would prefer I wasn't here at all, so it'll be easier this way."

"I thought I was the only one." The snarky comment rolls off my tongue, but once it's out, I realize what Nevio has implied and am curious what he means.

Nevio grins devilishly. "Oh, no. He outright asked me not to come last night. Trust me, you're not alone."

I'm a little shocked. I knew the two weren't super close, but I didn't realize it was so bad that Zeno would keep Nevio from his own father's funeral. "That's awful. You have every right to be here." Not just the right, he should be welcomed home by his family. Is Zeno that jealous of his brother's easy nature that he can't stand to be civil even at their father's funeral? The absurdity of it balls my hand into a fist tight enough to risk leaving crescent-shaped marks in my palm.

Nevio takes my hand in his and coaxes my fingers to open. "I don't let him get to me, and you shouldn't either. Let me run up and put my bag in my room, then we can visit." He brings my hand to his lips, placing a tender kiss on my knuckles.

Butterflies tickle the inside of my chest, causing my breathing to stutter. "Yeah, you get comfortable. Then you can tell me what you've been up to lately."

"Be right back." He winks, then strides swiftly up the stairs.

He's only out of sight for a matter of seconds before the front door opens, and Elena De Rossi enters with Zeno towering behind her. Her eyes are glassy and tired, and her poor nose is red. I can't imagine how hard it would be to lose a husband so suddenly. How heartbroken she must be.

"Elena, I'm so incredibly sorry." I greet her with a hug, hoping she feels the sincerity in my condolences.

"Thank you, Luisa. It's been quite the shock, but it's

lovely to see you." She pulls back and smiles, sorrow staining her features.

"You just missed Nevio. He ran upstairs to get settled." My eyes flick to Zeno, curious for his response, but his face is inscrutable. Not a lick of emotion. I'm not sure what I expected—maybe a hint of strain from mourning his father. Perhaps irritation that his brother has come despite his wishes. *Something.* They say everyone grieves differently, but I'm not sure Zeno De Rossi has sufficient human emotions to grieve. I always thought he looked up to his father, which would make this all that much more painful, but on the surface, Zeno is all business.

"Oh, that's great news." Elena gently touches my arm. "Everything here going okay?"

"Perfectly smooth. A few guests have already begun to gather out back. I was going to help receive people while Gia kept an eye on the refreshments."

"You don't need to do that," Zeno announces. "I'll stay up here and greet people. You two head outside and mingle."

"Are you sure, dear?" his mother asks.

Z places a kiss on her cheek and offers her an uncharacteristically gentle smile. "Yes, I'm fine. You two go on." No matter how detached he may appear, he has a soft spot for his mother.

Seeing the briefest glimpse of his armor slip tugs at my conscience. He may have hurt me in the past, but his father just died. I would never be so uncaring toward anyone else in such circumstances. No matter how thoroughly he attempts to suppress his emotions, I know he has them. I know who he used to be underneath the stoic mask. He used to be my friend, and while I can't write off his mistreatment toward his brother and me, I also don't want to believe he's totally heartless. Maybe it's naïve of me, but my common sense of decency demands I show some compassion.

"You want me to bring you a drink and maybe a plate of food?" The offer tumbles from my lips without thought. It's the least I would have offered to anyone else who lost their father, and Zeno should be no different.

"Some water would be appreciated ... thank you." He seems almost as surprised by my offer as I am.

I nod and flee toward the kitchen to escape his penetrating gaze. Bottles of water sit on the counter, but they're warm. After a little digging, I'm able to find a chilled bottle in the back of the fridge. I wrap a paper napkin around the cold plastic to help with the condensation and head back to the front of the house. Zeno is greeting two couples, both in their mid-sixties by the looks of it. I pause, tucking myself away where I can watch them without interrupting.

Z shakes hands with the men and smiles appreciatively at their wives, accepting their condolences graciously. One of the gentlemen pats him heartily on the back while saying something they all nod to in response. Zeno motions toward the back of the house, and they wander off to join the gathering. When they are out of sight, his head falls back, and his chest heaves on a tormented breath.

His unguarded display of weariness draws out my own breath until my chest feels hollow and cold. My inner skeptic whispers that Zeno is simply annoyed at the imposition of hosting, but my gut is convinced that's a lie. Zeno isn't as immune as he'd like everyone to believe.

I step forward, drawing his gaze. Blue eyes, infinite as a clear summer sky.

"Here's your water. Are you sure you don't want anything else?" I extend the bottle, and our fingers brush in the exchange. Ribbons of electric current unravel up my arm and bury themselves deep in my belly, where a pool of warmth gathers. I do my best to ignore the sensation.

"No, nothing else." His voice is the gentle rumble of distant thunder, sending a chill down my spine.

I offer a thin smile and turn to leave.

"Luisa," he calls, hailing my attention.

I pause and peer at him over my shoulder.

"Thank you … for being here."

I don't know what to say. Shock ties my tongue. Instead, I nod and flee from the confusion that threatens to overthrow my system. I don't know what's going on. Why did he thank me if he doesn't want me here? Is he merely out of sorts, or maybe he's playing games with me? No, that doesn't seem right. I saw him moments ago when he thought no one was watching. He wasn't in a place to be playing games.

Even if it isn't a game, that doesn't mean he won't go back to being his aloof self as soon as his grief passes. He's shown me over and over who he is through the years; I won't let a couple of days of civility dupe me into believing he's something he's not.

I shake my head, trying to clear my jumbled thoughts. Stepping onto the flagstone patio, I spot Grace talking with

Gia and make my way over. Respectful of the somber mood, we greet each other quietly and fall into light conversation. In half an hour's time, the patio is teeming with people, all talking amongst themselves in a mostly reserved fashion. I spot a number of familiar faces—the governor and his wife, a woman I believe to be one of our senators and a handful of B actors and singers. I'm sure other famous people are present, but I'm not the best at names and faces. Regardless of who they are, there is one commonality among them all. Everyone around us reeks of money. Having grown up around the wealthy, it normally doesn't bother me, but even I feel out of place in this setting.

"Can you guys believe this turnout?" Livia hisses when she joins our circle.

I cringe. "Liv, it's a *wake*, not the red carpet."

"I *know*." She rolls her eyes and crosses her arms over her chest. "That doesn't mean it's not a great place to meet people." Her irritation suddenly fades, and her eyes brighten. "Look over there, by the pool. See that gorgeous guy with the tattoo on his neck? That's Renzo Donati, underboss of the Moretti family and *totally* available."

"How do you even know that?"

Liv shrugs. "I asked Daddy."

"Asked me what?" Dad appears unexpectedly behind us with Mom at his side.

"The names of the available deep pockets here tonight. I've got my sights set on Renzo. Think I'll go introduce myself." Her eyes are glued to her target, and I'm already feverish with embarrassment.

"Livia Banetti, don't you dare!" I hiss, then look at my dad for reinforcement.

Dad purses his lips and rolls back on his heels. "Livy, this really isn't the place."

Not exactly the admonishment I was hoping for.

"Come on, Tony," Mom cuts in. "If not here, then where? It can hardly hurt for her to say *hello*. Here, Liv, take my drink. It's always easier to flirt with a drink in your hand."

Jesus Christ. How do I share DNA with these people?

Dad says nothing as Livia strolls coyly in the direction of her target. I'm contemplating crawling under a table when a microphone clicks on, and tapping resonates across the crowd. We all turn toward the house, including Mr. Donati's group, effectively cutting off Livia's access to him. I breathe an enormous sigh of relief. Her efforts won't be thwarted so easily, but for the time being, it's safe.

"If I could have your attention, please." Zeno's commanding voice lassos the crowd, and I am no different.

My eyes are drawn to him and greedily consume his suited form. My ears strain in curious anticipation of what he might say. My heart falls to my feet when his searching gaze locks on mine.

One second.

Two seconds.

Three seconds.

The evening breeze tugs at strands of my hair, but Zeno's gaze is unnervingly steady. Only after the crowd has quieted does he clear his throat and release me from his hold. I take a shaky breath to center myself as he begins his address.

"On behalf of my family and me, I want to thank you all for coming here tonight to celebrate the life of my father, Silvano De Rossi." He pauses, his throat bobbing as if he's struggling with his words. "I didn't always agree with my father, but my respect for him was immeasurable. He was insightful, clever, passionate, and his loyalty was beyond reproach." Zeno's gaze drifts back to mine, his features hardening before he looks away. "He has touched all of our lives in ways we will never forget. But if he were here with us tonight, I'm confident he wouldn't want us to mourn. 'Life is about finding the silver lining,' he'd say. So please, raise your glasses with me in honor of a man who lived life with abandon and who will never be forgotten." He lifts a crystal champagne flute in his hand, the crowd mirroring his movement in a choreographed wave. "To Silvano." His voice thunders overhead.

"To Silvano!" A chorus of voices cheers to the memory of a cherished family member, friend, and associate. The voices are mostly buoyant, but sniffles can be heard all around. Nothing blurs together gratitude with sorrow the way death does. Even for those not particularly close to the deceased, the mix of emotions is unavoidable. I grieve for the family who is clearly hurting, but I am so grateful it's not my father dressed in his best suit, laying stiff in a silk-lined casket. The emotions are so intense that I even take a long look at my mother and say a silent word of thanks that my time with her is not yet over. These not so gentle reminders of our own mortality are a blessing in that way.

I wonder if Zeno feels the same. If this display of the fragility of life will spur him to embrace his brother and heal old wounds. I could only imagine that would be the ultimate silver lining for Silvano. For his death to unite his children. What father wouldn't want his sons to be close?

Judging by the way Zeno purposely ignores Nevio's presence as the family accepts condolences, not even death will bridge these troubled waters.

CHAPTER 7

"Gia!" The excited cry draws my attention behind me to where two kids have ambushed my sister in a double hug, a girl clinging to her middle and a boy giving her a shy one-armed side hug. The joy on Gia's face warms me from the inside out.

"*Boston, Emily,*" Cora Bishop hisses. "What did I say about behaving yourselves?" She yanks at their arms, tugging them away from Gia.

G tries to discreetly assure the kids that she appreciates their affection without further upsetting Cora.

"They're only children, Cora," Carter says in a soothing tone. "No one will begrudge them a little happiness at seeing a friend."

"They need to learn to be respectful at times like these.

They can't grow up laughing and giggling at funerals and such."

Carter's eyes darken unexpectedly. "They know all too well about loss and funerals, in case you've forgotten. Let them be." His clipped warning is the first backbone he's shown in my presence and helps raise him, in my estimation. His children lost their mother, so it's imperative that he protect and nurture them. The hole in their hearts will never fully heal from that loss, but the wound may be less destructive with the right influence.

I peer at my sister and the adoring way she gazes at the Bishop kids. Her forgiving, loving nature would be the perfect balm for their souls ... if fate would give them that chance.

"Gia, I think I need an introduction." I raise my brows at the two blond children.

"Of course! This young man is Boston, and he turned twelve last month."

I extend my hand with a broad smile. "Hello, Boston. It's lovely to meet you."

He grins bashfully, eyes flicking up at his father's approving smile.

"And this," continues Gia, "is Miss Emily. She is ten and going into the fifth grade in the fall." She says the last part with emphasis to impart the impressive nature of such an accomplishment.

Again, I extend my hand. "How exciting! Will that be your last year of elementary school?"

Emily shakes her head. "No, at my school, sixth grade is the last year of elementary."

"Ah, very good. You'll just get more homework once you move to middle school, so no rush," I assure her.

"That's what I keep telling her," Boston pipes in with the puffed-out chest of authority.

All of us adults, except Cora, of course, smile at the innocence of youth.

"Have you two had a chance to get some food?" Gia asks. When the two shake their heads, she scoops their hands in hers. "Come on, I'll take you over to the food table."

The three disappear into the crowd, giving room for Zeno to slip into our circle. I'd been too distracted to notice his proximity and wonder how long he's been standing there.

"Zeno!" The scowl falls instantly from Cora's face, which is now alight with devoted concern. "How are you holding up?"

"I'm fine, thank you." His response is respectful, but I get the sense he's growing tired of issuing the same assurances. "I hope everyone is enjoying themselves as much as can be expected. Did you try any of the champagnes?"

"Yes, and your toast was so touching." Cora's hand comes to rest over her heart.

Her antics make my skin crawl. I itch to scream at her to have some self-respect and stop throwing herself at the man. Instead, I down the remainder of my drink and let the bubbles burn all the way down.

"I see you were able to get a glass," Zeno directs at me.

Cora scoffs. "Not everyone knows how to appreciate a good vintage."

If it wasn't for your ridiculous simpering, I could have sipped the champagne as it's intended. "Who says I didn't appreciate it?" I shouldn't make a big deal about her rudeness, not here in the middle of a wake, but I never could keep my mouth shut when it came to standing up for myself. Cora may have learned she can push my sister around, but I am not my sister.

"It's not your fault." There's condescension in her tone, and I can't wait to hear what she says next. "How often could you possibly have had an opportunity to drink a good Dom Perignon?"

I flash my teeth in a caustic grin. "Fortunately, I don't have to have it often to appreciate it. In fact, I'd say the opposite is true. Being accustomed to luxury would likely make a person more apt to overlook it, whereas someone who has little access would cherish the tiniest taste of opulence."

"Don't look now, Z, but I believe Miss Luisa is calling us spoiled." She cups her hand around his bicep and leans against him to emphasize their mutual station in life. And the manner in which she used my name is not lost on me either—patronizing, as though she's referring to a child. She believes herself so far above me that I'm surprised she can see me at all.

Zeno chimes in before I can shoot back a reply. "I'm not so sure that she did, but either way, she's free to think of us as she will. People have always assumed a great many things about me. That doesn't make them true." He makes his statement without looking at either of us. His comment was technically directed at Cora, but I take it upon myself to respond.

"People have to formulate their own opinions when questions go unanswered."

Zeno's arctic eyes collide with mine. "And that is an unfortunate consequence over which I have no control."

"It's not in your control to correct them?" I should stop and leave him alone. His father died, for Christ's sake, but words leap from my mouth without my consent.

"No," he bites. "It's not."

A sweltering tension descends between us, making my skin too tight for my body. Only Cora is left standing with us, and she fidgets as though our exchange has made even her uncomfortable. Seconds tick by in silence until someone swoops in and saves us.

Nevio, the antithesis of awkward discomfort, uses his superpower of congeniality to lift the oppressive tension from around us. "I saw you three from across the way and thought I'd join your little conversation, but now, I'm not so sure."

I flash him a relieved grin. "Oh no, now that you're here, you're stuck." His levity is exactly what we need.

Nevio drapes his arm around my shoulders and tucks me into his side. "I can't think of anyone I'd be more delighted to be stuck with. Right, Z?" He's being sweet, yet I get the sense he's also goading his brother.

My smile falters a touch.

Zeno's lips never even twitch. "I'm sure you'd love to catch up, but I believe Luisa has responsibilities to tend to."

His dismissal stuns me. I'm not even a paid employee, and we were encouraged to mingle tonight, but he's sending me to work? Is this some kind of reminder that I'm beneath him after I challenged him before?

"Well, then"—Nevio's tone is laden with defiance—"I'll just have to help her with whatever she needs to do."

"I'm afraid that won't work. Too many important people are here who we need to talk to."

Nevio chuckles darkly. "You're the one poised to fill Dad's shoes, brother. I'm nothing but a mere soldier in this organization. You've seen to that. Nothing I say to anyone here will be of consequence."

"We are not discussing family matters here." Zeno's words bite like the end of a whip. He's growing noticeably more agitated, and I am increasingly more uncomfortable being used to come between the two men. This is not the time or the place.

I pull out from beneath Nevio's arm and rest my hand on his chest. "There's no reason to argue. I'll be here for the rest of the week, and these people are only here tonight. I wouldn't be comfortable keeping you from them. Do what you need to do, and we'll catch up later."

His eyes are as dark as the starry sky overhead and equally as fathomless. Nev may be more charismatic than his brother, but both are endlessly complicated. I can't tell if he'll push the issue further, and my nerves fray with the uncertainty.

Eventually, he offers a regal bow. "As you wish." His nod to my absolute favorite childhood movie, *The Princess Bride*, earns him a beaming smile. I can't even believe he remembered. Nevio winks, allowing me to relax, then follows his brother's lead into the crowd.

As soon as they go, I escape toward the kitchen, breathing a deep gulp of cleansing air. The tension from multiple awkward conversations has seeped into every part of my body, including my lungs. I've been taking shallow, measured breaths like a rabbit caught between two wolves. The replenishment of oxygen makes me slightly dizzy. I smile at the feeling. Maybe it's the champagne. Or a little of both. Either way, I'm free for a moment, and that's a relief.

I coast slowly past the refreshments table on the way inside to assess what needs to be restocked. When I enter the kitchen, Cecelia has retired for the night, and the place is empty. I load up a tray with provisions and make my way back to refill the food table. Once I've returned to the kitchen and rinsed the tray, I drift to the window where I can watch the party rather than rejoining the guests. It's peaceful in the kitchen. I can only hear a faint murmur of voices over the hum of the refrigerator. The lights strategically placed throughout the landscaping make a stunning nighttime scene. There aren't any houses right on the waterfront, so the lake disappears in the dark, especially when the moon is new as it is tonight. It's a perfect evening for a gathering. The stars are extra vibrant in the black velvet sky, and the evening air is a comfortable reprieve from the heat of the day.

At least one-hundred and fifty people are scattered

about the flagstone plaza. I'm pleased that so many of Silvano's friends and family could come together. A man who impacted so many people should be honored properly. I recall a time when I was maybe six years old and had wandered over to the De Rossi house in search of the boys after Gia and I had gotten into a fight. Nevio and Z weren't home at the time, but instead of returning to my own house, I wandered onto the Hardwick plaza to entertain myself. I wasn't ready to go back and face my sister, so I used water from the stone fountain to finger paint fading designs on the flagstone. Silvano must have noticed me playing alone, which was unusual when so many kids lived nearby, and joined me by the fountain.

"I believe there's chalk in the garage somewhere—that way, your drawing doesn't disappear quite so quickly."

I've heard Mr. De Rossi yell at his boys, so I know he can be scary, but right now, his voice is calm and soothing, so I'm not worried. If anything, I'm surprised he's come out since he's usually busy with work.

"I like the way it fades. That's the cool part," I tell him.

He nods as though he understands now. "What are you drawing?"

"A house for myself without my sister where I'm the only one who gets to play with the toys. She says I mess up her doll's hair and won't let me play with it, but I don't. I always brush her hair carefully."

"Ah ... now I understand."

"Gia's just being mean cause she's older than me."

"Well, I suppose you could move into my house. It would mean never seeing your sister again—no birthdays or Christmas

mornings with her. No riding bicycles or painting with her. And you two share a room, right? You'd have to sleep all by yourself."

I look up at his huge house behind us. It's fun to play hide-and-seek in, but I'm not sure I want to be there all alone. No more Gia? No cuddles at bedtime. No singing while we clean up our room together. No sharing treats or laughing at cartoons together. No more Gia hugs.

When I look back at Mr. De Rossi, I can barely see him through the tears.

He squats until his eyes are right in front of mine. "Sometimes we get angry, but we forgive our family. Always. They are the best part of our lives."

I nod. "I'm gonna go home, now."

He smiles, and I take that as my cue to leave. I run all the way back home. When I step through the doorway to the room I share with my sister, she's on the bed, crying.

"What's wrong?" I ask, confused why she'd be upset.

Gia sits up, eyes round. "I'm sorry I got mad. You can play with my dolls."

Dolls forgotten, I run to the bed and climb on, wrapping my arms around my big sister.

Mom found us an hour later, asleep on the bed in each other's arms. It wasn't the only fight we ever had, but it was the last time I wished away my sister. Silvano had a way with people, even children. He was good at hearing people, which is a rare quality to possess.

Lost in the memory, I don't notice someone entering the room until a throat clears behind me. I startle, hand on my chest, when I whip around to find Zeno leaning in the kitchen doorway.

"I'm sorry to frighten you. I just wanted to see if you needed any help."

"I thought you and your brother had to mingle with your guests." *Away from the help.* My sympathy for his loss shrivels as I recall his arrogant refusal to allow Nevio time with me.

"Whoever thought it was a good idea for a grieving family to host a party was a masochist." His lips thin with the attempt at a smile. "It's fine if I'm gone for a few minutes." He's allowing me to witness how drained he's become over the past few days, a glimpse into his struggles. It's been unquestionably challenging, and I realize I haven't given him much grace. Someone in the midst of a crisis should not be judged according to their behavior during that time.

Yes, but why would you cast me away to the kitchens in front of my friend, then sneak away to help me?

Confusion puts me off balance, so I say the only thing that comes to mind. "I don't think I told you yet, but I'm sorry about your dad."

Pain, unfettered and raw, lances through him. "I've heard that so many times tonight, and every time I express my appreciation, put on a brave face, and assure people we're managing well ... that everything is fine. But it's not. There's nothing fine or fair about this." His agonized words hang in the quiet between us, filling the gaping distance. Neither of us moves to step closer to one another, though we are at opposite ends of the room. There's a safety to our distance as if a protective bubble exists around us and neither of us wants to risk upsetting the balance.

I can't tell what's unfolding between us, but I'm entranced and don't want it to end. No matter how angry he makes me, there will always be an even larger part of me that desperately wants to call him a friend again. I can't fathom why after so many years, but it's the truth. The hint of an olive branch from him assuages years of hurt and confusion.

"You're right. It's not fair at all," I say softly. "Life is utterly unpredictable—that's why we have to make the most of each moment we have." To forgive and forget. To embrace our families and hold them close even when we're angry. His father was the one to teach me that.

"And what would you have me do to make the most of this moment?"

My eyes glance out the window to the gathering of people. "You could take advantage of the opportunity to see family."

"And if I don't want to go out there?"

I peer at the pile of bowls and flatware in the sink, then bite my lip with a smirk. "There's plenty of dishes to be washed."

Zeno huffs an almost laugh, then slips his suit jacket off his shoulders. He deposits the jacket over the back of a chair and rolls up his white shirtsleeves to his elbows before ambling toward me.

I can't believe this is happening.

Have I stumbled into some alternate universe where my life is unrecognizable? A week before, if I'd been told I'd be back home doing the dishes with Zeno De Rossi, I would have fallen over laughing at the absurdity. Yet here I am, sliding on an apron before handing Z one of his own.

"Can't have you getting all dirty."

"A little dirt never hurt anyone," he murmurs. "Now, where do we start?"

We work in companionable silence for a half hour. Even if I knew what to say, I wouldn't want to interrupt the moment. I'd planned to leave the mess for Cecelia to clean in the morning, but there'd been something compelling in Zeno's manner that overrode my petty grievances. He'd offered up a rare showing of vulnerability. I hadn't stolen this knowledge by watching him covertly. He'd come to me with his shields lowered, something he hadn't done for years.

We get most of the dishes either loaded in one of the two dish washers or cleaned and set on towels to dry. No one interrupts, and for once, our history is forgotten. We are simply two people helping each other complete a necessary task.

Once I've hung up my apron, I wander back to the window. "People will start leaving soon. You should be there to say goodbye."

He's quiet, so I turn back to see what he's doing and find him staring at me. The intensity radiating off him sends a zing of adrenaline through my veins.

"You have your father's smile," he rasps softly. "You don't much resemble him otherwise, but when you smile, it's impossible to miss."

It's such a random comment, I'm not sure how to

respond. Since I adore my daddy, I choose to take it as a compliment, which draws out the very smile he mentioned … that is, until Zeno winces in response.

"I need to go." He slips his jacket back on without looking at me. "Thank you for the distraction." His eyes flit to mine just briefly before he flees the room.

I'm left in utter dismay, totally at a loss.

CHAPTER 8

"Isa, honey, it's time to get up."

My eyes feel glued shut, heavy with sleep. If light weren't pouring in through the windows, I could swear I'd laid my head on the pillow only minutes before.

Gia is sitting on the edge of the bed wrapped in a towel with wet hair hanging limp on either side of her face. "It's time to get ready, sleepyhead."

"Ugh," I groan. The funeral. "I hope you have something for me to wear because I got nothin'."

"We can scrape something together. Now get up before one of the others beats you to the shower." Her reminder of our limited bathing resources spurs me into action. Two bathrooms for a single family may sound reasonable, but when four sisters are trying to get ready at once, it's a nightmare.

I manage to snag the bathroom, still steamy from Gia's shower. The scalding water brings me back to life, especially when I run through all that happened the night before. I told Gia the basics of what had happened after we'd curled up in bed last night, but talking it through with her hadn't provided any further insight into the situation. Zeno's contradictory behavior has left me even more confused than ever. I don't know what to think, but I decide that maybe there is no conclusion to draw. Maybe this is a time of grief, and there is no logic or reason to anyone's actions. I'd like to believe his attitude toward me is changing, but that may not be the case.

No matter the source of his behavior, my visit home has become more than I bargained for—confrontations with the man who broke my heart as a child, and now, a funeral. Will the good times ever end?

We load into Mom's 4Runner, and everyone's remarkably quiet. I give thanks for small miracles because I'm not up for drama. After Livia threw a fit about having to change when Dad rejected the short skirt she'd picked out, we are all running a bit late and low on patience.

The church parking lot is already packed when we arrive. Cars will be parked down the street for blocks once the service begins. That's the way it is for someone of such importance as a Mafia underboss. Silvano's death will draw in family, both blood and otherwise, from all over the country.

We make our way into the sanctuary and select one of the few remaining pews with open seats. Mom is seated next to me, and I notice she keeps scanning the crowd, craning her neck to look at new arrivals every few minutes. Her odd behavior sets me on edge. I find myself peering over my shoulder without any idea why.

"Who are you looking for?" I ask in a whisper, growing irritated.

"Huh? No one. Just curious who came." She sits back casually, but I don't buy it. With Mom, there's no telling.

I glance around one more time and note many of the faces from last night, but the service today includes even more people, most of whom are unfamiliar to me. The procession to the gravesite will require a large police presence to navigate traffic, which is always odd because families like ours don't mesh well with cops. Sending Silvano off with a police escort seems wrong, but our funeral train will be far too long to execute without assistance.

Within minutes, it's standing room only in the church. The mood is somber with a respectful undercurrent of reunion as many people greet old friends for the first time in months or even years. Sorrow and gratitude, hand in hand, make yet another appearance.

The ceremony lasts almost an hour. Zeno speaks briefly, along with his mother. Yet again, Nevio does not say a word, and I wonder if that is his choice or if Z refused him the opportunity.

A priest conducts a short Mass, and Christiano De Bellis, the boss of the Giordano family, gives a respectful speech about his former second in command. He's somber, but I don't get the sense he caters much to emotion. He rose to become boss for a good reason—ruthless power resounds in every word he utters.

Eventually, we all filter back into our cars and take the slow, winding drive out to the cemetery. Marca and Livia chatter in the car, but I hardly pay any attention. I'm lost in a sea of my own thoughts.

As we exit the vehicle at the graveside, I swear I see my mom take a swig from a flask. If she were truly struggling with grief over Silvano's death, I could understand, but I've watched her over the past couple of days and know she isn't overly affected.

"Mom, are you drinking?" I ask once I've got her out of earshot of the others.

She shoots a glare at me. "That's not any of your business." With her attention fixed on me, she stumbles in the grass, catching her footing before she falls.

I help steady her, recalling when she slipped away during the funeral service to go to the bathroom. She'd also been surprisingly quiet on both car rides. "Exactly how much have you had?"

She yanks her arm from my grasp. "I'm allowed to be upset. It's a funeral."

"Everything all right over here?" Zeno appears from thin air, his voice a quiet warning. "Of course, Z," Mom gushes, suddenly all sunshine and rainbows. "We were just talking about finding the Larsons. Luisa here has always been such good friends with Grace, the poor girl." She leans in as if imparting a great secret. "She would be such a cutie if she wasn't so chunky."

"*Mom*, that's enough." Mortification isn't sufficient enough to describe how I feel. If I could, I'd jump into Silvano's casket and let them bury me with him. Judging from the heat blazing across my cheeks, they have to be bright red.

Swallowing back any semblance of pride I may have had, I turn to Zeno and attempt a smile. "Everything is fine. I'm sorry if we were drawing attention." I tug my mother toward the crowd and pray he doesn't realize she's tipsy at his father's funeral. I don't know what's gotten into her, and I'm afraid to find out.

We manage to locate the Larson family among the crowd and stand with them beneath two majestic oak trees. The graveside portion of the service is short, with only a few words spoken by the priest, yet somehow, it makes me even more heavyhearted than I was at the church. So few can witness a casket perched above a deep hole in the ground while grief-stricken families struggle to breathe without sharing in the pain of the experience.

Once the elegant silver box is lowered beyond our view, Elena steps forward and tosses a single red rose to be buried with her husband. The act reduces her to sobs, her face crumpling with heartache. Zeno places a hand on her shoulder, a surprisingly cold gesture considering their relationship and the circumstances. Nevio, with tears in his own eyes, pulls Elena against his chest, wrapping her securely in his arms.

Was Z trying not to look soft in front of his fellow made men? I can't imagine why he would be almost robotic with his mother when she was so distraught. Last night, he'd been almost tender with her, but now there's no sign of that Zeno.

The crowd slowly dissipates over the course of a half

hour. Some people feel the need to pay their respects to the family, while others simply drift back to their cars to leave the family in peace. Daddy makes no move from our spot beneath the trees, so neither do we. I've peered at him countless times throughout the morning and can't fathom what he must be going through. He looks ten years older than usual today, but there is no other trace of emotion. It's almost as though the loss has overwhelmed him to the point of emptiness. The sight makes my heavy heart break wide open.

I go to his side and take his warm, calloused hand in mine without saying a word. His fingers squeeze mine in return, assuring me that he's in there … somewhere.

The Larsons stay with us, along with Carter and Cora Bishop. They all talk quietly, but I stand silent in solidarity with my father.

Nevio is the first of the family to free up and come our way. His bloodshot eyes draw me toward him for a hug. I don't want to sever my connection with my dad, but Nevio is just as troubled. He was there for his mother, and I want to be there for him because Lord knows his brother won't be.

"I'm so sorry," I whisper.

He nods and pulls back, taking my hands in each of his. "I just wish we'd been closer while he was alive." His soft words are directed at the ground, only loud enough for the two of us. "Zeno found ways to make sure that never happened. He was even the reason I was sent to boarding school. Did I ever tell you that?" When he peers up at me, there's turmoil in his mocha irises.

I'm stunned—at a loss for words for several seconds. "No, I had no idea. I thought it was all about grades." How could this be the first time I'm hearing about this? Why hadn't he said something long ago?

Because he was gone before you knew what happened, then your paths rarely crossed.

I suddenly feel like a wretched friend.

He smiles, but there's no humor in it. "Grades were the story they told everyone. It's only ever been about Zeno. That's why I'm rarely ever here anymore; no point in coming home when I'm unwelcome here."

I have so many questions, but this isn't the time or place to pick at old wounds. He's suffered enough today. All of them have.

I squeeze Nevio's hand and look back toward my family to discover Zeno has joined them, and to my horror, Livia is chattering his ear off.

"I told Mom last night that it was so great having such a large gathering at Hardwick that you should have them more often. Maybe a Fourth of July barbecue or something."

Holy shit. Did my little sister just tell Zeno she had fun at his father's wake?

I cannot even begin to understand how her mind works. All she thinks about is what Livia wants and what's best for Livia. She doesn't care that others are grieving, and her petty machinations are beyond embarrassing. Her words are out faster than I can apologize on her behalf. And if that isn't bad enough, my mother voices her hearty agreement.

I glance at Gia in a silent plea for help. Her eyes slowly drift shut with embarrassment.

Zeno may have no tolerance for his brother, but he manages to remain polite, if not a touch austere, with my family, though heaven knows they don't deserve it.

"The house hasn't seen company like that in a while. Next time, hopefully, we'll be celebrating something much more uplifting." His eyes drift to mine, an inscrutable energy passing between us before his gaze drops to where my hand still clasps his brother's. When his stare reconnects with mine, the link is no longer present, and I'm met with cold indifference.

I feel cut off and dejected in a way I can't explain. A part of me wants to yell at him and demand an explanation. Why should it bother him if I hold hands with his brother? He couldn't possibly be jealous. He's never shown the slightest sign of interest in me. How can you be jealous over something you don't want?

"Zeno, Nevio, Antonio." Christiano De Bellis joins our circle and nods at each man in greeting. "And this is Gemma if I recall correctly." He extends a hand toward my mother, who tosses her red curls and grins.

"Yes, it's lovely to see you."

"And these are your girls, Antonio?" Christiano peers at all of us.

"The four here, yes. Gia, Luisa, Livia, and Marca. And these are our neighbors, the Bishops and the Larsons."

We all smile and wave.

"Lovely young ladies, wouldn't you say, Savio?" He draws a finely dressed young man into the group, who smiles graciously and nods his greeting. "This is Savio, my nephew. Antonio, you haven't been to the city in a while, but Savio is one of the young men looking to take over the most recent organizational vacancy." He's being vague because outsiders are present, but the rest of us are all aware he means Silvano's role as underboss. Someone will need to take over soon.

"That would be quite the honor," Livia says with a coy smile, seemingly oblivious that Zeno is the other capo vying for his father's old job. For those of us who know, the situation is endlessly awkward. Why bring up something like that at a funeral? Either Christiano was insensitive or he'd done it on purpose to goad Z. Either way, it makes him look like a jerk.

Savio nods and smiles but doesn't say anything further about his ambitions. Instead, he offers Zeno a private word and a handshake of condolence. He appears to recognize how uncouth his uncle's statement was and doesn't wish to dig the hole any deeper. My first impression is that I'd like him if we ever had the chance to talk. Some of the Mafia sort can be self-important, but I don't get that sense with him. I'm not sure how that would bode for a future as boss. A certain degree of arrogant ruthlessness is central to the role.

"The whole family appreciates you both coming out," Zeno interjects. "I hope you'll be staying for lunch at the house."

"We have to get back to the city, I'm afraid," Christiano says. "I've got a meeting with some important people, and

I'd like Savio to join me." He looks smug, and it makes me want to knock him on his ass.

Zeno's eyes blaze with intensity, but I'm not sure if it's anger, jealousy, or grief stoking that fire. When he speaks, his words give no hint at emotion. "I'm sure he'll be an asset at any negotiation."

"Yes, and it's important I give thorough consideration to all my options before I make a decision."

"I know you'll do what's best for the organization. Now, if you'll excuse me. I need to get back to the house and check on our guests." Zeno's words are clipped, as though he's reached his capacity for tolerance. Without waiting for an answer, he turns to collect his mother, who had migrated to the grave for a final private moment with her husband.

The rest of us offer our goodbyes to Christiano and Savio before returning to our cars. I am bone-weary as I plop into the back seat, but our day isn't even half over.

CHAPTER 9

"You okay, Daddy?" I had thought I'd run upstairs and freshen up after we made a brief stop at home before going over to Hardwick, but when I spot my dad standing on our porch, staring into the trees, I have to check on him. He hasn't been himself all day, even taking into account his grief.

He's quiet, and we both listen as a breeze rustles the leaves on the trees around us.

"These past couple of days, I've been thinking a lot about how I've led my life and the things I could have done differently." He gives me a sad smile and wraps an arm around my shoulders. "I ever tell you how we ended up here at the cottage?"

I rack my brain and realize he hasn't. "I guess I assumed Silvano needed someone, and you offered to take the job."

"Not exactly. We were young when we got married—your mom especially. I was twenty-three, and she was only eighteen. Nowadays, having a baby before you're married isn't uncommon, but back then, it was still frowned upon. Your mom got pregnant after we'd been dating for only a couple of months."

My jaw grows slack as my father proceeds to rewrite the history of their relationship, erasing the doctored story I'd been told while growing up and had believed wholeheartedly.

"I had no money and was new to the family, but Silvano took me under his wing. He'd moved up the chain of command quickly and had become a top-ranking capo in his mid-thirties. He'd gotten married two years earlier, in part to position himself to be underboss. He bought Hardwick to solidify his roots and give his new family a place to grow up alongside the other powerful residents at Tuxedo Park. Zeno was born close to the time they moved in, and Silvano recognized his need for help at the house. He wanted someone who was connected and knew I was in a situation. He approached me one day and said that if I planned to marry your mom, we could move to the cottage rent-free and work for him. I love the city, but I couldn't pass up the opportunity for my kids to grow up in a place like Hardwick." Dad pauses, turning his sad eyes to meet mine. "Who knows what would have happened without Silvano's intervention. He changed our lives, and ... I ... I'm not sure I showed him the gratitude he was owed. Now he's gone, and I can't do anything to right the matter."

I'd been told from the time I was little that my parents

were madly in love, so much so that they'd eloped only months after meeting. Gia was born within a year, but it had never occurred to me to question the timeline. To question whether they'd ever loved each other in the first place.

I feel like time and space are colliding to warp the world around me until things I've known all my life suddenly look unfamiliar.

"Did you want to marry Mom?"

Dad's face softens. "Your mom has a vivacious spirit that's infectious, even more so when she was younger. I knew she'd always keep things interesting, and I got you out of the bargain, so I have no regrets."

That wasn't exactly a yes. My parents' relationship was never one I would strive to replicate. They lead mostly separate lives, and Dad usually can't be bothered to deal with Mom's antics. They aren't partners so much as roommates, but that didn't seem so problematic when I thought the relationship had originated out of love. Now, I wonder if my dad has lived his entire adult life in misery.

"I just want you to be happy, Daddy."

"I am, Lulu. Especially when you're here." He squeezes me affectionately as Mom steps out the front door in leggings and a T-shirt.

"Are you not coming to the lunch?" I ask with surprise.

"I'm not feeling so great, so I'm gonna stay home and rest. Elena won't miss me with so many others there, but you can call if you need me." She crinkles her chin in a show of remorse, eyes dancing between the two of us before she slips back inside.

I look at Dad, my brows tightly knitted. "What's going on with her?"

Dad sighs. "No idea. Come on, let's get the other girls and go."

ELENA HAD INSISTED on a catered lunch so everyone could attend the funeral without worry. Gia can't help but check on things as soon as we enter the house, but otherwise, we are off duty. The luncheon is elegant yet casual. White linens hang from round tables set up all over the plaza. Each table is adorned with an artfully designed floral centerpiece and eight flatware settings. A buffet table sits at the far end of the plaza along with a drink station and a small table filled with desserts. Some people eat while others mingle, and a few children play in the grass off to the side.

Carter and Cora are already seated at a table and wave us over when we step onto the plaza. More precisely, Carter waves us over while Cora sips on her water and pretends not to notice us.

"Have you already had a chance to eat?" Gia asks, accepting the seat Carter pulls out for her next to him.

"No, we wanted to wait for you all."

"I'm so sorry you had to wait, but that's very thoughtful of you. We ran home to freshen up. Mom wasn't feeling well, so she stayed at the house."

Carter's brows furrow. "I hope she's not sick."

I'm pleased to detect genuine concern. He isn't simply

saying the polite thing or feeding Gia what she wants to hear. He really cares about people, which is an unusual quality in my experience.

"I think the past few days have overwhelmed her. Nothing to worry about." Gia smiles. "Let's get some food. You've waited long enough!"

He helps her again with her chair, and I exchange a glance with my dad. He shrugs, and I stifle a laugh. We each fill our plates, then return to the table and eat. Conversation is easy, which is a relief. With Mom absent, both Livia and Marca manage to be on their best behavior. That or Liv is simply preoccupied scoping out the guests for potential dates. Either way, lunch is a pleasant change of pace, and I'm thoroughly grateful.

Livia is the first to finish and excuses herself from the table. I'm not sure where she's hurrying off to, but I'm afraid to ask, so I don't question it. Marca stays seated with a frown. I get the sense she wanted to follow her sister but was refused. I have no doubt Marca is much better off right where she is.

Minutes after Liv disappears, Zeno wanders over to our table.

"Z, we have a seat open here. Why don't you join us?" Carter stands and motions to the unused place setting Mom would have occupied had she been with us. The seat next to me.

His eyes shift from my father to me before he stiffly lowers himself into the white folding chair. My teeth grind together at his palpable discomfort. After witnessing his ability to be civil, his irritability toward me feels like an even greater affront.

Maybe you should sit next to Cora, who is equally as disappointed with her present company.

"I can't stay long. I'll need to check in with my mother. Today has been exceptionally hard on her."

I could tell you were worried by the way you didn't comfort her at the funeral. I have to bite my tongue to keep my thoughts to myself. I'm tired of the whiplash I get trying to keep up with his moods. One minute, he's opening up and helping me, and the next, he can hardly stand to occupy the same breathing air as me. My patience is wearing thin far faster than it should, considering he just buried his father.

"Surely, you have enough time to get a plate of food," Carter says.

"No, I'm not hungry. I hope you've enjoyed everything, though."

"Of course," Cora coos from across the table. "Everything has been lovely today."

"Excellent," Z murmurs. His eyes lift to mine but slice away as if I've somehow sent him a telepathic electric shock. "I have to get going, actually. Make sure you get some dessert before you go, and if I don't see you before then, thank you all for coming."

"You're leaving?" I blurt, my control finally shattering.

I'm sick of feeling like a leper in his company, especially when we're around anyone else. He can't get away from me fast enough. And if that isn't bad enough, he forces his brother away as well, like he doesn't want my taint to spread to anyone in his family.

"I have over a hundred people at my house right now. I have obligations," he says tersely.

I lean in and whisper, "I don't believe it has anything to do with that."

Zeno turns to the others with a tight smile. "If you'll excuse us, please." He stands and wraps his long fingers around my upper arm, carefully tugging me along with him as he leaves the table. He doesn't stop until he's dragged me through the French doors of his office and tucked us away from prying eyes. We stand inches away from each other, his towering form caging me with my back to the drapes.

The waters in his oceanic eyes are raging when he blasts me with his stare. "Do you have something you'd like to say to me?"

My chest rises and falls as I struggle to catch my breath—not from the walk but from the adrenaline surging in my veins. A cataclysmic storm has been brewing between us since the moment I came home.

Maybe even for years.

I've tried to be tolerant and understanding, considering he lost his father this week, but my own hurt has grated away at my patience. "Your need to escape our company ... *my* company ... has nothing to do with checking on your mother or any other responsibilities." The bottled-up emotions I've been carrying spew out with my words.

"Then what exactly are you implying?" He's so close. Close enough for me to smell the spice of his cologne and feel the fiery heat radiating off him. He's nearly as furious as I am, but he's doing his absolute best to rein in his temper.

Good. Let him be angry.

Let him show me proof that the friend I grew up with is still in there somewhere behind the heartless machine he claims to be.

"I think you're arrogant—too proud to be seen with the help. *That's* your problem—your damn pride. You want to become king of the Giordano family and can't possibly associate with a lowly soldier and his family. You're hardly near us for two minutes before you can't wait to get away. *That's* what I think."

I expect my attack to instigate an all-out war, but it has the opposite effect.

A veil of placid indifference falls in place over Zeno's features. The tendons no longer strain in his neck, and the fine lines of fury gathered at the corners of his eyes simply vanish.

The change is instant and absolute.

When he finally responds, his words are a jagged cliffside, coarse and brutally sharp. "I don't want to be your family. You're absolutely right. But if I'm to blame for the situation, then it is my *loyalty* rather than arrogance at fault. Loyalty drives me to forgive when I cannot forget because family is everything. If you think me weak because of it, that is *your* problem. Do not pretend you are without flaws of your own. Your intentional ignorance keeps you from seeing life's truths. If our mutual shortcomings combine and lead you to conclude that I am something I'm not, then little can be done to correct the matter."

Zeno takes a slow step back before turning and stalking out of sight into the hallway.

I feel as though his departure has stranded me alone on a small island. I am bereft, and I don't know why. My hands tremble as I look around with unseeing eyes and attempt to sort through what happened.

He mentioned forgiveness, but what had been done to him to require his forgiveness? Who had hurt him? Surely, he couldn't mean me. I'd done nothing but act as a punching bag for his bad temper.

I think back to that painful week when our friendship ended, but just as I have tried countless times before, I can't identify the reason for his rejection of me. He insinuated I was failing to recognize something obvious, but how could I possibly change that if he didn't give me a hint? If arrogance wasn't behind his behavior, what was?

I slump helplessly onto the worn leather sofa in his father's office. It may be Zeno's office now, but the room hasn't been touched. It holds tight to his father's memory. Mementos sit on shelves along with books and framed photos of a happy family. The essence of him is so strong in this room that I almost feel like he's still here. Still alive.

"What am I missing, Silvano?" I whisper, only to be met with silence.

CHAPTER 10

Zeno, Age 14
Luisa and Nevio, Age 11

"Why do you guys always have to play Halo?" I groan, *flopping onto the sofa in the game room at Hardwick. The boys got a new Xbox 360 for Christmas and have been glued to it ever since. Some of the games advertised on TV look fun, but I don't like any of the games the boys have—mostly shooter games and race cars. Blech.*

"Because it's awesome," Nevio says without taking his eyes *from the screen. "Why don't you go play with Grace if you don't like Halo?"*

"She went to Connecticut for Easter to visit her aunt. The whole family went."

"And Gia?"

"She asked Mom to show her how to use the sewing machine." No idea why. I'd rather do a million other things before I'd ask to learn how to sew. So dumb.

"Hey!" Nevio cries. *"Why'd you pause it?"*

We both look at Zeno, who stands and tosses his controller on the couch.

"How about I go find the old Game Boy for you, Isa? I think we still have the Mario Cart game with it. Would that work?"

I grin so wide my cheeks ache. "Yeah, that works." Z is the best. If I had a brother, I'd want him to be exactly like Zeno.

He gives me a knowing smirk and jogs out of the room. For the next several minutes, I deal with Nevio moaning about his game being interrupted. I throw a pillow at him, which instigates a pillow fight. We shriek and chase each other around the room with sofa pillows clasped in our hands. I get a particularly savage strike in and laugh hysterically as Zeno returns in the corner of my vision. When I look at where he stands frozen in the doorway, my grin melts from my face.

"What's wrong?" I ask, ignoring Nevio's return strike to my gut.

"You need to go home." Zeno's body is rigid, and his angry glare makes me feel six inches tall.

"But the Game Boy? I thought we were all hanging out." My voice is barely a whisper because I don't understand what I've done to be sent home.

"Now, Luisa!" he yells, pointing at the door beside him.

Zeno is scaring me. I glance beside me at Nevio, who looks confused as well. There's an apology in his eyes, but he doesn't argue with his brother. All I can do is tuck my chin and slink from the room, hoping his bad mood passes quickly.

I want to cry as I walk through the spring grass on the way home, but I don't. Instead, I veer from the worn path and walk down to the lake. I need to be alone. I spend at least an hour skipping rocks along the smooth surface of the water, wondering what I did to upset Zeno. Whenever I think of how he glared at me, my chest feels hollow, and I want to curl into a ball.

Midmorning the next day, I walk to Hardwick and slip in through the kitchen door like I always do, making sure to tell Cecelia good morning. I'm equal parts nervous and hopeful about seeing Zeno. Even when Nevio makes Z really mad, it only ever lasts a day. I have convinced myself that whatever got into him will have passed, and we'll all hang out today like usual.

I find the boys together in the main family room, watching TV. "Hey, guys. Can I watch with you?" My gaze darts warily back and forth between them.

Nevio turns to smile at me briefly. "Sure. The Scorpion King is on."

Zeno doesn't tell me to leave or acknowledge my presence at all, for that matter, so I find a spot on the large sectional away from him and turn to the screen. Not even five minutes later, Z pushes off the sofa and storms from the room.

"He still upset?" I ask Nevio.

"Yeah, he's been extra quiet. No idea why, but I wouldn't worry about it. He can be moody like that."

I wish it were that easy. I can tell in my gut that Z is upset with me, and I want to fix it. Zeno's anger feels so much worse than when Gia or Grace get mad at me. Maybe because he's older and cooler. I don't know. I just want to make it better.

We continue watching the movie for almost an hour before I can't stand it any longer. I have to go find Z and apologize.

Nevio doesn't take his eyes from the movie as I slip from the room. The house is quiet, especially once I'm upstairs away from the sounds of the TV. The silent hallways at Hardwick are always a little creepy, but I'm more scared of Zeno staying mad at me than anything.

When I get to his room, the door is shut. I knock softly, not wanting to bother him but knowing I have to do something so that we can be friends again.

"What?" Z barks from inside.

"It's Isa. Can I come in?"

I stand in the huge hallway while a nearby grandfather clock ticks away the seconds. Could Z be so mad that he'd never talk to me again? I wait long enough until I begin to give up and am about to leave when the door creaks open.

Zeno stands tall above me. Taller than I remember him being, though I see him all the time. His anger makes him look enormous and a little scary. "This isn't going to work anymore, Luisa. I'm not interested in hanging out with the housekeeper's daughter. Plus, you're a kid, and I'm a teenager. That's the way it is, so you need to get over it." His voice reminds me of a dog's warning growl. There's no hint of teasing on his face or in his words.

Zeno is telling me he's done being my friend.

I blink back tears and push past the ache in my chest. "But ... what about this summer—bike rides, and hide-and-seek, and climbing trees, and..."

"That's not my problem. Maybe Nevio will play with you." Zero emotion. In fact, the more upset I become, the angrier he gets. Too angry for me to argue with him.

He's cutting me from his life the way Daddy trims weeds from our garden, and I can't do anything about it.

I turn and walk toward the stairs, speeding my stride with each step I take. By the time I make it outside, sadness leaks from my eyes in heavy droplets. I walk home, each step heavier than the last. It takes me a full half hour to make the short walk. By the time I reach our front door, I want to crawl under my bed and cry for days.

Z NEVER FORGETS HIS ANGER, *no matter how many times I try to reach out.*

One week later.

One month.

One year.

I've lost my friend forever, and though I don't cry about it anymore, the loss of his friendship is like a broken bone that won't heal. Reminders of him are everywhere, stirring up a dull ache when I let myself remember how much fun we used to have. Sometimes, I wonder what would have happened if I'd simply played Halo *with them instead of fussing. But it's pointless to think about because I did fuss, and nothing has been the same since.*

CHAPTER 11

"Mind if I join you?" Gia pokes her head out the door to where I'm sitting on the back porch.

"Not at all. In fact, there's something I wanted to tell you about."

"How intriguing. I'm all ears." She sits on the bench next to me with her knees angled toward me.

"I was talking with Nevio after the funeral today, and he implied that somehow Zeno was responsible for him being sent to boarding school. Do you know anything about that?" I'd been thinking about what he'd said all afternoon and about Zeno's comments as well.

"No, but I wasn't ever as close to them as you were. Zeno had already graduated and moved out when Nevio went away. How could he have been responsible?"

"I'm not sure. I could have sworn I was told he left

because of grades, but he said it had nothing to do with that. He didn't say anything more, and I wasn't going to push him while we were standing at his father's graveside."

"Of course, not. I'm surprised he even mentioned it."

"He was upset about not being closer with his father. Says he blames Zeno."

Gia sighs into the night air. "Those guys were always competitive, and Z was Silvano's mini-me. I could imagine that was hard on Nevio. He and his dad butted heads all the time—Silvano never could understand Nevio's laid-back temperament. Look at their positions in the family. Z has advanced faster, and Nevio probably feels like he lives in his brother's shadow. I can't imagine my father being my boss and knowing he refused to promote me above an entry-level position while my brother was poised to take over."

"Very true. Though, that doesn't exactly explain how Zeno could be responsible for Nevio being sent to boarding school. I don't know what happened, but I hate that something obviously came between them." *Between all of us.*

"Maybe when the time is right, you can ask one of them."

"We'll see. It's a conversation that needs to take place in person, and I'm not here very often. Who knows what kind of mood they'll be in over the next couple of days."

"Speaking of moods, you never did tell me what you and Z talked about after lunch. He sure seemed upset."

My shoulders sag. "I lost my temper and made some

accusations. He said words of his own. It wasn't particularly pretty."

"Oh, Isa. I'm sorry." Her delicate hand comes to rest on my forearm, and I appreciate her understanding.

Unfortunately, her empathy connects with the emotions I've been battling to keep suppressed and enables them to push to the surface. My chin quivers, and tears pool in my eyes.

"It's just been a crazy couple of days, and I wasn't prepared." The words are spoken on a breath because my voice has abandoned me.

Spending time with Zeno after only the briefest of encounters for years is an emotional landmine. To learn he's pushed Nevio away as well makes me want to rage at him even more. Then there's my family. The issues beneath my parents' roof are so vast I want to run back to the city to hide from the oppressive weight of it all. Gia and her hopeless longing. Livia's inability to consider anyone but herself. And now, my parents' marriage was little more than a sham.

Coming home has been so disheartening that I'm already dreading future visits. I'll still come back, but the thought is daunting, and I hate that. I want to look forward to spending time with my family.

Gia scoots closer and pulls me into a hug. "Don't cry, Isa. Everything will work out, I promise." She's using her most comforting mom voice, and it's almost enough for me to believe her. I desperately want to believe her.

"I'm okay, just tired." I squeeze the last of the tears from my eyes before pulling away and wiping the moisture from my cheeks. "Thanks, G. You always find a way to make me feel better."

"I'm glad because I can't stand to see you cry."

I smile reassuringly. "Such a softy."

"Guilty. Now, if you're okay, I'm going to head to bed. You coming?"

"Let me text Grace, and I'll be up." She'd reached out hours ago, but I'd been too distracted to reply.

"Sounds good." Gia kisses my forehead and disappears inside.

The woods are dark, but the kitchen light casts a soft glow on the patchy grass beyond the back porch. Most of the other lights in the house are off. Mom and Dad went to bed an hour ago, and Livia has yet to come home from wherever she disappeared to.

After checking my phone, I respond to Grace's message asking about the day without going into detail about Nevio's comments or my encounter with Z or my father's revelations. Those are conversations better had in person, but I'm not sure I even want to do that. Partly because I fear giving voice to my worries will make them all more real. Other parts simply feel too personal. Maybe once I sort things out in my head and figure out how I feel about it all, I can share, but until then, the things I learned today will stay with me.

I stand and stretch, my body tight from sitting on the hard bench for so long, then quietly make my way inside. As soon as I shut the back door, I hear whispered voices coming from the living room. I strain my ears and realize there's only one voice—my mother—and she's talking frantically to someone on the phone. Unable to help myself, I silently move closer until I can make out her end of the conversation.

"I told you, I'll get the rest ... No, you don't need to do that ... but ... I'm not being difficult, I swear ... Okay ... A week? ... There's no way ... Please, Aldo ... Aldo?" She's quiet for several counts before her fist pounds the sofa, and she hisses a string of curses.

I peer around the corner at where she sits perched on the edge of a sofa cushion, her small body forlornly curved in on itself with her head dropped back, eyes cast skyward. She looks despondent, but it only makes me angry. I hate that she's the reason Gia can't move on with her life. If my mother could get her shit together, maybe she could have been a real mom and not leave that for her eldest daughter to take on. The daughter she'd never meant to have.

"What was that all about?" My voice is a deadly blade slicing through her moment of self-pity.

Mom shoots upright, her face sculpted in innocence. "Hey, Lulu. I didn't realize you were down here."

Obviously. "What was the call about, Mom? It have anything to do with why you've been selling things?" I'm not letting her leave this living room until she tells me the truth.

She stands and waves a hand at me as though I'm being silly for asking questions. "It's nothing. I borrowed a little money from a friend, and she needs it back sooner than I expected."

"How much?"

"How much what?"

"*Jesus*, Mom! Don't be difficult. How much damn money do you owe?" I want to smack the wide-eyed look right off her face. It's an act, and it's wasted on me.

Like any animal being forced into a cage, she lashes out. "Don't act all high and mighty around me. Just because you're getting some fancy degree doesn't make you better than us."

"And you're not going to redirect this conversation. Tell. Me. What. You. Owe."

Her lips purse and eyes narrow as she studies me, weighing her next move. My inflexibility on the matter must register because her chin lifts defiantly in preparation for her surrender.

"Originally, it was fifteen, but I paid off five, so now it's down to ten." She straightens a stack of magazines nonchalantly on the coffee table as if she's just told me about tomorrow's breakfast options rather than unloaded a financial bomb in our living room.

"Are you talking … thousands?" My mind is utterly blown. "You owe ten *thousand* dollars to someone?" How does that even happen? They don't pay a mortgage or rent. Three of their daughters are grown and should be independent. They have one car between them and never travel. Had Mom racked up ten grand in debt from merely buying shit?

My legs want to give out, but I have the upper hand and refuse to hand it over to her by looking weak.

"You never worried about my finances before, so there's no reason to start now. You'll go back to the city and your fancy life in a few days, so it's not your problem anyway. Forget about it."

I want to listen to her. I don't want to make this my problem, but I have to. Something about the way she panicked worries me. Mom gets herself into all kinds of predicaments and always brushes them off. This is different. Something about this debt has Mom worried.

"Who lent you the money?" This time my words are eerily soft.

I know I've hit the crux of the problem when her lip trembles. She slowly sits down on the sofa, her eyes intently studying her fingers as they fiddle with a hole in her leggings. There is a sincerity to her actions, but it won't gain my sympathy. Whatever mess she's in, she got herself there. I may assure her and even help her, but I won't feel sorry for her.

"His name is Aldo Consoli. He's ... he's a bookie. I make a bet here and there, nothing major. I gave it a try one time because there was this Fendi purse I *really* wanted, but I knew we could never afford it. I figured, what does it hurt to chance a couple of hundred on a bet? Instead of buying a crap purse I didn't want with the money, I'd use it to at least try to get the bag I wanted. And I did it—I made five grand from nothing. It's the most incredible feeling, Isa, like winning the lottery. I got the purse then made a couple more bets with the rest of the money. I won three more grand and felt like I was on top of the world, but then I had a bit of a dry spell. Things didn't go so well for my next few bets, but a race was coming up that I felt great about. I *knew* that would get me back in the money. I felt so good about it ... I still don't know what went wrong. One minute, I was swimming in cash, and the next, I was fifteen k in the hole."

A bookie. There never was a friend. She owes money to a *bookie*.

Fuck.

Fuckfuckfuckfuckfuck.

This is so much worse than I assumed. Ten grand is a lot, but ten grand to a bookie is serious trouble. My stomach churned into an angry knot as her explanation unfolded, and now, there's a real chance I might vomit.

"This ... Aldo—he's associated with *the family*, isn't he?"

She nods, and I have to keep myself from lunging at her and wrapping my straining fingers around her throat.

When someone on the street doesn't pay their bookie, they can end up dead, but Mom is technically a part of the family—she's protected as Dad's wife—but that means Dad assumes her debt. They won't kill a member of the family over a debt, but they could easily rough him up. And maybe even worse, he'd be disgraced forever. As if not advancing past soldier at his age wasn't bad enough, my dad would be labeled a deadbeat.

"Does Dad know?"

"No, and he doesn't have to." She jumps up and rushes over to me. "I'll find a way to pay it off. I'll ... I don't know, but I'll find a way."

"*How*, Mom? How the hell are you going to come up with ten grand in a week without Dad knowing?"

Her brows knit together as she chews on her bottom

lip. "I don't know, Lulu." Her helpless whisper claws at my skin. I'm so angry I could scream.

"Don't call me that. Don't you ever call me that again." Lulu has always been my father's nickname for me. That's how Gia pronounced my name when I was born, but it became my dad's term of endearment for me. I don't want her tainting something so special. "This conversation isn't over, but I'm going to bed. I can't deal with this right now."

I've had more than I can take for one day.

I leave the room without waiting for a reply. There's nothing for her to say. When I finally make it upstairs, Gia is already in bed, sleeping peacefully.

I envy her. Sleep won't come easily for me tonight.

Needing to at least try to relax the tension now coiled in my muscles, I take a hot shower. The heat soothes my body, but it does little to wash away my fears. I can't bear to let my dad suffer such a disgrace. The thought alone sends a bolt of searing pain through my chest. He's only ever done what he thought was best for his family; he doesn't deserve to be humiliated, no matter what the family code of honor says. It's not his fault my mother is irresponsible and selfish.

Once I'm dried off and in an oversized pajama shirt, I crawl into bed with my worries. They haven't subsided, but at least I'm more disheartened than angry. Unfettered rage makes for a poor bedtime companion.

I close my eyes and try to drown out my thoughts when I hear a sound in the hallway. The only people upstairs should be us girls, so I immediately assume Livia has finally come home. She's old enough not to have a curfew, but I wasn't crazy about her disappearing without a word. I tell myself that arguing with her now is beyond my capacity, and it's best if I let it go. Then I lay, straining to hear more sound, wondering if it was her at all. Maybe it wasn't, and she's still out. Maybe she's been hurt.

I sigh deeply and slip from the bed. At some point, I'd think my brain would be exhausted with itself and quit, but no such luck.

The bathroom door is shut with the light on. I test the knob and find it's unlocked. When I open the door, Liv is sitting on the side of the tub, half-naked with her red curls plopped in a messy pile on her head. She looks so much like Mom and is equally as bad at making decisions for herself. It hurts my heart to witness.

"Lu-*ees*-a," she hiccups with a blinding grin. "What are you doing up?" Her words are slurred but not enough for me to worry about alcohol poisoning. Some of the scathing comments I'd considered die a quick death when I realize she's drunk. No point in arguing with a drunk Livia.

"Hey, little sister," I whisper. "You been having fun?"

She puts her finger to her lips as if telling me to be quiet when she's the one with the volume problem. "I've had such a lovely night." Her eyes drift shut as she smiles again.

"I'm glad to hear it, but you never told anyone where you were going. That's not safe, you know."

"Don't be such a Worry McWorry Face. Everything is going to be fine. You … you take my word." She struggles to take off her bra and put on a sleep shirt as she talks. Watching her is rather entertaining, but I give in and help.

"Some of us have to worry because *others* of us don't worry enough."

"There's no need, silly. I'm going to marry someone rich, rich, rich! So why worry?"

"Orrr," I draw out. "You could make your own money and not rely on someone else to take care of you."

Livia collapses into a fit of giggles, snorting, then snickering some more. "You're so funny, Lulu."

Apparently, everyone was going to resurrect that nickname tonight.

"All right, Livy. Let's get you to bed."

I help her up and get her tucked in before returning to the bathroom to tidy up. When I crawl back into my own bed next to Gia, I am well and truly exhausted. My worries finally coalesce into a fat, gelatinous blob in the back of my brain, enabling me to hide from them for the moment. I focus on Gia's slow, even breaths, and before I know it, I'm drifting into a deep, dreamless sleep.

I HAVEN'T FELT *this well rested in ages.* It's the first thing I think as I stretch in bed. I must have slipped into a coma because I feel like I've slept for a week. When I open my eyes, I confirm that the sun is well into the sky. I've slept much later than I intended. Now that the funeral is over, I don't need to help my family with work, but I still hadn't meant to sleep half the day away.

After I roll myself out of bed, I pull on a pair of booty

shorts and give my teeth a quick brush before confirming I'm alone in the house.

Thank God. I need a few minutes of peace and quiet. No drama. No more surprises.

I slip a pod in the Keurig and open my phone to start scrolling on social media when a knock sounds at the front door. My parents don't get many visitors, especially unexpected visitors, since guests have to be approved at the gate. Assuming it's probably Mrs. Larson stopping by to see my mom, I open the door wide. Only, it's not Mrs. Larson. It's not anyone I know.

"Can I help you?" I ask warily, crossing my arms over my chest when I remember I don't have a bra on.

The man on our front porch grins the most seedy, serpentine grin I've ever seen. His black hair hangs down over his forehead, and his eyes are a smidge too close together. He's not big, but somehow, he's not any less intimidating for it. If he were walking toward me on a sidewalk, I'd find a reason to cross the street.

"That depends. I'm looking for Gemma, but judging by those eyes, you must be one of her girls."

Most people don't think I look a ton like my mother because I don't have her billowing red curls, but my eyes and nose are just like hers. That never bothered me before as much as it does right this second. I don't want this man to find me familiar, and I especially don't want to bear any resemblance to the woman I call a mother.

"They're at work right now." I study the man to sort out who he is, but in my gut, I know. This is the bookie my mom owes money to. The reason she was scared out of her mind. "Are you Aldo?"

He rocks back on his heels with a grin that makes me want to pumice my eyeballs. "Hey, look at that. It's like I'm famous. Your ma tell you about me?"

"Not exactly. How did you get past the gate?"

His tongue plunders his teeth like he's got the holy grail stuck back there. "You got a lot of questions for a girl. You wanna go on a date, we can *talk* all night long. Right now? I got some business to handle."

I say nothing. I certainly don't want to go on a date with this creep, nor do I want to piss him off. He accepts my silence for the rejection it is, shrugs, and continues.

"I've been in the area for three days for this damn funeral, and I wanted to get this shit with your mother finished by the time I went home, only she's managed to avoid me at every opportunity. I'm gettin' real fuckin' sick of chasing after her."

So that was why Mom was so out of sorts the past few days. That was why she was drinking and why she bailed from going to the luncheon. She was hiding.

"I heard her talking to you last night on the phone. I thought she had another week to pay you."

The corner of his mouth fish-hooks up in a smirk that bleeds into a snarl. "No, sweet thing. She was asking me for another week. I told her she better get my money by to-fucking-day."

"And if she doesn't pay you?" I can't totally irradicate the fear from my voice.

"I suppose that's between your pops and me."

"Look, he doesn't know anything about this, and I don't want him hurt because of it. What if … what if I helped my mom pay her debt? If I promise I'll get you paid by the end of this week, would you give me that time?" I'm not sure what I'm doing, but I have to at least try to buy more time.

Aldo's lecherous gaze drifts down my body, my skin itching with the invisible stain of his touch.

"I'd give you all sorts of things if you asked nice enough."

I desperately want to slam the door in his face, but I know I can't. "Time. All I need is a little time, and you'll get your money."

"Suit yourself. End of the week, no more extensions." He winks and turns away, calling over his shoulder. "I'll be in touch." He doesn't have a car in the driveway, but he could have parked it down the street to catch Mom off guard. Or maybe he jumped the wall around Tuxedo Park, and that was how he got in. All I know is I'm glad he's gone.

I shut the door and bolt it, leaning back against the aged wood and sliding down to my bottom. My knees bend up toward my chest, and I hug my legs as though I'm a little girl again. I feel like I could be. These mounting problems weigh too much for my shoulders—as though I need an adult to come rescue me. But it's an adult who got me into this mess. My own mother. Now, I have to find a way out for all of us.

CHAPTER 12

I NEED TO FIND GIA AND TELL HER WHAT'S GOING ON.

Forgetting all about my coffee, I throw on some clothes and start toward the back door. It feels safer, like Aldo might still be waiting for me out front. And with that thought, I detour to my parents' bedroom and grab one of my dad's pocketknives. I can't be too cautious where Aldo is concerned.

Fucking creep.

I open the back door and almost pass out when there's someone on the other side. Nevio's fist is raised as though he were about to knock, but my already frayed nerves elicit a momentary panic that I'm about to be attacked. I shriek and flinch, slamming the door shut in his face. Recognition registers seconds too late, and when I open the door to apologize, poor Nevio is still wearing a look of shocked confusion.

"Oh my God, I'm so sorry!" I start to laugh at the absurdity of my morning.

"You okay? I didn't mean to startle you." He flashes that signature smile, brows drawn up good-naturedly.

"Yeah, I'm totally fine—just didn't expect someone to be standing there." And now that my brain has caught up with real time, I process that Nevio has come by the house. Not only has he stopped over for an unannounced visit after years of not seeing each other, but he's come to the back door, which all strikes me as a tad unusual, but not totally out of the question. When we were kids, we always let ourselves in and out of the back of our houses because it was easier than walking around to the front, and as children, we weren't encumbered with a need for formality. But we're adults now, and as far as I know, Nevio hasn't been to our house in ten years.

"I thought I'd stop over to visit. I would have called, but I don't have your number."

"You're right. I don't think we've ever exchanged numbers." I pull out my phone. "What's yours? I'll shoot you a text."

He reads off the digits, and I'm hopeful we'll stay in better contact.

"I was about to walk over to your house in search of Gia. You can keep me company on the walk."

"Absolutely."

I make sure to lock the door behind me before

following Nevio into the grass. "I didn't get a chance to ask before. How long will you be staying at Hardwick?"

"I suppose that depends on a couple of things," he muses.

"Like what?"

"Like how long you'll be here." The honesty of his answer startles me, and I'm not certain if he's sincere or merely being his flattering self.

"Oh, yeah?" I glance over to find his warm brown eyes already watching me, and I can't help the smile that creeps across my face. "Surely, I'm not the only factor in that decision."

"You play a bigger role than you might think. I spent a lot of years trying to get you out of my head, but after seeing you again, I'm not sure what I was thinking."

My stomach bottoms out with his words.

Am I reading into his meaning? Did he mean to imply he had a thing for me back then? That he *has* a thing for me now?

I'm stunned speechless for a solid minute. "Nev, what are you saying?"

We slow to a stop, my eyes searching his face for a semblance of understanding. Growing up, we'd been close, but it never went beyond anything but friendship. When he left for boarding school, I didn't have a cell phone of my own yet, so we couldn't text, and we didn't call or write very often. I missed him, but my life was full with friends and school such that I moved on quickly. It never occurred to me he harbored deeper feelings for me.

I don't know what to say. Ten years is a long time. I'm

not as idealistic as I was as a girl, but he still seems to be the same carefree playboy he's always been. That's not exactly the type of man I go for at this stage in my life. Maybe back then, if I'd known how he felt, but now … I'm not so sure.

Nevio raises his hand and gently guides a lock of hair behind my ear after it escaped from my hastily plopped bun. "I'm saying I've missed you and would love to spend a little more time with you. I normally don't like coming home, but with you here, I don't want to leave."

I smile and look anywhere but at him as I'm engulfed in an ocean of awkwardness. "I'll only be here for a couple more days."

"It's a chance to reacquaint ourselves. That's all I'm asking." He eases us back into our walk, which is not overly hot now that a line of clouds has overtaken the sun. "I'd love to hear more about your life in the city. Where did you end up settling down?"

"Over in Brooklyn. I'm finishing my degree in English lit at St. Joseph's. I'm a little older than the average student, but I've been paying my own way, so it's taken me some extra time. Not to mention, I got a late start."

"Hell, I'm impressed you went after what you wanted and are achieving it. Not everyone can say they've done that." He smiles warmly at me. "I remember how much you loved reading. English lit sounds perfect for you. Are you wanting to teach one day?"

"That's the part I haven't totally figured out. I've been so concentrated on getting through school that I haven't had a chance to fully consider what I'll do once I'm done." That's not totally true. I know what I want to do, but I'm just not sure how to make it happen. I want to write my own stories—create my own characters and watch them evolve into multidimensional people—but the process is daunting, and I'm not sure I want to tell anyone until that first book is complete. The pressure I put on my own shoulders is more than enough. I'd rather not have to bear the expectations of others as well.

"That sounds perfectly reasonable. I don't believe anyone can truly know what they want from their lives until they've lived a little. If I'd gone to college, I wouldn't have had any idea what degree program to pick. That was one of the perks of having my life already decided for me."

Both De Rossi boys had followed in their father's Mafia footsteps, but I'd always assumed that was because they wanted to and not for any other reason. The suggestion that my assumption could be wrong shocked me.

"Were you forced to join the family?"

"No, not exactly. It was more like an expectation, and I wasn't a fan of school, so going to college was never an option. I could have lived off my father's money easily enough, but then I'd have felt like even more of a failure than he and Zeno already thought I was."

"Why would they think that?" I balk.

"Why were both of them always hard on me? My father didn't think I was tough enough, but Z just had a stick up his ass. He wanted to be the favorite and saw me as nothing but competition." His words are spoken with a cool impassiveness that reminds me of the hard layer of ice coating a frozen pond, hiding the treacherous water below. Nevio was concealing a world of raw emotion centered primarily around his brother.

"Yesterday, you mentioned something about Zeno being the reason you were sent away in high school." I'm feeling a little awkward about pushing for an explanation on such a delicate subject, so I technically don't ask a question. I figure he can take the hint and offer an explanation or sideswipe the issue entirely if he chooses. He was the one who brought it up in the first place, but still, I don't want to intrude on a private matter.

Nevio shows no signs of being uncomfortable, launching into his account of what happened so many years ago. "Z started acting funny his senior year of high school. He was distant and more uptight, but he also began to work for the family, so I assumed he was acting tough to fit in. He wasn't around much, and while I missed the friendship I'd had with my brother, there was little I could do to change matters. You and I were only around fourteen at the time and starting our sophomore year. After Christmas, everything got so much worse."

"I remember that Christmas. Mom let us have Bailey's in our hot chocolate—it was the first time I got a little drunk. Or at least, what I thought was drunk. Now, I'd say I was barely tipsy. I remember laughing our asses off." The memory brings a broad smile to my face.

Nevio smiles as well, but his eyes bear a sadness to them at the same time. "That's one of my absolute favorite memories. Unfortunately, it's followed by one of my worst. Two months after that, I overheard Z talking to Mom and Dad about me. He insisted that I needed more discipline and that the only way I'd stay out of trouble was to be sent away to school. He argued specifically for a military school on the West Coast. I couldn't believe what I was hearing. My own brother was trying to exile me from the family for no good reason. I wasn't getting in trouble at school or making bad grades; *he* was the sole instigator. It's the same reason he didn't want me here for the funeral and asked only this morning when I'd be leaving." Nevio looks at me, pleading in his eyes. "Can I be totally honest with you, Luisa?"

"Of course, you can."

He glances up at the house looming before us. "He's never said anything directly, but in my gut, I'm certain it's always been about you."

"Me?" I blurt, totally caught off guard.

"I don't want to put you in an awkward position, but I want you to know the truth. To understand. I think you and I were getting close, and he saw that, so he found a way to keep me away from you. It didn't click with me until years later. I had a lot of time to think while I was away at school, and it's the one thing that made sense. He wanted a clear line drawn between our family and anyone he deemed *lesser* than. I told him once that I wanted to ask you out, and he told me I was a fool. That I'd end up like your dad, stuck at the bottom of the organization with no hope of success. I told him he was being absurd. I think he was stepping in to make sure nothing developed between us. He probably thought he was protecting me, but it wasn't his call to make."

I'm dumbfounded. It makes sense in a way, but it's still

hard to imagine someone could be so shallow. "Why would he be so narrow-minded? Our parents are friends. We grew up together."

Nevio shrugs. "Dad groomed him from the day he was born to lead the Giordano family. There's no telling what he said to Zeno to warp his thinking. Being friendly with a soldier's family is one thing but marrying into it is another."

I shake my head in wonder that anyone could cling to such archaic principles. I wonder if that's what happened that day so many years ago. Had he run into his father and been given a reprimand about hanging out with me? It's all so odd. People marry whoever they want—Mafia jobs aren't some makeshift caste system. At least, I'd never gotten that impression. But once I start thinking about it, I wonder why Dad never did advance to a capo's rank. If Silvano saw him as inferior due to his job and hasty marriage, that could explain it. It's a question I've never considered, but now, the need for an answer feels imperative.

"It's strange to think I could have been so wrong about people. Your dad was always kind to me, and I thought he and my father were friends, but I'm starting to wonder if I knew anything at all."

Your intentional ignorance keeps you from seeing life's truths. Is that what Zeno had meant when he'd said those words? That I was turning a blind eye to reality in regard to our stations in life?

"Dad wasn't all bad, but he wasn't always a good man, either. Now that he's gone, I hope his influence will fade.

He's the one who set in motion the plan for Zeno to marry the boss's daughter. Although Z will probably go through with it to honor Dad." He shakes his head incredulously.

My steps falter. "Christiano? *That* boss?" It's a stupid question—there's no other boss to speak of—but I'm so surprised that the words tumble from my lips.

"That's the one."

"Huh." The news is so shocking that I have no emotional response. None. Only confusion. What did it mean that there was a *plan* for him to marry someone? Was there an actual arrangement, or was it more of a matter of vague hopefulness? Surely, the two aren't in a relationship. She would have been at his father's funeral, and I never saw him with a woman—not in that way.

"Yeah. I can't say I envy him. I wouldn't want Christiano breathing down my neck every day of my life."

"The only time I've ever met him was briefly yesterday at the funeral." I didn't form the greatest initial impression, but I've tried not to let a quick conversation at a funeral color my perceptions.

"Consider yourself lucky. He's one ruthless bastard."

"Nevio! He's your *boss*. You can't talk about him like that." I can't help smiling a little, though. It's just like him not to care about protocol and speak his mind.

"It's the truth." He grins. "So, are you working at the house today?"

"No, I just need to talk to Gia. Any idea where she was when you left?" The reminder of my original purpose drops a wet blanket on any light-heartedness I'd found on our walk over. My steps are suddenly leaden as we walk up to the side entrance nearest the kitchen.

"No clue, but I'm happy to help you look."

My lips thin as he opens the door for me. "Actually, I need to talk to her in private. It's sort of a family matter."

He raises his hand. "Say no more. I don't need to intrude."

I appreciate his understanding and am relieved to find Gia in the kitchen, irradicating any need to go searching for her.

"Hey, you two," she says warmly. "What's up?"

"Mom here?" She tends to spend her work hours talking with Cecelia in the kitchen, so I'm surprised to find Gia instead. Her absence makes me wonder where Livia and Marca are as well since they weren't at home when I woke up. I'd been too inundated with chaos to question the matter until now.

"Dad had some appointment to go to, and Mom dropped the girls at the mall before going to lunch with a friend."

The mall. Great. I'm freaking out about how to pay Mom's debts, and the girls are at the mall.

"Gotcha." My eyes cut to Nevio, who gives the back of my neck a gentle squeeze.

"I'm going to make a couple of calls, but I'll see you later, right?"

"Yeah, sure." I smile half-heartedly, and when my gaze drifts from his retreating form to Gia's bulging eyes, I shrug. "It's been a seriously crazy morning."

She dries her hands on a dish towel and removes her apron. "I need details."

"Oh, you'll get details, but not the kind you're hoping for. Where can we go where we won't be overheard?"

"I know the perfect place. Come on."

She leads me to the old chapel—a tiny prayer room that's rarely ever visited. Two small benches are centered in front of a podium holding a gold cross backlit by a vibrant stained glass window. The room is good for the devout Catholic or a game of hide-and-seek, but that's about it. The air is musty, and only one of two lights flicker on when we enter.

Gia closes the door behind us and stares at me expectantly. "Start talking, lady."

"I needed to talk to you, but it's not about Nevio. I have no clue what's going on there. He indicated he had feelings for me when we were growing up, and they've come back. I'm not sure what to think, but none of that is important at the moment."

"It's not?" she gawks, confused.

"You know how you were worried about Mom selling stuff?"

Her lips thin, and wariness hardens her gaze. "Yeah?"

"Well, a guy showed up at the house earlier demanding money. She owes ten freaking grand to a bookie," I hiss the last part, my anger reigniting.

Gia's jaw falls open. "No," she breathes. "Please tell me you're joking."

I shake my head sadly. "I wish. She knew he was in town for the funeral and was avoiding him. He wants his money. I told him I'd help find a way to get it paid if he'd give me until the end of the week."

"Luisa, where the hell are you going to find that kind of cash?"

"That's why I needed to talk to you! I've got some, but I was hoping you could help too. This guy is a Mafia bookie. If we can't find a way to pay him, the debt falls on Dad."

My sister visibly deflates, overcome with dismay. "What do we do?" she whispers, eyes searching mine for answers. "I don't have that kind of money, Isa."

"You don't have anything saved?" She lives at home with hardly any bills. How could she not have any money?

She chews on the inside of her cheek, eyes dropping to the floor. "I used a bunch of my savings when I bought my car a year ago. Then there was an incident. Mom told me their credit card got hacked, and someone had spent a bunch of money on it. She said the credit company was demanding they pay for it and was going to file criminal charges. I had the money, so I gave it to her. I'm wondering now if she may have lied. I've barely put anything away since then."

"What's barely?"

"I have two thousand in savings." She grimaces. "I could sell my car, I guess."

She'd do it, too, but I can tell how much the idea pains her. She needs her vehicle just as much as Mom and Dad need their 4Runner, maybe even more because that's her sole source of freedom. And my parents' old SUV wouldn't help—I doubt we could get a solid five grand for it. Plus, if we sold the car, we'd have to tell Dad, and I'm not even sure we could sell it before the end of the week. Gia didn't say how much she gave to Mom, but it had to be sizable to empty her accounts. She's done so much; the last thing I want to do is ask her to forfeit the car she spent years saving to buy. Livia and Marca don't have any money, and I can't think of anything else to sell.

No matter how I look at it, I'm left with only one option.

My eyes close, heavy with the weight of my decision. "You've already helped her enough. I'll handle it." The hollowness of my voice is an outward reflection of the emptiness I feel inside. Too many emotions war for dominance—rage, desperation, anguish. I can't process them all at once, leaving me in a vacuous darkness.

"What does that mean, Isa?"

I open my eyes and meet her concerned gaze with resignation. "I'm going to use my school money to pay her debt. I have just enough saved to cover what she owes. Then I'm telling Mom we're done bailing her out."

"Should we tell Dad? I feel like he should know."

"He would be humiliated if he knew we'd been covering for her, but I don't want him hurt because of her either. If he doesn't know what's going on, he can't protect himself." A pounding headache starts to pulse at my temples. "We have a little time to think it through. Let's not make any decisions on that yet."

Gia pulls me into her arms, but I can't hug her back. A tidal wave of emotion threatens to drown me, and her affection will only draw it closer.

"What does that mean for you and school? Will you still be able to finish?"

I pull away and shrug. "It's taken me forever to get this far. What's one more year?" I put on a strong front because I have no other choice. On the inside, a part of me wants to scream and rage about the unfairness. "I'm going to head out and let you get back to work." I need to be alone. I need a moment to come to terms with my decision because that's what it is—a choice. I don't have to pay off Mom's debt. It's my choice, and that means I can't blame anyone but myself. That won't be easy, but it's necessary. I don't want to carry a chip on my shoulder for the rest of my life, and the only way to be free of that is if I believe the decision was mine.

"Okay, honey. We can talk more this evening."

I offer a broken smile before walking numbly from the room. I'm halfway to the lake before I even realize where I'm going. Nevio had talked about hanging out, and I have his number, but that's not an option at the moment. I have no capacity to even think about Nevio or Zeno when my entire life is in the process of derailing.

I have twelve thousand in savings—some from student loans, and some I've stashed away from each paycheck I've earned waitressing. Without that money, all my earnings would have to go toward rent, leaving me nothing for school. I would need all of my savings plus the three months of summer earnings in order to cover school and living expenses. There's no way I can make ends meet now. I could look into getting more student aid, but I've tried so hard to keep my loans at a minimum and already stress about repayment. Not only would this add more debt to my total but I'd have to take out my standard amount plus a bunch more to cover the money I'd earned at work. I'd have to spend an entire year working to replenish my savings enough to take classes.

The serene waterfront comes into view as something my sister said the first day I arrived plays in my mind.

I could get used to working with you. With Anna gone, we'll need to take on someone new.

If I moved back home and worked at Hardwick, I'd be able to save up twice as quickly. I could take a single semester off and be back in classes by January. But at what cost? I'd lose my fucking sanity living with Mom and Livia, not to mention I'd run into Zeno on a regular basis and have to deal with his infuriating arrogance.

Isn't finishing school worth it? It's not forever.

I heave out a breath, my shoulders slumping.

My internal monologue leads me to the only logical decision. I have to suck it up and do what is needed to get me back on track as quickly as possible.

I have to make Hardwick a part of my life again.

CHAPTER 13

THE GLASSY SURFACE OF THE DARK BROWN WATER SHINES with sunlight, reminding me of a storm cloud's silver lining. The water isn't crystal clear like the shores of the Caribbean. There's moss and silt, and the fish within wouldn't wow any children with their lackluster scales if displayed in an aquarium. But the lake is beautiful in its own way. The tall trees standing watch at its borders protect the water's edge like soldiers out front of Buckingham Palace. They seem to recognize the intrinsic pricelessness of the water, though they have no eyes with which to experience its beauty.

I lose myself pondering the wonders around me in an intentional effort to focus on the good parts of life so that I will not sink deep in the quicksand of despondency. Its spindly claws tug at my body each time my mind drifts back to my situation. Each time I think of calling my would-be roommate and letting her know I have to back out of my promise to sublet the room in her apartment. Each time I consider calling the school registrar and asking for a hold on my status as an active student. Each time I resolve to ring my boss and inform her that I won't be coming back.

Disappointment lives and breathes inside me, but I will not let it take over.

Something about the permanence of the lake gives me a wealth of reassurance. These few months that I'm stressing about are but a single season of rainfall to a body of water that has existed for possibly centuries. It's a welcome reminder that a handful of months out of what I hope will be a long and happy life will hardly be memorable in the long run.

Performing mental gymnastics to keep the proper perspective helps to some extent. I have assured myself that the world isn't ending, but I'm still not in a great headspace.

"Please, don't."

The rumbling command startles me for the hundredth time today. If this keeps up, I'm going to need a pacemaker to keep my heart from giving out.

I whip around to find Zeno standing not ten feet behind me. "What?" He's clearly talking to me, as there's no one else around, but I have no idea what he means.

"If I didn't know better, I'd say you were contemplating drowning yourself in the lake."

My eyes drift back to the surface of the water. "I'm surprised you wouldn't cheer me on," I mutter.

"Why would you say that?"

The frustration I'd had on a leash is suddenly wriggling free, hissing at me to say brash, hurtful things.

"Because every time I'm near you, I get the sense you wish I'd disappear." Tears burn at the back of my eyes. I try to regain the control I thought I'd mastered minutes before, but I'm swimming out of my depths with no idea where the shore has gone. "I'm sorry," I clip, attempting to minimize the damage I'm doing. "I've got a lot going on."

Why is he suddenly interested in starting a conversation? Of all the times to play nice and talk civilly, he has to choose the moment I'm at my lowest. I can sense the heat of his gaze studying me—assessing and analyzing—when all I want is to be invisible.

"Is everything all right, Luisa?"

Do I detect a note of genuine concern in the mellow hum of his voice? I look back at him, but his face is stoic as ever. Why is he even here? I can't imagine he was walking by the lake in the middle of the day and just happened by me, though no *other* explanation appears any more or less probable.

"I'm fine." I wave him off, then peer back at him. "But since you're here, I have something to ask you." Might as well hit him up for a job while he's in a relatively decent mood. "My plans have recently changed, and I'll be staying with my parents a while longer than expected. Gia mentioned that Anna would need to be replaced, so I was wondering, if you're okay with it, if I could take the job. It wouldn't be forever, but I could really use the money until the end of the year." I struggle to hold his gaze. It shouldn't matter what he thinks, but it does. I hate for him to see me moving back with my parents and groveling for a job.

Z steps closer; his position uphill from me magnifies his already imposing height. Light reflects off the water, making his cobalt eyes almost cerulean. His irises have always had a touch more green than mine, and the effect in this light is breathtaking.

"Has something happened?" His assertive nature urges me to spill my guts. It's tempting, but word of my mother's debt getting out is exactly what I'm trying to avoid.

"No, it's nothing to worry about. Some things didn't line up as I'd expected." Maybe I'm reading into it, but I swear his face is lined with conflict, as though he's torn about helping me. The resistance I detect raises my defenses. "Look, you don't need to feel obligated. It's not a big deal. I can find a job somewhere else."

"*Stop.*"

Zeno's barked command silences me instantly.

"Don't assume to know what I'm thinking because you don't. I want to help you, but I'm concerned about my brother."

"What about him?" Is it true? Is he worried Nevio might form an attachment to me and shame his family?

Z moves even closer until only a foot of space remains between us. His nearness sucks up all the oxygen in the area, leaving me breathless and dizzy.

"I've seen the way he watches you. His track record with women is ... let's say he's not great at sticking around.

I don't want you to get swept up in that." He wants me to think he's protecting me, but is that the truth? Or are his motives more selfish?

"I appreciate you trying to protect me, or whatever this is, but your concern is unnecessary." And unwanted. "Nevio is a friend, and that's it. But even more importantly, I'm an adult who can make relationship decisions on my own."

The slight furrow of his brows and pursing of his lips tell me he's not convinced. My threadbare patience unravels along with my hold over my emotions. I sense tears threatening on the horizon and know I need to get away from him before the storm hits.

"Look, you can trust my judgment and give me the job or not, but whether I do something with your brother is none of your damn business."

Zeno stiffens at my rebuke. "He's my brother and a soldier under my command. I don't need you to tell me what is and isn't my business."

My lips snap shut. "You're right. He's your family, despite how you treat him."

"Do you want the job or not?" Each word is clipped and sharp, spoken between clenched teeth.

I hold my ground, not allowing my gaze to waver, but I realize I'm jeopardizing the plan that will get me back to school the quickest. With that in mind, I inhale slowly before speaking calmly. "I do."

"I'll tell my mother you're staying on." The bitter cold of his reply stings, though I brought it on myself. I can't be angry because it achieves what I need. Our conversation is over.

I hold perfectly still as he turns and walks away. A sob is clawing its way up my throat from deep inside me, and if I make the tiniest move, it will burst free while he is near enough to hear. Using the last of my mental energy, I hold tight to my reins until I'm certain he's gone, then I allow the emotions to drag me under.

Hiding my face in my hands, I attempt to suffocate the sound from my uncontrollable weeping. Heaving breaths wrack my chest, and my shoulders curve in as my legs threaten to give out. For long minutes, I come undone.

Six years of hard work, and I was so close to being done. So close to achieving my goals. It's only a delay, but no matter how much I try to package the turn of events in shiny paper and colorful bows, it still sucks. And no matter how many times I tell myself this is my choice and it's what I want, I'm still heartbroken over it. Someone has extended the finish line of my marathon, and after all the running I've already done, those last few meters feel like an eternity.

I cry—long, and hard, and ugly.

The cleansing wash of emotions leaves me ragged and bleary-eyed. I do my best to wipe away the snot and tears before making the slow trek back to the cottage. I give myself the afternoon to wallow in bed, only leaving my room for bathroom breaks and a single stop in the kitchen. I don't want to eat, but after not having anything all day, my stomach insists.

When Gia returns from work in the evening, she comes

straight to our room and curls up with me in bed. She doesn't ask questions. She doesn't give empty assurances. Gia's most innate skill is intuiting how to provide the perfect form of support and comfort to those she loves.

"I'm so sorry, Lulu," she whispers.

"I know, G. Me, too."

A few sounds filter in from downstairs, but otherwise, the room is quiet. My sister's presence is enough to give me more mental strength than I've had in hours, enough that I can pretend to function for the evening.

"I made arrangements with Z to stay on and work."

"Have you told Mom?"

I shake my head. "Tomorrow. I'm not up for it today."

"Totally understandable. You know, maybe she still has some cash stashed away. If we used my money and hers, maybe you could still swing school." The hopefulness in her voice is why it's impossible not to love her. Gia will always hope for the best and explain away the worst.

"No, G. She already paid what she could."

My sister lifts her head to look at me in surprise. "If she already paid some, how much was the debt to start with?"

"Fifteen," I say dryly.

She falls back down onto the soft mattress. "Jesus," she breathes.

"Yeah."

"Well, on a totally selfish note, a part of me is glad I'll get to see more of you. I know that sounds awful, but it's true."

It's probably the most selfish thing I've ever heard my

sister say, and it makes me smile. "I love you, too, G. And I'm glad we'll get to spend some time together."

We're both quiet for several long minutes before Gia speaks again.

"How was talking to Zeno?"

I huff out a dry laugh. "I might have been a little short with him. He didn't catch me at the best time." I tell her all about our conversation and what I'd learned earlier in the day from Nevio.

"I'm not sure what to think of all that—any of it," she muses, staring blankly at the wall.

"You and me both."

"So, Zeno followed you down to the lake—"

"We don't know that," I cut her off.

She shoots me a critical look from the side of her eye. "Right. He just *happens* by you at the lake—the same as he just happened by you in the kitchen the other night. Are you sure Zeno doesn't have a thing for you? Maybe that's why he doesn't want Nevio around you."

"Gia, you know Zeno as well as I do. Do you really believe he's so shy he couldn't make a move on a woman if he wanted her? That he's wanted me all this time but was so meek he couldn't find a way to tell me? I'll admit that his behavior is confusing, but I'm not about to read into it."

"Now you sound like me," she teases. She's right, and it draws a reluctant smile from me.

"Oh, G. You're the only reason these next few months are going to be remotely tolerable." I pick up my phone after ignoring it all afternoon and find I have a missed text from Grace.

Grace: The Bishops want to have you all and the De Rossis over tomorrow night for dinner. That work?

I shoot a sly grin at my sister. "Looks like we're all having dinner at the Bishops' tomorrow night."

As I'd hoped, her face lights up like a kid at Christmas.

Realization dawns that I have a secondary purpose for my stay here at the Hardwick estate. I'll do my best while I'm here to help my sister make a move on her crush. Considering how into each other they both are, it shouldn't be all that hard. Helping her find her happily ever after would make every minute here worth it.

Me: Sounds wonderful! We'll see you then.

Gia and I both get up to go downstairs for dinner, and as I freshen up after a day in bed, I start to wonder if fate has kept me here for a reason. I'm still not thrilled with delaying my graduation, but my perspective begins to shift. I have the next six months to play matchmaker for Gia, guidance counselor for Livia, and spend some precious time with my father. Knowing my sacrifice serves more than one purpose is gratifying enough that I'm able to refrain from strangling my mother at dinner. That alone is proof that miracles happen.

CHAPTER 14

THE NEXT MORNING, I FIND MYSELF ALONE WITH MY MOM IN the kitchen and decide it's time to have a talk. Gia is finishing in the bathroom, and the younger girls were still asleep when I came down, so I've got some time before we're interrupted.

I walk to the coffee maker, right next to where she's peeling an orange.

"Aldo came by yesterday while you guys were out." I impart the information with perfect calm and quiet enough that we can't be overheard, just in case.

Mom drops her orange.

"He wasn't going to give you more time, but I told him I'd get it paid, so he's giving me until the end of the week." I place a mug under the coffee spout, not meeting her stare, though I can feel her wide eyes gaping at me. "I understand

Gia has already helped you recently. You've cleaned her out, so she has no more to give. I'm doing my part to help this *one* time. You hear that?" I finally lock eyes with her. "Once, Mom. That's it. After this, you will be on your own. Gia and I have agreed."

Mom flings her arms around me, crushing me in a hug that I want no part of. I stiffen, but she doesn't catch on to my irritation. All she can focus on is how she's miraculously escaped yet another shit situation.

"Oh, sweetheart, thank you so much. I swear, it won't happen again." She pulls back and looks at me with earnest hazel eyes that I don't trust for a second.

"Don't thank me. I'm not doing it for you. I'm doing it for Dad. You know damn well what they'd do to him if we don't get this paid."

She finally shows a hint of the remorse that should be eating her from the inside out. "Are you going to tell him?"

I lift my now full coffee mug up and breathe in the caffeine-laden steam. "Probably, but not until this has all settled down. In the meantime, I suggest you find a new damn hobby besides gambling and shopping."

"I will—I am," she stutters. "I swear."

I'll believe it when I see it.

"In order to make this happen, I'm moving back home for a while. I already talked to Zeno, and he said I can take Anna's place."

"Oh! Well, doesn't that work perfectly!" She grins, tossing her orange peel scraps in the trash. "Gia will be especially happy to have you here. And your dad. You stay as long as you need, honey."

Who cares about the life I'm putting on hold, so long as you get your debt paid? So much for mothers putting their children first.

"Hopefully, it won't be too long. A few months, maybe more."

"Are you starting today?"

"I suppose I will, but I have to make a few calls first. You and Gia can go on without me, and I'll catch up." I make myself comfortable at the kitchen table and pull out my phone.

"No problem, I'll leave you to it, then. See you at the house!" She wiggles her fingers at me, and I flash a thin smile to get her to leave.

I spend the next thirty minutes making arrangements to put my life in the city on hold. I'll need to retrieve some of my belongings from storage at some point, but I have a little time. The girl I'd planned to live with is clearly upset when I inform her that I'm backing out, and rightly so. I hadn't signed a lease yet, so I could legally back out, but it was a shit thing to do when she counted on me. I feel horrible, but my family comes first.

"What's this I hear about you not going back to the city?" Dad is leaning against the doorframe behind me, studying me curiously.

"Morning, Daddy. I figured you'd gone to the house with the others." I get up and give him a hug, loving how my head rests at the perfect place over his heart.

"I was down by the water when they left, then I overheard the tail end of your call there. What's going on, Lulu?"

"I ran into a bit of a snag with my job and decided it would be best to stay here for a bit and save up before jumping into my last year of school." I try to weave in as much honesty as I can so that the lie feels real. I *will* tell him the truth, and soon. Just not quite yet.

He pulls back, and while there's happiness in his sloping brown eyes, there's also a touch of hesitation. "You sure everything's okay?"

"Absolutely! And don't you worry, I one-hundred-percent will finish school."

"No worryin' here—not about you. If you tell me you're okay, I believe you. And I certainly won't complain about having you around." He lightly pinches my chin and grins proudly. The sight fills me with conviction that I'm doing the right thing. My dad is unquestionably worth whatever sacrifice I have to make.

"I told Mom earlier that Zeno is letting me take Anna's position. I thought I'd spend the day getting acquainted with what I'll be doing. If you can wait a minute for me to throw on some clothes, I'll head over to the house with you."

He waves a hand and strolls to the coffee maker. "I'm in no hurry. Take your time."

MY FIRST DAY goes as smoothly as I possibly could have hoped. Cecelia is thrilled to have a dedicated hand back in the kitchen rather than relying on my mother when she happens to be around. We discuss my duties, gossip about the gardener having an affair with a maid from another house, and I help her plan the meals for the following week. Gia stops in several times to visit along with Laney, Mom, and even Nevio, who pokes his head in after hearing of my change of plans.

The one person I don't see is Zeno.

Overall, I'm relieved because my day was emotionally draining enough as it was. However, a niggling seed of guilt has sprouted in my mind over the way I'd spoken to him the day before. I need to apologize and plan to do so when we're at the Bishops' for dinner. Cecelia told me earlier in the day that the De Rossis would all be attending, but she and Laney already had prior engagements. Zeno would be present and hopefully receptive to an apology. He's my boss, and no matter how much he frustrates me, it's the right thing to do.

We are able to get home in time from work to clean up before going to the neighboring estate. Grace has assured us that dinner won't be formal, but I can't imagine dining as a guest at one of these magnificent homes and not stepping up for the occasion. She may be used to the house and its family, but I've never been to the Bishop home.

I straighten out the frizz that has blossomed around the crown of my head and give my hair a controlled wave with a flat iron. I've always been grateful that I didn't get Mom's kinky red curls. Livia is the only one who got the full brunt of Mom's genetic blessings. Marca's hair is similar to mine in texture, but the color is a deep auburn. Sometimes, Liv tries to tame the curl with a flat iron, but it takes ages, and if there's any humidity at all, the resulting frizz is hardly worth her effort.

I hadn't put on any makeup in the morning since Dad was waiting on me, so I remedy that with some eye shadow and mascara. I rarely mess with foundation. I'm fortunate enough to have good skin and am fine with a few imperfections showing.

After asking Gia what she's going to wear, I choose a sundress appropriate for dinner. It's a soft cotton fabric, green with small yellow flowers, and wraps in the front in a way that teases at my cleavage and the side of my leg when I walk or sit. It's feminine and classy, yet sexy at the same time. I add hoop earrings and a delicate gold chain with my favorite pendant—a golden rose in full bloom.

We drive to the house even though it's not far. None of us care to walk home in the dark. There is a third row of seats, but no one wants to climb over the back seat, so Marca sits on Gia's lap for the short ride. The sun is still out when we arrive, though settling low enough on the horizon to soften the evening light. Carter Bishop's home is much newer than the Hardwick mansion, so it doesn't have the same majestic feel, but it is impressive in its own way. A huge fountain in front of the house welcomes visitors as they enter the circle drive. The landscaping is perfectly manicured, thanks to Mr. Larson, and the home itself is stunning—three stories of cream-colored stucco with cornerstones cut at alternating lengths lining each corner. It's a beautiful example of architectural design, and while it's larger than anything I could ever imagine owning, it's quaint compared to Hardwick's sprawling thirty-five thousand square feet.

"Hello, everyone!" Carter greets us at the front door. "I'm so pleased you could join us. It's been such a trying week."

Dad extends his hand to shake Carter's. "We appreciate the invitation."

Carter smiles broadly before his eyes are drawn over our shoulders to the driveway. "Ah, it looks like the rest of our party has arrived as well."

We all turn as Zeno drives up in a black Range Rover with Elena in the passenger seat. The two exit and join us at the front door, everyone greeting one another.

"Will Nevio be joining us?" Carter asks Zeno as we make our way inside.

I wave to Grace, who approaches from the living area, but my attention is focused on hearing Zeno's answer.

"No, I apologize for the late notice. He had something come up." He doesn't sound particularly upset about Nevio's failure to attend, making me wonder if he played a role in his brother's change of plans.

I hate to think Nevio can't enjoy an evening with his family and friends because his brother is so impossible to be around. When I saw him earlier in the day, he'd sounded like he fully intended to be present at dinner. In fact, he had sounded excited enough about seeing me that I'm surprised he didn't text to tell me he wouldn't be here.

Grace and her father join us at the door while her younger sister and mother are back in the kitchen. Cora is also present, but she keeps herself apart, only offering cordial smiles from a distance.

"Not a problem at all. This wasn't meant to be anything formal, simply a friendly gathering after a trying week." He leads us into the elegantly arranged dining room, despite his assurances of a casual affair. "I believe Mrs. Larson has dinner ready, so have a seat."

Carter sits at the head of the table with Cora at the opposite end with the two children.

"Livia, Marca, you can sit with Boston and Emily," Mom says.

Liv gapes at her. "I'm twenty-three, Mom. Did you really just put me with the kids?"

Marca stills while holding the back of one of the chairs as though she were going to sit until her sister balked at the suggestion.

"I don't mind sitting down there," Gia offers.

"Oh, but I'd love to have your company on this end," Carter says hopefully.

Irritated that Livia is acting like the child she claims she isn't, I hiss at her under my breath. "*Sit*, Livia."

She rolls her eyes at the indignity but does as she's told. Mom, Dad, and the Larsons fill the middle of the long table. I find myself sandwiched between Grace and Gia, who has been encouraged to sit on the end next to Carter, across from Elena.

The arrangement suits me perfectly, except that Zeno is seated directly across from me, making it almost impossible not to accidentally meet his gaze. He's left his suit jacket at home and rolled up the sleeves of his light gray dress shirt to expose his tanned forearms. His right wrist is adorned with a platinum watch, accenting his deep olive skin tone. Over the course of dinner, I practically memorize the contours of his strong hands in an attempt to avoid meeting his eyes. Every time my eyes raise from my plate, they snag on his hands or the buttons of his shirt instead of risking an inadvertently awkward collision of our gazes. The only times I openly peer at him is when Carter speaks, and I'm assured Z's eyes will not stray to mine. I study him during those brief moments, especially the way he watches Carter interact with Gia. His eyes shift back and forth between them, and I wonder what he's thinking, especially when his gaze wanders over to his mother before he appears to grimace and shift in his seat.

Curious if I missed something that would have caused such a response, I attempt to jump back into the conversation. I wasn't paying a lick of attention, so now I struggle to catch up.

Gia is laughing after Elena commented on something she said.

Carter wears an enchanted smile. "I'd say that's a perfectly reasonable response. Just the other day, I held an entire conversation with someone talking on a Bluetooth earpiece. I thought she was talking to me. It took a full three minutes before I realized."

"Well, I couldn't believe I'd done that." Gia blushes softly. "But now I know."

"That's one of the best things about our Gia," Mom cuts in. "She can brush things off when they don't go as planned. She'll make a wonderful mother someday. Don't you agree, Mr. Bishop?" The meaningful glint in her eyes leaves no one to guess at her insinuation that it's *his* children Mom has in mind.

I'm hideously embarrassed, but poor Gia looks like she wishes the floor would swallow her whole.

"*Mother!*" I hiss around Grace, who flattens herself wide-eyed against the back of her chair to stay clear of my rebuke.

"It's the truth." Mom shrugs with a smirk. "There's nothing wrong with being honest." She looks back at Carter and grins. "This has been such a lovely evening. We'll have to do this again but at Hardwick next time." She turns an expectant gaze to the De Rossis, and I can't bear to witness their expressions at her presumptive offer.

"Yes!" Livia cheers from the other end of the table. "And maybe we could invite a few others. Zeno did say the other day that it would be good to entertain some more." She grins, totally oblivious of the imposing nature of her request.

It's as if Livia and Mom have launched an all-out smear campaign to embarrass us until our family is left without a shred of dignity.

Elena smiles graciously as ever. "I think that can be arranged."

I look over to offer her an apologetic smile. Fortunately, she's known Mom forever and can't be too shocked at the behavior. Elena is an exceedingly patient woman, which is the only explanation I can find for her enduring tolerance of my mother.

"Wonderful!" Mom cheers while Liv silently claps her

hands together. I take a giant swig of my wine and pray that the worst is over.

The remainder of dinner goes relatively smoothly. The food is delicious, and I'm able to tell Grace about my plans to stay, keeping to the massaged truth I told my dad. Even if I was going to tell her about Mom, which I'm not sure I will, I certainly can't do it at dinner in front of everyone. Much like Gia, Grace expresses how sorry she is that my school is delayed but can't hide her pleasure at having a friend nearby.

After dinner, Carter turns on the speaker system to play some light pop music while everyone takes their wineglasses onto the back veranda. Gia helps the kids set up a backyard game where participants throw two balls connected by a thin rope at a ladder and try to get the rope to wrap around one of the rungs. Carter plays with them, and everyone laughs heartily at their attempts.

About thirty minutes in, I notice Zeno slip back inside, and I decide to take the opportunity to apologize. Two oversized glasses of wine and plenty of laughing have relaxed me enough to take the leap. He's in the bathroom when I step inside, so I refill my glass and wander to the adjacent sitting room to admire the artwork while I wait.

"Did you need something?" Z asks when he reappears.

"Not exactly. I, uh … I wanted to tell you I'm sorry for how I acted by the lake yesterday. You caught me at a rough moment. I really do appreciate you letting me work, especially when I was so short with you."

He stares at me for agonizing seconds that stretch an eternity, wreaking havoc on my nerves.

Not a word. Not a hint of emotion.

"This is where you tell me it's fine. No need to worry," I tease with an uneasy smile, giving into the pressure to fill the silence.

"And what if it's not fine?" he finally asks, his voice coarse as volcanic stone. Affected and raw. "What if none of it's fine—your anger at me or your prolonged stay at Hardwick?"

I'm so stunned by his words that I nearly spill my glass of wine as I lower it to the table next to me. "I'd ask for an explanation." I can't fathom why my presence would be so damn upsetting to him.

"And if I refuse?" He steps closer so that I have to crane my neck to keep my eyes on his.

I don't understand this game he's playing, but I won't let him win either. "Then I'd say *you're* the one with a problem."

Before I know what's happened, he's spun me around to face the wall behind me. He keeps his strong fingers firm around my waist, holding me in place when his mouth lowers to my ear. "What if I make it your problem as well? I see the way you look at me, Luisa. I'm not the only one who's torn."

I place my hands on the wall to ground myself. His grip assures he won't let me fall, but the world suddenly tilts on its axis. "I wouldn't be torn if you wouldn't be such an ass." My words are breathy, more so than I'd like, but his nearness has made my entire system unsteady.

I have no idea where any of this is coming from.

Why, after so many years of stilted encounters, is he changing the rules?

"I wouldn't have to be an ass if you weren't so *fucking* beautiful." He spits the words with savage hostility. An admission ripped from deep within him against his will. "This ... *this* is what you do to me." His right hand snakes farther around toward my belly, his palm pressing flat against me and tugging me flush against his rigid frame.

The length of his impossibly hard cock molds itself into the soft flesh of my backside. Words escape me. My lungs no longer expand and contract in a proper rhythm. Every ounce of blood in my body rushes to my core for a mindless moment. A handful of seconds when need consumes me, but my thoughts begin to return after the initial rush.

Zeno wants me, but he's conflicted. Why? Why does his desire make him so angry?

Because you are nothing but the help. Always have been, always will be.

I flinch at the sting of my own thoughts because I know they're right. Despite his attraction, Zeno wouldn't want me because he thinks I'm unworthy. Between my family's behavior, economic situation, and Mafia rank, I am nothing but a pretty face and potential disgrace.

In a matter of seconds, I run an emotional gambit that leaves me spinning. Anxiety, shock, desire, elation, confusion, then blinding fury. I would be hurt if there were any room left for the emotion, but my skin is now tight with righteous anger.

I press off the wall in one swift motion, forcing him to

release me and stumble back a step. When I whip around to face him, my eyes impale him with shards of jagged ice.

"Thank you for making your *uncomfortable* situation so clear. I had no idea my presence was such a problem for you."

He scowls with irritation. "You're putting words in my mouth, yet again."

"Only because you haven't done any explaining of your own. But then again, I don't know why I expect civility from you when you can't even be kind to your own brother. Did you keep him from coming tonight just so you wouldn't have to be near him?"

A mask of indifference settles over Zeno's face. The swift and complete change at the mention of his brother causes goose bumps to dance along my arms.

"I didn't say a word to him," he clips. "But I would have if he hadn't backed out of his own accord."

"You know, in a twisted way, I get why you push me away. I think it's shitty, but there's logic to it. Nevio is your *brother*, though. He's kind and decent, and there's no excuse for hurting him like you have."

"I lost all respect for my brother long ago, and he has failed time and again to earn it back. Any rift between us lies squarely on *his* shoulders, not mine."

I scoff on a dry, humorless laugh. "I'd say your refusal to even entertain a relationship reveals that you're equally as flawed. He's your *brother*."

"Exactly," he barks. "He's *my* brother, and our relationship is none of your damn business."

"You make it my business when you try to keep Nevio

and me from being friends. If you had your way, he wouldn't get within six feet of me."

"You're *goddamn* right he wouldn't." He slams his hand on the table beside us, rattling my wineglass.

The sound of his palm slapping against the wood resounds in my head long after the room has stilled. We stand in that vacuum of time, our eyes locked in an unspoken battle until my heart begins to ache.

"I don't understand what's happened to you … to the boy I used to know." My confession slips quietly from my lips on a wisp of uncertain air.

It's a final plea that goes unanswered.

"Life happened." The arctic touch of his voice stings my skin.

Zeno leaves the room without another word.

Tears sting at the back of my eyes for the second time in two days. This time, I'm able to use my anger to successfully ward off the threat, but I can still sense the emotion fighting for release.

I say little more than a word the rest of the evening. Zeno is equally withdrawn, though his quiet nature makes the change harder to discern. I don't want to discuss the incident, and fortunately, Gia is so wrapped up in Carter that she fails to notice my silence. Dad, however, has a keen eye, especially where I am concerned. He pulls me aside not long before we call it a night.

"You all right, Lulu? I noticed you and Z were both inside for a while. Neither of you seemed very upbeat when you returned."

I try to smile reassuringly, but judging by his expression, I fail miserably. "Yeah, it's fine. We had a bit of an argument, but it was nothing. All we do is butt heads anymore."

"Zeno is complicated. Unlike Carter, Zeno has a role to play in a demanding organization. He can't be relaxed and friendly, but that doesn't mean he isn't a good man underneath."

"I'm not so sure, Daddy. He's definitely not the same person I used to know."

Dad wraps his arm around my shoulder and pulls me in for a side hug. "Well, at least this is only a pit stop in your journey. You won't have to be around him for long."

Even less if he avoids me as I suspect he will now.

That should be a good thing, so why do I feel like I have an ice pick buried deep in my chest?

CHAPTER 15

Zeno, Age 19
Luisa, Age 17

If Elena hadn't offered up her house as an escape, I might have strangled one of my sisters by now. Not Gia, of course, but a thirteen-year-old Livia is more than I can take. It's only early July, but I'm certain I wouldn't have survived the summer if it wasn't for Elena and Hardwick. Thanks to her generous offer, I find myself tucked away in the TV room most weekends with my nose buried in a book. The comfy sectional sofa is hardly ever used now that Zeno and Nevio are both gone.

It felt strange at first to be here alone. Nevio has been away at school for almost a year. I thought he'd come home for the summer, but he didn't. Poor Elena practically begged me to come over and keep the house from feeling so empty. It works for me. I'm away from my family, out of the heat, and free to read uninterrupted—Saturday afternoons don't get any better than this. If I'm not working at the local library, which is the summer job I was lucky enough to score, then I'm usually here. The Hardwick library would be a fabulous place to read, but that's Elena's space. Faced with choosing another hideaway, I naturally gravitated to the media room. I suppose it felt the most comfortable after so many years spent playing in here with the boys. The smell alone fills me with warm familiarity.

After an hour or so of reading, I slip away to the bathroom. The house is silent, but that's nothing new. Even when the boys and I were little, the stately mansion was a vacuum of sound. Elena and Silvano are here, somewhere, along with Cecelia and one of the housekeepers, but the place is so large that sound doesn't travel, and it's easy to feel alone.

I find the solitude cathartic.

In the month since I started coming here to read, I've learned to embrace the seclusion, which is why I squeak in surprise when I return to the media room and find a half-naked man holding my book.

Not a man.

Zeno.

I've hardly seen him in a year, and he's done a lot of growing in that time.

My mouth fills with cotton at the sight of him. Broad, sculpted shoulders glisten with droplets of sweat that run down muscular arms. Arms now adorned with artfully drawn black ink. I desperately wish I could move closer and study the details of his tattoos. Explore the thin trail of hair leading down beneath the low-slung waistband of his athletic shorts. Lose myself in the aquamarine eyes now staring me down.

Zeno is absolutely breathtaking, and I might be mesmerized enough to tell him if I thought my confession wouldn't make him angry.

"Were you reading here?" he finally asks while I still openly gawk at him.

"Yes ... um, your mom said I could. I didn't know you were here." As the shock of seeing him settles, a sense of unease creeps beneath my skin. Zeno made it perfectly clear in the past that he didn't want me in his house. I try to squash the self-doubt. I am an invited guest, whether he likes it or not.

"I got in this morning. Just went out for a run."

"I see that." I swallow at my own semi-admission that I've been ogling him.

Z's hypnotic gaze holds me captive until he peers down at the book in his hand. That's when I remember what it was I'd been reading. Of all the books he possibly could have caught me with, and I cruise through nearly one a day, it had to be the one time I was scratching an itch for a historical romance. The book is the epitome of bodice-ripping, virgin-snatching, rake-filled smut, complete with a shirtless man on the cover. The novel is every stereotype and cliché in one printed paperback, and I was loving every word.

That is, until the book found its way into Zeno's hand.

Now, I'm utterly mortified. I rush over and try to take it from him, but he stubbornly refuses to hand it over.

"Just give me the book, Z, and I'll get out of here."

His head tilts to the side a fraction. "Is there a reason you need to leave?"

My lips part, then snap shut before repeating the process. "Are you serious?" I've felt unwelcome in his presence for nearly two years, and he wonders why I'd run the second he shows up? Is he screwing with me? I have no idea what to think.

Zeno's full lips thin and brows knot while his eyes sweep the room. "Why are *you reading here?"*

I stand a little taller, raising my chin. "It's a hell of a lot more quiet than my house. When I mentioned to Elena ... to your mom ... that I never had any peace and quiet at home, she suggested I come here." I pause before adding, "I think she likes the company, even if we aren't hanging out together."

His eyes drop from me to the book still clasped in his hand before he gently tosses it onto the sofa. "I suppose there's no harm in you reading." He steps around me, but before he's out of reach, he pauses and turns back. I get the sense he's about to say something when his father's voice booms up from the stairwell.

"Z, I've made arrangements for dinner at seven. It's your birthday, son. Are you sure there isn't anyone you'd like to invite?"

His birthday, of course. How could I have forgotten? That's why he's come home.

Zeno stares at me as though his father had never spoken, though a barrage of questions quickly pass behind his ocean eyes. Their meaning is completely lost on me.

Instead of pushing for answers, I offer him an uneasy smile. "Happy Birthday, Z." The words drift between us, a white flag raised in the air, only to hang limp when Zeno's thunderous look sucks all the oxygen from the room.

His brow looms heavier, and the cut of his jaw sharpens like a knife's edge. "Seven is good," he calls out to his father. "And no extras."

He doesn't tell me I need to leave, but he doesn't have to. I feel his sudden animosity in every fiber of my being. His dismissal cuts open the old wound, especially when seconds before, I'd started to wonder if we might have a normal conversation. If maybe, just maybe, we might work toward being friends again.

But I'd been delusional.

Zeno De Rossi wants nothing to do with me, and I'm only too happy to comply.

CHAPTER 16

Rain falls in sheets on Saturday. It's the perfect excuse to hide at home and do nothing. However, my day is less than ideal, considering six of us live in this small cottage. Solitude is hard to come by.

I try not to dwell on my exchange with Zeno at the Bishops' house, but the scene plays over in my head the second my mind wanders. Even reading doesn't hold my attention. Watching television would require me to join whoever is in the living room, and I'm not in the mood to be around anyone.

A brief reprieve in the afternoon weather allows Gia the chance to run some errands. She drags me with her, and I'm surly about it, but I appreciate the chance to get away from the house. The outing lifts my spirits enough that I agree to play a game when we get home. The four of us girls get out our old Sorry board game and sit around the kitchen table. For a precious hour, we are girls again. Gia doesn't mother anyone, and Livia has no reason to act out. Marca giggles at all of us while I fall into my natural place as the ringleader. We are a team, enjoying our time together, despite the battle of our game pieces. With every laugh between us, the bond of sisterhood reforms and solidifies. Livy and I may never be close, but I appreciate these times when we can connect. She needs that. I need that.

"Who's going to Mass with us tomorrow?" Mom asks from the doorway behind me after Gia steals the win, and we pack up the game.

"I'm about to go to Claudia's house for the night, so I won't be here," Livia responds.

"Do you need a ride?"

"Nah, she's coming to get me." She checks her phone and stands. "Damn, it's later than I thought. I better go up and get ready."

Mom's eyes fall on me. I find it ironic that she goes to church since I'm not sure she lives by any of the principles, but it's one of the few rituals she has clung to over the years.

"Luisa, what about you? Gia and Marca will be going. You want to come with us?"

If they're all going to church and Liv is out, that means the house will be empty. I would have the place to myself—it's too good an opportunity to pass up.

"Sorry, I'm going to pass. Maybe next week."

She shrugs. "Suit yourself."

I will, thank you.

I wake when Gia does the next morning, but I don't budge until she and the others bound out of the house. They go to the late service, so it's a good time to get up—I never could sleep in very long.

The rain has subsided since yesterday, but the sky is overcast, and the air is still and peaceful. It's the perfect morning to recalibrate myself after the week from hell. I take out a journal I brought with me and open it to a fresh page. I title the page *New Goals*. Number one is, "Save all the money I can." Next to the number two, I write, "Enroll in school for the spring semester." I'm not certain this is attainable, but these are goals, not blood oaths. The third is, "Commit to a first novel plotline by the end of summer." I've considered so many ideas over the years that it's hard to know where I should start. It's time to get over that fear and go for it.

Three things. That's it. And all three should be feasible.

It reassures me to see my plans in black and white.

Feeling empowered, I jump in the shower. I don't want to waste precious alone time in the bathroom, so I make it quick. Once I'm dry and dressed, I feel like a new woman. Downstairs, I brew a cup of coffee and admire the scene from the kitchen window. The leaves and grass are all still damp, making them look even greener than normal. Moisture is heavy in the air, at least, until the rich scent of coffee permeates the house. Then all I can smell is encouragement and optimism. For a moment, I'm confident things are going to be okay. Like really, truly believe that things will work out for the best.

Then there's a knock on the door.

My heart lurches in my chest, but I admonish myself for being paranoid. The chances are slim that Aldo has found his way back to our house. He told me he'd give me until later this week for the money. And besides, it's Sunday morning. Surely, even bookies take off Sundays.

To be safe, I sneak to the window beside the door and peek past the edge of the curtain. The chances weren't slim enough, apparently, because Aldo, dressed in a leather jacket and a ridiculous chain draped from his pants' pocket, is standing on our front porch.

Blood races through my veins until my pulse pounds in my ears.

"Little Miss Banetti, open up. I see you in there." His sing-song voice mocks me, helping me regain clarity through my anger.

I debate not opening the door, but I don't want him to think I am reneging on our deal and go after my dad. With a slight tremble to my fingers, I undo the deadbolt and open the door a few inches.

"What are you doing here, Aldo?"

His arms splay wide, and one corner of his lips smirk while the other holds a toothpick in place. "Jesus, that's some fucking hospitality you got here. I just came to talk to you about easing your burden." His foot scoots backward as if to steady himself.

I take a more scrutinizing look at his face and note his bloodshot eyes. Is he drunk? He may be slightly unsteady, but he's not totally trashed. Maybe he's still riding a binge from last night. Whatever is going on, I want no part of it.

"You shouldn't be here. My dad could have seen you."

"I saw the rest of you Banettis get out at St. Luke's, so relax. That's why I'm here. I wanted to talk to you because I know you're in a rough place." He steps closer until his face is only a foot or so from the door.

I don't want to retreat from my position against the door because it gives me leverage to slam it shut if needed, but I hate his face being so close for many reasons, the least of which is the stench of liquor wafting from him. I pull my face away as much as I can without conceding my position.

"I told you I'd get you the money. I'm going to the bank tomorrow."

"Yeah, but what if I made a deal with you to ease the terms? I can be a real generous guy, you know." His voice drops to what I suspect he intends to be soothing, but it's only that much more grotesque.

I can't stop my lip from lifting in a snarl. "No, *thanks*," I grit, then go to slam the door, but nothing happens.

My eyes widen, and a vile grin creeps across his face. We both peer down to where his foot has wedged its way between the door and its frame.

In one swift move, he lunges forward on the leg, flinging the door open. I stumble back against the hall closet door with a gasp.

"There's no reason we can't talk. I never got to tell you about my discount program. And since your delay is keeping me from getting back home, it's only fair that you give me a little of your ... time."

"I don't need a discount. I have the money ... I'll have it

to you tomorrow, every cent." I don't want to sound scared, but I'm terrified. I'm no match for his strength, even in his inebriated state.

Aldo places his hands on the door beside my head, caging me in. "How do you know what you want when you haven't heard the terms? Maybe you'd like it a whole lot."

His noxious breath makes me sick to my stomach. The walls close in around me, and adrenaline floods my veins with the need to fight for my life. I know down to my bones that if I don't do something, this man will take what he wants. He'll take a part of me that I won't ever be able to get back. I'm no virgin, but what he wants would tear my soul to shreds. I can't let that happen, not without a fight.

I don't plan my actions. They simply happen.

My knee flies upward with every ounce of my strength, smashing up into his crotch. He instantly folds over, giving me the leverage I need to shove him out the front door and slam it behind him, deadbolt clicking into place.

"*You fucking* cunt!" His enraged scream chases me back to my parents' bedroom, where my father keeps his guns. I grab a nine millimeter and take off the safety as I rush back to the front of the house.

Aldo raises himself enough to pound a fist against the door before catching sight of me in the side window, gun raised.

"I'll have the money tomorrow, asshole," I call through the window. "You can come back at three in the afternoon, no earlier. You'll take your money and get the fuck out of here."

"You think you can fucking *threaten* me?" He pounds a

fist against the door. "Your debt just went up twenty fucking percent, you *bitch*. Have every dime in cash, or I take your dad with me when I leave." He hawks up a loogie and spits it at the glass.

I blink, but I don't flinch, so I take that as a win.

Aldo walks away, his body still curved in on itself despite his efforts to disguise his pain. Again, there's no car in the driveway. He disappears behind the thick brush by the street, but I can still feel him all over me.

I shudder and hurry to the kitchen, where I set the gun on the counter and scrub my hands, splashing water on my face as well. My body begins to shake uncontrollably. I lean my hands on the counter and bend at the waist, hanging my head to catch my breath. When the world slows its spin, I put the safety back on the gun and pour myself two fingers of my father's scotch to settle my system. I down it in one breath, the burn giving me focus.

Holy shit, I can't believe that just happened.

I sit at the kitchen table and thank God I used to love target practice with my dad and am comfortable with guns. I'm not sure I could have pulled that off without the confidence that I could shoot if I needed to. I roll the black gun around in my hands, appreciating its heavy weight. The security.

Heading back to my parents' room, I open the drawer where Dad's guns are kept and swap the nine millimeter for a small thirty-eight. He rarely carries a gun on a daily basis anymore—there's no need at Hardwick—so I don't think he'll notice it's missing. Even if he does, I'll make up an excuse. Until things are settled with Aldo, and maybe for a while after, I'll feel safer with protection.

I breathe deep, in through my nose and out through my mouth.

It's over. Everything is going to be okay.

I would tell my mom what happened, but I'm not sure it would make a difference. I'm not sure anything will push her to change until she has to face her consequences. And she will ... next time. Once Dad is safe from the effects of her fuckups.

THAT EVENING, Dad and I sit on the porch together. I've spent days thinking about my parents, and after witnessing firsthand the nightmarish culmination of my mother's carelessness, I have questions that have to be asked. My dad may not know about Aldo, but he sure as hell knows who my mother is at this point. He sees the way she behaves, and I can tell he doesn't approve. I'm not even sure he likes her all that much. So, why? Why continue to put up with her?

"Daddy, can I talk to you a little more about Mom?"

His smile bears a sadness even his dimples can't erase. "Of course, sweetheart. You can always talk to me about anything."

"I can't help but ask myself why you stick around. Don't you think, if you guys aren't happy together, that you'd be better off separating?" I'd love for my parents to be a happy couple, but that's simply not the case. It serves no purpose to pretend otherwise.

"It's complicated, Lulu. And I don't hate your mother. If I was miserable, that'd be different. This is simply how things played out for us." His complacency baffles me, but that's my father. Dad is so much more laid-back than I am. I could never have tolerated Mom's hot mess express.

"You know she spends way too much money." I decide to extend feelers and test the waters.

"I do, but she's a grown woman."

"Yeah, but her spending impacts you too. What will you do when you can't work anymore if she's blown all your savings?"

Dad smirks. "Fortunately, the family doesn't exactly force us into retirement." He's laughing off my concerns, and while I'm glad he's not overly burdened, I wish he'd take the matter more seriously.

"It's not just money—she has responsibilities. Livia and Marca need a good role model."

"Your mom did fine with you and Gia. I can't imagine two more perfect girls."

I nudge his chest with my shoulder. "Daddy, stop. You know Livia especially is a whole other monster. She's following in Mom's footsteps, and I hate to see that."

"As you get older, Lulu, you come to accept that you can only do so much for people. Even your children. We've done the best we can, and at some point, a parent has to let their kids lead their own lives. Livia will find a man who thinks she walks on water. He'll provide for her, and even though they may not have a relationship you would find fulfilling, it'll work for Livy. She'll be fine, you'll see."

I hear the truth in his words, but I'm not totally sold. At only eighteen, Marca is still malleable. Mom's and Livia's influences are still shaping my youngest sister, and I hate to imagine where that will leave her. I don't want Livia to think she has to rely on a man. I don't want Mom to put my parents in the poorhouse. But like my dad says, if I can't change any of it, getting upset over it is pointless.

Ughhh.

I sigh deeply and lean back against his warm chest. Once I get the debt paid, I'll find a way to tell Dad about it, and maybe then he'll change his tune.

Please, God, let him see reason.

CHAPTER 17

First thing Monday morning, I arrange to take a late lunch and borrow the car. I tell Mom my plans and enlist her help making sure Dad doesn't wander back home while I'm at the house. When it comes time to leave, I grab a canvas tote bag to take to the bank and make sure the gun is in my purse. I won't take it into the bank with me, but with Aldo keeping tabs on us, I want to at least have it in the car.

Walking into the bank with a tote for money and a gun in the car is the strangest feeling I've ever experienced. I have to actively remind myself I'm not robbing anyone. I explain to the teller that I'm buying a car, feeding her the story because I am self-conscious about cashing out so much money. I have no clue how often this kind of thing goes on at banks. Would a twelve-thousand-dollar cash withdrawal raise any flags, or is that an ordinary Monday for them? It feels like a ton of money to me, but I'm guessing it's not as much as I think.

My hunch is confirmed when the teller hands over a stack of bills about an inch tall, and that's being generous. She counts out the hundreds, and I realize my tote bag was a gross miscalculation. Clearly, I watch too much television because I was envisioning stacks of cash in a duffel bag like in one of the *Ocean's* movies or something.

It's actually kind of sad when I think about it. A year of savings—enough money to get me through my last year of school—and it fits in a damn greeting card envelope.

I take the cash and toss it in my purse, clutching the leather bag against my chest when I step outside. With my luck, some giant bird of prey might swoop down and mistake my Coach knockoff for lunch, and I'll be screwed. I'm not taking any chances.

Once I'm back in the car, a tiny trickle of relief eases the vise clenched around my chest. I drive extra slowly the whole way home. I should get there with another twenty minutes before Aldo is supposed to arrive. As I drive, I decide to sit out front and wait for him. I'm done with surprises.

The ironic part is, I keep expecting to have some semblance of control when fate is hell-bent on stealing the reins. I might as well sit back and enjoy the ride like Dad suggested because I clearly am nothing but a passenger in this shit show my life has become.

When I pull up at the house, Aldo is already there, and he's with Grace. Sweet, unsuspecting Grace, who smiles at the wolf in sheep's clothing as though his claws are not hanging out for everyone to see.

Frantic to get him away from her, I toss the gun back in my purse and rush from the car.

"Hey, Grace. What are you doing over here?" My greeting is less than cordial, and her face registers the surprise.

"Um, your mom borrowed my mom's sewing scissors a while back. Mom is trying to mend one of the drapes that got sucked up in the vacuum and sent me over to get her scissors back."

"Yeah, no problem. Let me look for them, and I'll bring them over in a few minutes, okay?" My eyes cut over to Aldo, who is openly enjoying my discomfort.

Grace smiles politely at him. "It was good meeting you, Aldo."

"It's been a pleasure." His gaze follows her as she leaves, making my fists clench with the need to claw those black eyes right out of his skull.

I pull the money from my bag, leaving my right hand in my purse, gripping the gun. "Here's your money," I hiss, tossing the thick envelope at his feet. I'm not letting my manners put me within ten feet of him. Not again.

Aldo's eyes cut down to the money before flicking back up at me. He stares, the hint of a snarl rippling his lips. He's trying to intimidate me, and it's working, but I try not to show it. Eventually, he bends and retrieves the money.

"It better all be here."

"It is. The ten plus twenty percent, like you said. Now, take it and leave."

His beady eyes narrow. "You got a real fuckin' attitude problem. You know that?"

I purse my lips as I remove my hand from my purse, clicking off the gun's safety without taking my eyes from Aldo.

A slow Cheshire grin spreads across his face as he slides a toothpick back in the corner of his mouth. He raises the money to use in a salute at his temple. "So long, Banetti. It's been a pleasure doing business with you."

I keep his retreating form in my sights so long as I am able. Only after he disappears onto the main road do I hurry onto the porch and nearly break off my key trying to get inside, suddenly wishing I hadn't locked the door when I left.

It's over. You can breathe now.

I rush inside when the lock gives, then re-lock the deadbolt and fall back against the wood door. I take in several lungfuls of air with my eyes pressed shut to calm myself. Once my heart has slowed from its sprint, I get out my phone and text Mom that I'm back and tell her about the scissors. She offers a guess as to where she may have left them, which is enough for me to track them down. I put the safety back on the gun but leave it in my purse, then head out to find Grace.

I meet up with her at the rear entrance of the Bishop house. "Grace, I'm so sorry about that. I know I was rude, but that guy gives me the creeps, and I didn't want him bothering you."

"He was definitely on the slimy side, but he wasn't being rude or anything."

"Well, you're lucky then because he's a real asshole. If you happen to see him around again, please stay away from him."

Her brow furrows, and she glances around before responding. "He said something about you guys owing him a little money. Is everything okay?"

That cocksucker has a big mouth.

"Yeah," I assure her. "Just a little loan, but I got him all paid off. It's nothing to worry about. And look! I found your mom's scissors." I hold up the heavy silver sheers.

"Perfect! Thanks for bringing them by."

"Not a problem at all, but I better get back to Hardwick. Maybe we can hang out later this week—Wednesday evening or something?"

"Sure! That would be great. Shoot me a text, and we'll figure it out." Grace waves with a smile.

I return the gesture and begin my walk back to work. The sun is sweltering, so I do my best to stay in the shade. I walk straight past our house and continue toward Hardwick. As I near the open clearing of the main grounds, I spot Nevio walking toward me.

"Where are you headed?" I ask once we're close enough to talk without yelling.

He squints in the sunlight, narrowing his already hooded eyes to nothing but slits. I have no idea how he even sees out of them. He gives me a beaming grin, his half-dimpled smile causing a flutter to stir in my chest.

"I was just out getting some air. What about you?" He directs me back beneath the shade of a large tree. "It's too damn hot to stand in the sun."

"Welcome to summer." I wink. "I had to run an errand, so I took a late lunch. We missed you at dinner on Friday."

He flashes a lighthearted grimace. "Yeah, I'd thought I could stomach going, but then I reconsidered. I know what it's like to spend an evening with Zeno and have him constantly remind me that my presence is unwanted. I couldn't do it. We'd had a bit of an argument earlier in the day, so I knew spending any time around him would be extra miserable."

Nevio would have had enormous fun playing lawn games and chatting with everyone over wine, and I feel awful that his brother took that from him. That Zeno makes him feel like an exile in his own home.

"I'm so sorry, Nev," I offer softly. "I hate that he acts that way around you." I lean back against the wide tree trunk behind me and peer up at my childhood friend. "My sisters may drive me crazy, but I'd never treat them the way he treats you."

He eases closer and places a hand on the trunk above me so that he's leaning beside me. It's a position of familiarity that could easily morph into something more intimate, and I'm not sure how I feel about it. My pulse kicks up with uncertainty, but being near him doesn't light a fire inside me the same way being near his brother does. The realization is disappointing. Why on earth does the jerk turn me on more than the nice guy?

"I don't have to worry about him for a little while," Nevio continues, unaware of my internal conflict. "Z left for the city yesterday."

My suspicions had been correct. Maybe it's presumptive to think I'm the reason he left, but I had a feeling he'd avoid me after our confrontation at the Bishops'. His retreat to the city is remarkably coincidental.

"When's he coming back?" I ask absently. When I peer up at Nevio, he's studying me.

"I can't say. He doesn't tell me his plans, that's for sure. What I do know is that I've arranged to stick around for a while." He lifts his free hand and traces the angle of my jaw with a touch as gentle as a butterfly's wing. "Have dinner with me, Luisa. You name the night, any night this week, and I'll be there."

I don't know what to say at first. I enjoy being around him, but I remember his playboy history. I don't want to be just another good time.

Am I not willing to give Nevio the opportunity to prove he's changed?

Ten years is a lot of time to mature.

"Yeah, that would be great. How about Friday?"

Nevio's smitten gaze is so unguarded and pure that I'm mesmerized. He smiles as though I've offered him the world on a platter. I can't help but smile back, and when I do, his eyes darken. Ever so slowly, he leans down, one millimeter at a time as though I'm a fawn who might startle away at any moment. My eyes drift to his slightly parted lips, and I can almost taste him on my tongue when the crash of glass shattering pierces the air around us.

We both turn to the house where one of the windows on the main floor has been broken. Laney appears in the opening, and though she's some distance from us, I can see the whites of her wide eyes. She mouths what I'm guessing is a curse, then disappears into the shadows, undoubtedly cleaning up after herself.

Nevio and I exchange a look of surprise.

"I'd better go help her." I smile awkwardly.

He nods with a hint of irritation. "I suppose so."

He raises a hand toward the house to lead the way. We don't openly acknowledge what passed between us, but I can sense a shift in our dynamic. The ease of old friendship to the uncertainty of something new. Am I truly open to being with Nevio? He's everything his brother is not—exciting and doting and easy to talk to. I'm so angry with Zeno for so many reasons that it's easy to lean into my relationship with Nevio, but is that what's best? The two brothers are so overwhelming, it's hard to see beyond their enigmatic shadows. Is there light on the other side or just more darkness?

CHAPTER 18

Tuesday is blissfully uneventful, but the reprieve doesn't last long. I find my mother talking to Elena Wednesday morning and learn my aunt and uncle are coming from the city to visit. Emanual Gravina is my mother's older brother, and his wife, Chiara, is my favorite aunt. She's clever and loves a good laugh. Their five kids are close in age to me and my sisters, so we all grew up visiting each other frequently. I never got the sense Uncle E was overly fond of his sister, but he maintained the relationship for the sake of his wife and kids. Aunt Chiara gets along well with Mom, and us cousins always had fun playing together when we were little. Now that we are older, however, gatherings mostly consist of the two sets of parents.

"When are they coming?" I ask Mom.

She's sitting with Elena in the library, which is Elena's favorite haunt. She's managed well since Silvano's death, but her eyes don't light up the way they used to. I'm glad Mom is here to keep her distracted, something my mother excels at. The two have a friendly working relationship. They aren't best friends or anything, but they often talk about more than household affairs and even go to lunch occasionally. Elena has never displayed any hang-up over our disparate stations in life the way Zeno has. If Silvano was, in fact, the source of that mindset, it appears his eldest son was the only member of their family to subscribe to his beliefs.

"They'll get here on Friday. I thought I'd make a lasagna. It's such a process that I haven't done one in forever. Having them over will make the effort worth it."

I begin to chew absently on my cheek as I consider the fact that I've made plans with Nevio for Friday night. Dinner with him would be fun, but there's something about the first night when company arrives. Everyone is excited and catching up with drinks and laughter. I don't want to miss that.

"What?" Mom blurts. "Is there a problem?"

"No, it's just that I'd actually made plans for Friday."

"With who? Grace? She'll understand."

I glance at Elena with a touch of embarrassment. I'm not sure why. Nevio and I are adults, but I feel awkward admitting to our date in front of his mother. "Actually, I had dinner set up with Nevio. I'm sure I can reschedule, though."

When I peek at my mother, her eyebrows have

launched into space. For once in her life, though, she keeps her mouth shut, which I greatly appreciate. I have no doubt she'll grill me about it later.

"Of course, you can," Elena chimes in. "My Nevio is always understanding. You should definitely spend time with your family—you can see him around anytime now that he's staying for a bit."

I nod and smile. "You're absolutely right. Any idea where he's at this morning?"

"Oh, I don't think he's even up yet. He's always out late."

"No problem, I'll shoot him a text. You two have a good morning!" I offer a parting wave with a smile and flee from the room before there can be any more discussion about why Nevio and I would have dinner together.

I text him as I walk back to the kitchen, and once he gets back to me, we decide to move up our dinner by a night. That means we have our first date tomorrow.

My stomach dips and swerves, but I'm not sure if it's out of excitement or trepidation. It's hard to suss out my feelings for him when there's history between us. Not romantic history, but still enough of a past that it complicates everything.

I don't see him at all while I'm working. I keep busy, and he doesn't seek me out. I try not to read into any of it and am now incredibly relieved that I made plans with Grace for the evening. Hanging out with her will be the perfect distraction.

I go home at five to change out of my dirty work clothes, then walk the familiar path over to her family's cottage. When I arrive, she hauls me up to her bedroom.

Since it's only her and her younger sister, they each have their own rooms. I used to be jealous as a kid. Maybe I still am a teensy bit, but I also know that Grace has her own issues. No one's life is perfect.

"What's with the rush?" I ask teasingly, making myself comfortable on her bed next to her. "You didn't even let me say hi to your mom."

"I didn't want to risk her saying something before I got a chance to tell you."

"Tell me what?"

Grace flashes me with a smile so bright it could power the city for a week. "I'm making the move. I've got enough stashed away that I can get my own place in the city."

"That's amazing! I'm so freaking excited for you!" I give her a tight hug, and my heart fills with joy for my dear friend. Getting away from Tuxedo Park will be the best thing she could do for herself. "From the way you talked a few days ago, I thought you were looking at another six months or more." I sit back and look at her, ready to hear all the exciting details, but Grace's gaze has trouble finding mine.

"I wasn't sure myself, but I managed to scrape together a bit more than I expected."

I study her, really examine each of her movements and words. The result forms a knot of unease in the pit of my stomach. "Gracie, where did you get the extra money?"

"I'm twenty-seven, Luisa, and I still live with my parents. Your dad was able to help you when you left home. We don't all have parents who can afford to do something like that. If I didn't find a way myself, I'd never escape Tuxedo Park and make a life of my own."

Her defensiveness surprises me and solidifies my suspicion that something big has changed since we last talked about her plans. This is no adjustment in her budgeting plans. She's come up with new money somehow, and she's embarrassed to tell me the source.

An image of her talking to Aldo flashes in my mind.

No. She wouldn't ... couldn't have. They were only together for a handful of minutes.

He's a bookie—did he moonlight as a loan shark too? My eyelids drift shut with defeat because it makes perfect sense. She'd never be defensive about getting a loan with a bank or taking a second job. I know where she got the money, and it terrifies me.

"Please tell me you didn't borrow money from Aldo." The reality of her situation sucks all the joy from hearing she is moving to the city. Doing business with someone as dangerous as Aldo is no reason to celebrate.

Her chin is raised defiantly when I open my eyes. "You guys borrowed money from him, too. He can't be *that* bad."

Fuck! God-fucking-dammit!

I want to pound my fist into something so bad my fingers ache. "Grace! He *is* that bad! He's the reason I'm having to move back home. I had to get him paid off for my mom before he hurt my dad. I used all my savings—paying him off cleaned me out, but it was worth it because he's *that bad*."

A hint of worry softens her posture. I don't want to

scare her, but it has to happen. She needs to understand what she's gotten herself into.

"I appreciate your concern," she responds, "but I've got it all sorted out."

Until Aldo changes the terms.

"I know you want to hurry things along and move, but you'd be so much better off not relying on his money. Is there any way you can give it back?"

She visibly flinches at the suggestion. "Look, you're pretty and smart, and your family has enough money that you'll never know what it's like to be in my situation. I was hoping you could be happy for me, but maybe that was too much to ask."

I clasp one of her hands in mine, pleading in my eyes. "I know how much you want this, and aside from the Aldo part, I'm absolutely thrilled for you. I just want you to be safe, Gracie." I don't want to lose my oldest friend by pushing her away, but I can't ignore the mistake she's making. "Your life could be in danger."

"I appreciate you looking out for me." Her lips form the thin line of a forced smile, and she squeezes my hand. "But what's done is done. You can accept that and help me pick out a neighborhood to live in, or you can go. I'd prefer we didn't argue and for you to stay, but I understand if you need to leave."

Leaving her to manage the situation alone would only put her in more danger. Plus, I'd never forgive myself if something happened to her while my back was turned.

"You can't get rid of me that easily. We'll figure it out together."

A cautious smile tugs at the corners of her lips. "I'd really like that."

"Do you have any particular areas in mind?" I do my best to look excited when, in reality, my heart is weeping.

We spend the evening talking about apartments and where to look for work. I mention the possibility of her taking over the sublease I had to back out of, but the rent is more than she can afford. We talk budgets and expenses until well after dark. Painting a smile on my face for so long is exhausting. By the time I step outside to walk home, I welcome the blanket of darkness that wraps itself around me. Clouds choke out the moonlight, and the area is far enough removed from any city that light pollution doesn't cast its invasive glow. I am invisible in the night. No worries or expectations. No witnesses to my shortcomings. No need to laugh when all I want to do is cry.

My feels weighed down by the time I collapse onto my bed back home. Gia is already under the covers, but she's left the bedside lamp on for me. I slip off my shoes, then grab my pajama shirt before creeping to the bathroom. Light beams from beneath the door of the younger girls' room, telling me they are still wide-awake. It shouldn't surprise me. Without school or jobs, they can do whatever they like. It must be nice.

Once I've mechanically performed my bedtime routine, I return to our room and crawl under the covers. Something about sinking into bed is incredibly cathartic, as though the light blue duvet is an impenetrable barrier to the outside world. Beneath these down feathers, all is safe and warm and perfect ... until I hear a sniffle from beside me.

"Gia, you okay?" I whisper into the dark.

My words are met with silence for several long seconds.

"I made cookies this afternoon to have on hand for when Uncle E and Aunt Chiara come. I thought I'd take a few over to Boston and Emily, but ... but they're gone." Emotions choke the sound from her words.

"What do you mean, honey?" I move in close, spooning my body around hers.

"Cora was there packing up some of her things. She said Carter and the kids had already left for the city and that..." Her breathing catches on a sob that guts me. "That Carter decided to leave because certain *situations* had made him uncomfortable lately. She made it clear that ... that it's *me* ... he needed to escape." My sister has never spoken with such heartbreak, and in an instant, I am ready to ravage the world on her behalf.

"Oh, Gia. That's terrible, honey. I'm so, so sorry." I hold her tightly while she struggles to maintain her composure. I wish she'd let herself come undone, but that's not her way. Not even in front of me.

"I just thought ... but I must have imagined it. I mean, of course he wouldn't..."

"Gia, don't you dare doubt your feelings. That man was *clearly* into you, plain as day. You weren't misreading anything." I'd bet my life on the fact that his departure had everything to do with that bitchy sister of his. I'm not sure what her motivation might be, but she has to be behind this. "And maybe you misunderstood, and they're just leaving town for a long weekend. They aren't going to sell their house because of you." I try to assure her, but my sister rarely overreacts. If she understood they were leaving for good, she's probably right.

"I'm so embarrassed, Isa. I don't understand how I could have been so confused."

"Because you weren't. For once, I'm telling *you* that there's been a misunderstanding, and we'll find a way to fix it. I've seen the way that man looks at you. He is totally smitten."

She doesn't deny my claim, nor does she grasp at the hope I've placed before her. Instead, Gia lies silent in my arms as we both listen to the gentle murmur of Livia's and Marca's voices passing through the thin walls. After a while, I start to think she's fallen asleep when her voice carries back to me.

"How was your night with Grace?" It's just like Gia to ask about me when her world is collapsing around her. I've never met a more selfless person than my older sister. If Carter is dumb enough to walk away from that, then he's a bigger fool than I could have imagined.

"That depends. You've already had a rough day, so I hate to burden you."

Gia adjusts herself so that we are now lying eye to eye. "What happened?"

I sigh deeply, a practice that is quickly becoming a habit lately.

"The other day, when Aldo came to get the money from me, Grace happened to come by the house. They got to talking, and I guess he told her about Mom owing him money. Grace got it in her head that she could borrow money from him and be able to move to the city rather than having to wait to save more. She borrowed money from him, Gia. I can't believe she'd go and do something so reckless. I get that she wants to get out of her parents' house, but that's not the way to do it."

"I admit, it's not the safest route, but I'm not sure we can say what's best for her. We don't know what goes on under their roof. I'd like to believe the Larsons are kind people, but only Grace can decide what's best for her."

I sigh, yet again, at Gia's response because it's so completely *her*. "I cannot comprehend how borrowing money from a guy who may rape or kill her is ever the right move."

Gia props herself up on an elbow. "Rape or kill her? What on earth makes you say that?"

I realize I never told Gia about my close encounter with Aldo. I peer into her already swollen eyes and consider telling her, but I can't do it. She's already so broken up that burdening her further feels wrong.

"I just get a bad feeling from him, and it worries me."

She eases back down and pulls me into her arms. "It's hard to watch people struggle, but she'll be okay. Grace is a grown woman, and unlike Mom, she'll get this guy paid off."

I nod, but I don't believe it one bit.

"Where is he taking you?" Gia asks the next evening as she watches me put the finishing touches on my makeup.

"Stella's. Have you heard of it?"

"Of course! It's delicious, and they always have live music in the evenings. Makes it a little hard to talk over dinner, but the music is always excellent."

I shrug. "I guess we can talk anytime since we live next door to one another."

Gia's eyes fall to a loose thread she's toying with on the duvet, and I realize my comment has made her think of her own romantic estrangement with our other neighbor.

"Did you try to reach out to Carter today?" I ask softly.

She smiles and shakes her head. "No, not yet. Like you said, he may come home in a few days, and I'll have worried over nothing." Her tone isn't totally convincing, but I'm glad she's trying to stay positive. I'm also glad our aunt and uncle will be here to distract her.

"Luisa, Nevio is here for you," Mom calls up the stairs.

My face breaks out in a goofy grin. "Wish me luck!"

Gia gives me a warm hug before I clatter in my heels down the wood stairs. Nevio is standing in the front entry, dressed in slacks and a button-down shirt with the sleeves rolled up. He is incredibly handsome, and the grin he flashes me bathes me in adoration.

"Don't you two look lovely," Mom beams. "Don't worry about needing to be up tomorrow, Luisa. You guys stay out and have as much fun as you want." And then she does the unthinkable. My mother winks at Nevio suggestively.

If a person could die of embarrassment, I'd be six feet under.

"Thanks, Mom." I grab Nevio's hand and drag him out the door. At least my dad was absent to miss the absurd innuendo.

"Hey, hold up." Nevio chuckles, trying to slow me down. "I didn't even get a chance to tell you how incredible you look tonight."

"You can do it in the car where my family isn't watching."

He tugs me backward a smidge before I reach the passenger door of his car. "Let me." Reaching across my body, he opens the door and helps me inside, pausing to lean forward and catch my gaze. "You look radiant, Luisa."

I'm hidden from the view of my family, but I'm still a little embarrassed. My cheeks warm, and I drop my eyes. "Thank you. You don't look so bad yourself."

He smirks and closes the door. Our ride to the restaurant goes smoothly, if not a touch awkward. Like any first date, I'm hyper focused on every element of our time together. His choice of sensual music on the radio. The way his voice lowers to a rumbling purr in the confines of his car. The possessive feel of his hand resting on my lower back as we approach the hostess station in the restaurant. Every nuance of Nevio's being is crafted for seduction, and it puts me on edge. I don't even think he means to do it. In the same way charisma is a natural part of his personality, seduction is the way he shows interest in a woman. I have no doubt every other female on the planet must fall helplessly into his capable hands, and it makes me uncomfortable.

I'm able to ignore my unease during most of dinner. We

sit at a small table across from one another, and the live music that Gia had mentioned fills the air around us. I limit myself to one glass of wine. Nevio does the same. We catch up on our years apart, talking straight through dinner and long after about school, concerts, friends, and all other aspects of our lives. At the candlelit table in a crowded restaurant, we are merely friends talking, and I'm able to relax, though the nerves resurface the second we stand to leave.

Nevio walks me to the passenger door of his car, but instead of opening it, he stills, eyes seeking mine. "I would invite you back to my place, but it's not exactly private."

I gnaw on my bottom lip and smile awkwardly. "That's okay. I'm not quite ready for that."

"I didn't mean to pressure you. I just hate for our evening to end already."

"We do live next door to one another. I have a feeling I'll see you around plenty, although that might be more difficult when Zeno returns home."

He lifts his hands to cup my cheeks and pierces me with his stare. "I'm not afraid of Z. In fact, let him see us together. I'd love for him to face the fact he can't control everything."

His words snag in my ears, unraveling a thread of concern.

"That's not what this is about, though. Right?" I pull back enough to escape his touch. "You're not going out with me just to piss him off, are you?" It hadn't occurred to me before, especially when Nevio is so convincing with his admiration, but now that the idea has taken root, it makes sense.

"Of course, not!" he says adamantly. "I was only trying to say that I let you slip away once, and I'm not doing it again." His eyes soften before he leans in to place a gentle kiss on my forehead. "You are worth so much more than Z's petty wrath." His words are murmured against my skin, their heated promise coaxing goose bumps to line my arms.

I nod shakily, all the blood from my head rushing southward.

Nevio finally opens the door to the sleek black Mercedes. Our ride home is quiet, and I wonder what he's thinking. Mainly to distract me from my own confused thoughts. When we pull up at my house, he tells me to wait so that he can help me from the car. I let him because I recognize that the gesture has little to do with my actual need for assistance. This is about him showing me respect, and I appreciate his thoughtfulness.

His hand holds firmly to mine once I'm out of the car. "Tonight was absolutely perfect," he says quietly, chirping night insects providing a chorus to his murmured words.

"It was pretty great, thank you." I smile and drop my gaze, unable to overcome a shyness that creeps up in his presence.

Nevio doesn't seem to mind. If anything, the display of my demure side encourages him. He begins to move closer when the porch light flicks on, startling me. For the briefest second, my father's face peeks from behind the curtains in the side window. Despite my age and years of living away from home, I'm instantly transported back to my youth and take a lunging step away from Nevio.

"Looks like Dad is still up." I bite on my lips to hold in a laugh. I feel like I've been caught stealing from my parents' liquor cabinet as a minor. The absurdity of my response is endlessly funny to me.

Nevio smirks, seeing the humor, but I sense his disappointment at being thwarted. He lifts my hand and places a kiss on my knuckles. "Good night, Luisa. Sleep well."

"You, too. And thanks again for a lovely evening."

I slip away and hurry up the porch steps. Inside, the downstairs is now empty. I'm a little surprised Dad didn't stick around to ask about my date, but it's late, and we all have to work in the morning. He probably waited up to make sure I was alive and had already fallen into bed. I'm a little envious. The date has given me so much to think about, and it's going to take me ages to fall asleep. I'll survive, though I don't handle sleepless nights as well as I used to.

Maybe I should have indulged in another glass of wine or two.

I picture Nevio's sultry stare and know immediately that I made the right choice. I'm not ready to crawl into bed with him, but with a little more alcohol and his persuasive abilities, there's no telling what would have happened. I'd rather suffer insomnia than get carried away and make things even more complicated than they already are. Taking a friendship to the next level is one thing; getting drunk and fucking a friend is another.

In a moment of weakness, I picture Z as I walk up the

stairs. If things hadn't fallen apart at the Bishops' house, would more have happened between us? I can't deny the searing lust I felt when his body was pressed against mine. If I'd been on a date with him, and he'd said the things Nevio had said, would my night have ended alone?

I shiver at the answer resounding in every fiber of my being.

I would have given myself to him completely, but that scenario would never have happened. It's not even a possibility because Zeno is not like his brother. Not even close.

CHAPTER 19

Uncle E and Aunt Chiara arrive midafternoon on Friday, but I don't get to see them until I'm off work at five. By the time Gia and I get home, the house is filled with the delicious aroma of lasagna and the chatter of excited voices.

"There are my girls!" Aunt Chiara and my uncle, along with Mom and Marca, are sitting at the kitchen table with music drifting in from the living room.

I go straight to my aunt and wrap her in a hug. "It's so good to see you!"

"You, too! It's been ages. Come sit down and tell us what's going on with you two."

I swap with Gia to give Uncle E a hug, then retrieve one of the extra chairs Mom keeps in the living room. "Dad not home yet?"

"You know your father," Mom shoots back while scooting her chair around to make room for us. "It's just like him not to pay attention to what's going on in this family. He knows I'm making lasagna, so he'll show up eventually."

Chiara ignores Mom's fussing and places a hand over mine to get my attention. "Your mom says you're staying here for a while?"

"Only for a few months. I got a little short on cash, so I'm going to save up before finishing out my last year at school."

"Always so responsible and determined. We are so proud of you!"

"Thank you." I grin shyly because praise from her truly does mean the world to me. "Tell me what's been going on with you guys. I want to hear everything I've missed."

Aunt Chiara dives into a quick update on each of her children—three boys and two girls, all grown and living on their own. Gia and I contribute what we can about our own lives, but there's little to tell. Eventually, Dad and Livia both show up, and we all move to the dining room table and stuff ourselves with a delicious dinner. With food in our bellies and wine in our veins, we sit back and continue to talk through the evening.

About an hour after dinner, Mom slips away to the restroom, and Aunt Chiara turns to Gia with concern lining her face.

"Gia, sweetie, are you okay? I get the feeling something's off."

"Oh, I'm fine. Just tired. It's been such a busy couple of

weeks!" She attempts to infuse her smile with reassurance, but it doesn't reach her eyes.

"You know what you need?" Chiara perks up in her seat. "A vacation. When's the last time you got away from here?"

Gia chuckles. "It *has* been a while, but Luisa just got here. I'd hate to leave."

"I'm not going anywhere for a while," I remind her.

"See!" our aunt cries. "There's no reason you shouldn't come back with us and spend a week in the city. Everyone needs to get away from home every now and then. You'll feel so much better once you do."

This is perfect. If Gia goes to the city, she can find Carter and talk to him. In-person conversations are so much more effective than texting or even phone calls.

"Absolutely," I chime in. "You should definitely go. There's at least one friend you'd like to catch up with, and this would be the perfect opportunity." I infuse my stare with meaning to make sure she knows who I'm talking about.

"I don't know, Isa. Surprising someone out of the blue isn't always a great idea."

"Sure it is, especially when that person adores seeing you."

"What if you're wrong, and they don't feel that way?"

"G, you won't know until you try. Maybe you lost touch because of a miscommunication. This is the perfect chance to find out for sure and reconnect." More than likely, Carter's absence is owed to his sister, but arguing a miscommunication has a better chance of gaining Gia's favor. And I'm hoping that seeing her will snap him out of whatever brainwashing Cora has used on him.

Aunt Chiara's gaze ping-pongs between us with curiosity. "Who exactly...?"

I place my hand on hers and look at where Mom exited the room. "G can tell you all about it on your way into the city." It's not that Mom can't know what's going on with Gia, but Gia would prefer if Mom didn't end up in the middle of her business.

She nods with understanding. "I look forward to it."

"I'd like to go to the city," Livia cuts in. "Can I come, too?"

"Come where?" Mom asks as she enters the room.

Aunt Chiara sits tall and grins at Mom. "Gia is going to come back with us to the city. And as for you, Livy, maybe next time. This trip is for your sister."

Liv is unimpressed, setting her wineglass down with more force than necessary. "Gia and Luisa always get everything," she mutters.

Everyone ignores her, as usual.

"That sounds like a lovely idea," Mom says. "With Luisa here, we can definitely manage for a few days."

We spend the next thirty minutes planning Gia's upcoming getaway—how long she'll stay, activities to do, and people she might visit. I'm absorbed in the conversation when my phone buzzes in the back pocket of my jeans. I pull it out, expecting to see a text from a city friend but find an unknown number.

Unknown: Did you enjoy your dinner last night?

Heat blazes across my face as if I've been caught doing

something I'm not supposed to, and I have no clue why. I don't even know who is behind the text.

Me: Who is this?

Unknown: The man who had you panting against a wall less than a week ago.

Zeno. It wouldn't have been all that hard for him to get my number, but why would he want it? He acts like he hates me. I have no doubt he can get any woman he wants with a single look, so why is he texting me? Why flirt then push me away?

Me: Enormously. Enjoying your escape to the city? Irritated, I have to make a dig at his sudden disappearance.

Zeno: No. Not even a little. His admission catches me off guard. Considering how pompous he can be, I assumed he wouldn't admit to emotions that might hint at an error on his part. That might hint he regrets leaving Hardwick.

Maybe he's more self-aware than I thought.

Or maybe not. He's so damn adamant Nevio is at fault for the rift between them that he won't even entertain the idea he played a role as well, so it makes sense that he would believe our own tense exchanges are no fault of his own. Hell, maybe I'm reading into his meaning, and his remorse about leaving has nothing to do with me. Maybe he had a shitty meeting or was in a car accident. There's no way to know what this is about unless I ask.

Me: Why did you leave?

It takes three whole minutes for his response to come.

Zeno: I needed time to think. Not everyone manages their emotions as well as you do.

What does that mean? It's not exactly an apology, but it hints at reconsideration.

I'm not sure what to say in response. I feel a need to keep the channel of communication open, but I don't want to say the wrong thing.

Me: I'm not so sure. Sometimes, my head is messed up like anyone else's.

Sometimes, I crave the man I hate.

Me: Why are you texting me, Z?

Zeno: Because I can't stop thinking of the way you felt against me.

Zeno: Hearing about your date made me furious.

I'm speechless.

I glance around at my family, still talking about God knows what. "Um, I'm wiped out. Sorry to bail so early, but I'm going to head to bed so I have the energy to hang out tomorrow." I have to get away because they'll ask me why I'm so distracted, and I don't want to lie. Fortunately, Gia and I still have our bedroom, whereas Livia and Marca have been moved to the pullout sofa to give Uncle E and Aunt Chiara their room.

As I hurry upstairs, I wonder how Zeno found out about the date.

Me: How did you know we went out?

Zeno: Are you alone?

I close the door to my bedroom and turn on the bedside lamp, then sit on the edge of the bed, staring at his question.

Me: Yes, why?

Zeno: In your bedroom?

My chest stirs with a surge of tingling anticipation that radiates out to my fingertips. I should stop this—tell him it's none of his business—but I don't want to. I want to see where he's taking me. I want to get burned by the fire he stokes.

Me: Yes.

Zeno: Lie back on the bed.

Zeno: Imagine I'm pressed up against you like we were on Friday.

My breath escapes my lips on shallow pants. Just as he said I'd been breathing that night.

I know the second I do as he says, the sensation will swarm me because it won't be the first time I've sought out the feeling. Drawn it forth from my memories.

I start to move, then pause. My fingers tremble as I type.

Me: How did you know? Did Nevio tell you? Nevio said his pursuit of me wasn't derived from spite for his brother, but if he reached out to rub our night in Zeno's face, I'd have to wonder if he was lying. Why else would he intentionally anger his brother?

Zeno: Do you really want me to answer that?

Me: Yes.

Zeno: I keep tabs on everything Nevio does.

He keeps tabs on Nevio? What does that mean? Does he have his brother followed? Or does he just watch his credit card receipts and use GPS to track his location?

I couldn't be more surprised if Z had announced he was gay and carrying on a secret relationship in the city. I'm at a loss. Why the hell would Zeno need to monitor his brother's every action? Clearly, there's a lack of trust between the two, but tracking him? That takes things to another level. I'm not sure what to think.

Me: Why?

Zeno: Because it's my job.

As a brother? As Nevio's Mafia superior? What does he mean it's his job? Every text between us only makes me more confused.

Zeno: Are you going to do as I said? Because my cock is hard just reading the words you write.

Zeno: I need to know you feel the same.

If he only knew how his words were affecting me. I can't breathe or think. My thoughts are in shambles, and I don't know how I feel except that I want—I want him to want me. It's absurd and dangerous. He probably only wants me in order to keep me from Nevio, but here in the dim lighting of my bedroom, where only the walls can see me, I don't seem to care.

I want to be desired by him.

I need to feel that connection.

Glancing around the room, I slowly scoot back on the bed. My family will be downstairs talking for hours, so I don't have to worry about interruptions. I lean back on the pillows and soak in the nervous excitement lighting my veins on fire before I tap out an answer.

Me: Yes.

Zeno: Good girl.

Zeno: I want you to free your breasts. Expose those beautiful nipples, then give them a sharp tug because I wouldn't be gentle if I were there.

Jesus Christ.

I shudder with a wave of crippling hunger elicited from his words alone. He does something to me that no other man can do. Speaks to a primal side of me that I never knew existed.

I do as he says, moaning quietly when the sensation sparks a fire in my belly.

Me: Please tell me I'm not doing this alone.

I need to hear he's there with me, drowning in an ocean of desire as deep as the one pulling me under.

Zeno: I'm right here with you.

Zeno: My cock is in my hand, so angry and red. My fist can't grip tight enough.

Zeno: Are your nipples peaked and sensitive? Have you given them plenty of attention?

Me: Yes. God, yes.

Zeno: Fuck, I wish I could see you.

Zeno: Take your hand slowly down to your slit. Dip your fingers into your wetness, then roll them gently around your perfect clit.

Even if he hadn't instructed me to do it, I would have done it on my own. I'm so damn turned on I'm blind with need—that mindless place where nothing else matters but chasing the pinnacle of pleasure.

I use dictate to text him back now that one hand is occupied. Without having to text out each word, my messages become less guarded. Words tumble from my lips without fully thinking them through.

Me: Why are we doing this, Z?

Zeno: Because we want to—we want one another—

and because it feels good. Doesn't it feel good, Luisa?

Fuck, yes.

I start to lose myself in the sensation and forget to text him back until my phone buzzes again.

Zeno: Don't you dare finish without me, Isa. You hear me?

Me: Z, I need to come. I'm so close.

Zeno: WAIT.

Zeno: Imagine we're back against that wall, but this time, my hand slips down beneath the waist of your pants. Imagine my teeth grazing the skin of your neck and my other hand claiming your perfect breast.

Me: Z!

Zeno: NOT. YET.

Zeno: Feel my cock, hard and desperate to be inside you.

Zeno: Hear the way my breath shudders with each of your moans.

Me: I can't...

Zeno: NOW, Luisa. Come all over your hand for me.

I held off as long as I could so that when I read his text and release the flood of sensation, I'm completely swept away. In fact, I'm so lost in the cascade of pleasure that I don't realize I hit the text record button. Panting and moaning through the crescendo of physical bliss, I record the sounds of my release, and when my finger slips from the button, the recording is automatically sent to Zeno. I don't even realize what I've done until I regain my bearings and look at my phone again.

Zeno: Jesus Christ, you're killing me.

Me: Oh my God. I didn't mean to record and send that. I accidentally hit the button.

Zeno: Sexiest sounds I've ever heard. I only wish I was there to lick your fingers clean.

My mouth falls open in awe of his words and everything that passed between us.

I just sexted with Zeno De Rossi, the man who treats me like shit and makes me totally crazy. The man whose *brother* I went on a date with. What in the actual fuck was I thinking?

Me: I have to go.

I type the words as panic overrides my post-orgasmic chill.

Zeno: Luisa
Me: I'm sorry, I have to go.

I turn off my phone and bury my face in my hands, but that's even worse because I can smell the evidence of what I've done on my fingers. Needing to escape and clear my head, I right my clothes and hurry to the shower. I hope that getting the scent off me will help, but touching my naked body only reminds me of the way his words made me feel.

Zeno has injected himself into my bloodstream like a poison I can't escape.

I was confused before, but now, I'm utterly lost.

It takes me hours to go to sleep, and when I finally do, cobalt eyes are there waiting for me, feeding me dirty commands I don't hesitate to obey.

Zeno doesn't text the rest of the weekend, and I'm hesitant to admit how forlorn that makes me. I try not to let it show—my confusion and distress, longing and duality. Instead, I spend time with my family. We get in some shopping and play a few board games before Sunday rolls around, and it's time to say goodbye. I don't want them to leave, partially because I enjoy their company, but also because I'll have more time to think. About Nevio. About Zeno. About everything.

I keep Gia company while she packs Sunday morning. The Bishop house is still empty, making it look less and less likely that the family took a quick trip to the city. I catch her looking toward the house when she thinks no one will notice. The spear that pierces her heart with every glance passes straight through her and into me. Her pain is my pain. Maybe not to the same degree, but I abhor knowing she's so heartbroken.

"It'll all work out, G. You'll see," I assure her and myself. I desperately hope I'm right. Surely, Carter wouldn't be stupid enough to let his snobby sister keep him from someone as perfect as Gia.

"I suppose you're right, one way or another. I appreciate you encouraging me, though. It'll be good to at least get it over with."

"And if for some reason he's a total jackass, then I want you to spend some time thinking about moving to the city with me. Liv is a grown woman, and Marca is out of school now. Without Carter or the girls, there's no real reason for you to stay."

She starts to say something, but I cut her off.

"Just think about it. That's all I'm asking."

Gia shakes her head with a smile. "Okay, Miss Bossy Pants. Now, help me carry this thing downstairs. Uncle E wants to head out as soon as possible."

I give my sister an extra big hug before she gets in the car and make her promise to be in constant contact. Everyone else goes back inside when the car disappears around the corner, except for me. I turn and gaze at the trees in the direction of the Bishop house and swear to myself that if Gia can't resolve things with Carter, then I'll step up and have words with him myself. If he truly doesn't have feelings for her, I want to hear him say it with my own ears.

"Do you stare at the trees like that often?" Nevio's voice startles me from my reprieve.

"Hey! Um, no. Gia just left for the city with my aunt and uncle for a little time away. I guess I got distracted by the view. What are you doing over here?"

"It looks like your sister isn't the only one headed to the city for a bit. Zeno has insisted I join him for a few days, but I'll get back out here as soon as I can. I wanted to tell you in person."

Nevio has no idea, but I'd bet my life this is about Zeno keeping his brother away from me. But somehow, this time, I'm not as upset. I don't like that he's manipulating his brother's life to serve his own purposes, yet I'm also kind of flattered. Coming between Nevio and me to keep us apart is one thing, but pushing his brother out of the picture because he has feelings for me—that's very different. Surreal. Shocking, even. But not totally unwanted.

"That's sweet of you. It should be a quiet week, so you won't miss much." I smile, but it falters when I meet his steady gaze, full of desire.

"I'll miss *you*, and that's all that matters."

How did I end up in this dangerous dance between two brothers?

I don't want to lead them on, nor do I know exactly what I want. Who I want. They're both alluring in their own ways, though the two are complete opposites. If I'm going to entertain a relationship with one, I'll need to pick soon or risk losing both of them.

Nevio detects the swell of emotion I'm battling and mistakes it for passion. He's not totally wrong, but the feelings are far more complicated than that. He only sees what he wants to see and places his hands on either side of my face, bringing our lips together in a delicate first kiss rife with tenderness.

"Promise you'll keep in touch while I'm gone. I want to hear about everything I'm missing."

I nod, words escaping me.

Just when I think he's going to close in for another kiss, the front door barrels open.

"Oh, damn. Excuse me, I didn't realize anyone was out here." Dad waves a hand in the air, and I leap away from Nevio as though I've been electrocuted by his touch.

"It's okay, Dad. Nevio was just stopping by on his way out of town." The shrillness in my voice makes it clear that I would make a terrible criminal. The slightest hint of guilt, and I crumple completely.

Nevio grins at me, finding my reaction enormously

funny. "I'll be in touch, gorgeous." He winks, waves to my dad, then heads back toward Hardwick without the slightest indication of discomfort. Either he's damn good at hiding embarrassment, or he isn't the slightest bit fazed at getting caught by my father.

"Sorry, Dad. Didn't mean to make things awkward." I join him on the front porch, expecting him to tease me and laugh off the situation, but instead, an unusual wariness darkens his already umber eyes.

"I heard about your date the other night. I didn't say anything at the time, but I don't think Nevio is a good idea." Daddy's caution speaks louder in my ears than most. I'm surprised to hear him say anything against Nevio.

"I thought you liked him."

"I do. Nevio is a good man, but—" He looks around as if searching the trees for the right thing to say. "That doesn't mean I think he's good *for* you. I may not be an active part of the Giordano family, but I still hear things."

"You've heard something bad about Nevio?" He's always so pleasant and laid-back. It's hard to imagine he's capable of doing something my father would deem unworthy.

Daddy frowns, his eyes tracing soft lines across my face. "Would it be enough if I simply asked you to trust me?" He doesn't want to say, and though I'm endlessly curious, I adore my dad too much to refuse him.

"Of course, Daddy. I know you're only looking out for me," I say softly. After two days of uncertainty wavering between the two brothers and wondering what I should do, Dad's request is almost a relief. I'm even a little surprised at how easy I'm able to mentally set Nevio aside, at least as far as my feelings are concerned. Putting the brakes on a relationship between us will be a tad more difficult.

Dad's face melts with relief and pride. "That's my girl." He pulls me into a hug, filling my heart with joy. When he begins to release me, he pauses and stares deep into my eyes, down into the depths of my soul. "On the topic of looking out for you, I need to ask a question. And Luisa, I want to know the truth. Why are you moving back home? You're too responsible to have spent your school money. I want you to tell me why you're actually staying."

Shit. Shitshitshit. I'm not ready for this conversation.

I may not ever be ready, but I need to tell him at some point. Might as well be now.

"How about we walk for a minute?"

He nods, and I lead us down the porch steps.

"You're not going to like what I tell you, so just listen and try to understand. When I arrived home a week ago, Gia told me that Mom had been acting weird lately—selling things and behaving funny. I didn't think anything of it, but then a bookie came by when I was at the house one day. Mom owed him a lot of money. A *family* bookie. I was so worried about them hurting you and your reputation that I decided I wanted to take care of it."

Dad's gait becomes so stiff, I can sense his agitation without even looking at him. "Are you telling me you paid my fucking debt?" Never once in all my years has my father spoken to me with such disdain. His anger is a punch to the gut, but I keep going in an attempt to explain.

"It wasn't your debt. It was Mom's. And yes, I *chose* to

pay it. My choice. And before you get even more upset, let me finish. I didn't tell you about it because I knew you wouldn't let me do it. But the reason I'm saying something now is because I won't step in again, and I agree that you need to know what she's been doing. You need to protect yourself because Gia and I won't help Mom again—or at least, I won't. I guess I can't control what Gia does. I don't know if you can tell the family not to deal with her or if you have to … if you have to divorce her, but I don't want you getting hurt." Each word is harder to say than the last until my emotions have stolen my voice completely.

"And where does Gia fit into all this? Did she contribute as well?"

"Not this time, but it turns out Mom was in trouble about six months ago."

We walk for several minutes in silence. I feel like there are eggshells under each step I take, my shoulders tense with worry. Eventually, I give in and continue pleading for his understanding.

"I know it kills you to hear all this, but as much as you can't stand to hear that your daughter took on a burden you feel should have been yours, it would have killed *me* if you were hurt when I could have prevented it. Don't begrudge me for what I did. You would have done the same."

Dad stops and stares at me. His eyes are bloodshot and suspiciously glassy, piercing me with a flood of emotion. Once again, he pulls me into his chest. "Christ, I don't know what I did to deserve you." His pained words wrap themselves around my heart the same way his arms cradle my body.

"I love you, Daddy."

"Love you, too, Lulu. And you don't need to worry about me. I'll take care of everything."

CHAPTER 20

I don't hear from anyone for a day and a half. Not until Gia calls after lunch on Tuesday. I can't wait to find out how her trip is going, so I answer with an enormous grin.

"Hey, G! How's the city?"

"Not so great." Her broken whisper barely traverses the distance between us.

My heart crumbles to rubble at my feet. "Oh, Gia, honey. What happened?"

"I wasn't sure how to reach out to Carter, but I had his city address, so I wandered that way while I was thinking this morning. I ordered a latte at the coffee shop in the lobby of his building and sat down to get the courage to call him when Cora happened by." Her words grow unbearably full of emotion, making them thin and brittle.

"She came straight over and accused me of stalking her brother. Isa, I've never been more embarrassed in my life. I never was crazy about her, but the things she said … they were so hateful. I can't figure out what I did to deserve being treated like that."

If Cora Bishop were here right now, I'd break that snooty nose of hers and laugh while she bled all over her designer shoes. I'm so fucking mad that I'm shaking.

"You didn't do anything at all. She's a wretched, hateful human being. Please tell me you aren't going to let her win—that you'll keep trying."

"I can't possibly risk him thinking I'm stalking him like a crazy person. I've been praying all morning that she doesn't tell him. God, how embarrassing."

I want to fuss at her not to let Cora intimidate her, but Gia is too upset to see reason. "Maybe once things settle down, you can talk to him and explain. You two were friends, and at the very least, it's reasonable for friends to talk things over before they end a friendship. He can't leave without a word and expect you not to be upset. That's especially unfair to his kids—they adore you!"

"I'm not making any decisions right now. I just want to finish my trip and pretend none of this ever happened. I was almost too embarrassed to even tell you, but I knew you'd force it out of me."

I smile at the tiny ray of love warming her words, so grateful I can give her that when she's hurting. "Never in a million years. I'd make you tell me everything."

"I know, and since I had to call you anyway, I knew keeping it a secret was pointless."

"Why else did you have to call?"

Gia's voice drops to a whisper again, but in a different way than before. This is a whisper rife with secrecy. "I was looking to distract myself earlier and decided to go to a restaurant for lunch over in Little Italy that Anna used to rave about before she up and disappeared. It's owned by someone her parents know. I didn't end up going in, though, because I saw her inside through the window."

"The woman who used to work in the kitchen at Hardwick? The one who's job I took over?"

"*Yes!*"

"If she disappeared so suddenly, why didn't you go in and check on her?"

"*Because* ... she was inside with *Zeno*. They were standing together, almost intimately. His hands were holding her face while he talked to her, and she was nodding intently. It looked pretty serious, but I have no idea what could have been going on. Maybe he happened to see her as well and decided to confront her about leaving so abruptly?"

The food I ate for lunch solidifies in my stomach. I don't buy into coincidences. In a city of millions, what are the chances that he happened to run into his missing housekeeper? Practically zero. But what does that mean? Did he know from the beginning where she was, or did he track her down? And if so, why?

"That *is* strange." It shouldn't unsettle me, but it does. He owes me nothing and may have only been talking to the woman, yet I feel deceived. Or at least, I'm worried about being deceived.

I don't trust Zeno. That much is clear.

He hurt me years ago, and a part of me fears he'll do it again. Am I willing to take that risk?

"It's not like he was asking her to come back. Now that you're working at the house, they don't need any more staff. It was so intriguing."

Would Zeno seek out Anna to hire her back in order to get me away from Nevio? That would be crazy. It couldn't be ... could it?

"Yeah," I say distractedly. "Hey, I actually need to get back to work, but I'm glad you called."

"I'm glad I did, too. Just hearing your voice makes me feel better."

"Love you, G."

"You too, Isa."

We hang up, but I don't hurry back inside. I had stepped out the side door when Gia called, but now, I need a minute alone. Only, there are two dueling brothers who don't get that memo because two texts ping on my phone simultaneously.

Zeno: What's wrong?

Nevio: How has your week started out?

Zeno's unusual text draws my attention first.

Me to Zeno: Why would you think something's wrong?

Zeno: Because I'm watching you on the security cameras.

My heart leaps into my throat as my eyes dart up to the eves of the house. Of course, there are cameras. I knew that, but it never occurred to me he'd be watching. I slip back into the kitchen to escape his view.

Me to Nevio: All is quiet here. How about you?
Me to Zeno: Stop watching me! Everything is fine.
Don't you have meetings with other women to attend to? My insecurities flare to life in my head, begging me to lash out. I'm able to keep them caged, for the moment.

Nevio: This trip is a waste of my time, but I knew it would be. It's Zeno's way of exerting his power over me. He can call me to the city, but that won't keep me from you forever. 😉

Zeno: How else do you expect me to know what's going on when you never texted me back?

I scroll up to look at his messages and realize he's right. Technically, there was one last text from him telling me not to ignore him. I had ignored it.

I switch back to my conversation with Nevio and start to reply only to come up short. I don't know what to say to him. I want to keep things light because I don't want to lead him on. Judging by his comment, though, he already thinks we're … together.

Me to Nevio: ~~When do you think you'll be back?~~
That implies I'm here waiting for him.
Me to Nevio: 😶 **At least the city is never boring!**

Perfect. Neutral yet engaging. I'll deal with him later. Back to Zeno.

I imagine him with Anna. I remember the months of hurt and worry after he quit talking to me when we were younger, then I hear all the harsh words he spoke to me in the years since. He suddenly wants to connect with me, but only after years of pushing me away. He has no right to expect anything from me. Maybe I'd be better off walking away from both brothers—God knows it would be easier.

Me to Zeno: I don't have to tell you anything. It was phone sex between two people who had an itch to scratch. That's it.

Harsh but necessary. I'm tired of being blown around like a leaf caught in his turbulent winds.

Nevio: I'd still rather be with you. I'm coming back no matter what on Friday. Will I be able to see you?

I can picture his dimpled grin coaxing me to say yes, but I respect my father too much to ignore his warning. I don't understand it, but I don't have to.

Me to Nevio: I should be around. *That sounds vague enough.*

Zeno: Is that what you think?

Me to Zeno: What have you done over the years to suggest anything different?

Nevio: Knowing I get to see you once I'm back makes this trip tolerable.

Me to Nevio: See you soon!

Shit. Was an exclamation point too much?

Zeno: Nothing. I've done everything I could to push you away.

His words cut deeper than I'd like. So deep, my hand plants against my stomach to keep the bleeding at bay. The only consolation is that I now know he recognizes the way he's acted toward me. He knows exactly what he's done.

I stare at the screen of my phone for several agonizing minutes. Tears blur my vision, then retreat, but I can't force myself to text a reply. There is nothing left to say. Zeno must feel the same because my phone falls silent.

I force myself back to work, but I'm lethargic at best. Between the prospect of hurting Nevio and the pain of Zeno's confession, I fall deep into a melancholy haze. I find places to work in the house where I'm guaranteed to be alone. I'm even hesitant to answer the phone when Grace calls well into the afternoon, but I worry she could be in trouble, so I force myself to take the call.

"Hey, Grace. What's up?"

"I'm planning a trip into the city to look at apartments and wanted to ask if you'd come with me."

"When were you thinking of going?"

"I was hoping to leave Thursday and come back Sunday."

"I would, but I can't ask for time off when I've only been working a week." Although, having a break from the incessant drama here would be a welcome relief.

"I know it's a big ask, but I really need your help. I've never done this before, and I don't know anyone else who could help guide me through the process."

I don't have to hear the concern in her voice to feel compelled to help her. She is a fish out of water in the city, and if she doesn't have experienced help, she might end up in an even worse situation than she's already in. And I'm the reason she's in that situation—I invited Aldo to meet me at our house. If I hadn't done that, she'd never have run into him.

"Okay, let me find Elena and talk to her. I'll let you

know what she says." It can't hurt to ask. And after all, this isn't my forever job.

"Thank you so much, Luisa! You don't know how much this means to me."

"Don't thank me until I get the thumbs-up. I'll text you in a bit."

Grace will be on pins and needles until I text with an answer, so I go straight in search of Elena. I'm not worried about her being upset. I'm almost certain she'll agree, but I feel bad taking advantage of my situation. She's been so kind to give me a job on short notice, and now I'm asking for more.

I find her alone in the library, scrolling on her phone. "Hey, Elena. Do you have a second?"

She's a stunning woman, even in her fifties. With blond waving hair and green eyes that change in the light, she could be a model. Her cheeks are smooth and full above perfectly shaped lips that almost curve upward without her even smiling. Her hair is blond, which hides any sneaky gray hairs, and the few creases she's gained through the years are minimal. She's absolutely gorgeous, inside and out.

"Of course, come sit down." She motions for me to sit in the armchair across from hers.

"Thank you. I just got a call from Grace—the Larson's daughter."

"Of course, Grace is such a sweet girl."

I smile in agreement. "She's making the big move to the city and needs to find an apartment, but she knows nothing about the process or where to look. I know I just started, and I feel terrible for asking, but if it wouldn't be a huge inconvenience, I'd like to go to the city Thursday to help her. I'm worried if someone isn't with her, she'll end up in a bad neighborhood or a terrible lease."

"Oh! Of course! I can't imagine how overwhelming that would be." Her brows knit together, a sign that her beauty is a product of excellent genes and not buckets of Botox.

"I really appreciate it and want to assure you that I'm not going to run off every weekend."

Elena puts her hand over my knee and smiles warmly. "Life happens sometimes. And not always when we expect it."

"No kidding," I murmur with an apologetic smile.

I expect this to end our conversation, but Elena's head tilts to the side, and she peers at me questioningly.

"Luisa, would you be willing to talk to me about why you ended up back here?"

The silence in the library is suddenly deafening.

I'm not sure why everyone insists on pushing this issue when I have no desire to talk about it. However, I asked for a huge favor from my new boss, and I hate to deny her a simple request for understanding.

I look down at my hands pressed flat together, tucked between my thighs. "I just hit a bump in the road. I'm not thrilled to have to move home, but it's not forever."

"That's right. You know, life rarely goes as expected. I don't talk much about it, but many years ago, I had a miscarriage. I hadn't told anyone about the pregnancy, but I was *so* excited. That baby was a new life—a new beginning. I was devastated over the loss." The lingering sorrow in her voice is unmistakable.

"I'm so sorry, I had no idea."

"No one did. And the only reason I tell you now is because I want you to know you aren't alone. Just because people don't talk about problems doesn't mean they don't have them. I hated feeling like I was going through that alone, and I recognized the turmoil in your eyes. It may not be a lost baby you're dealing with, but life interruptions can be difficult no matter the source."

I nod because words escape me. I'm so touched by her sincerity and vulnerability. She didn't have to put herself out there, but she could see I was struggling and decided to forge a connection.

"More specifically," she continues, "if money is the reason you had to leave the city, I want to help. You are so close to your goal—your parents are always telling me about all your accomplishments. I have the means to get you back on track, and I'd like to do that."

I list backward as though the power of her words has physically moved me. Shock doesn't even begin to describe how I feel. Dumbfounded. Awestruck. Humbled.

"Elena, I don't know what to say."

"Just tell me how much—that's the only thing you need to say."

And it would be that easy. Her sincerity is plain in her loving green eyes. But I'm not the type of person who could take a handout like that. Maybe it's my father's teachings that nothing free comes without a price, but I can't do it.

I shake my head slowly. "You are giving me the money I need by paying me to work. It won't take but a few months, and I'll have what I need without owing you or anyone else. I am incredibly grateful for the chance to work at Hardwick, and right now, that's all I need."

Elena smiles affectionately, but there's a glimmer of sadness in her eyes. "You're an independent young woman, and I suppose I should have expected nothing less. However, in a world where women need to stick together, I hope you'll reconsider. My offer has no expiration."

Her generosity and solidarity nearly bring me to tears. It's true that as women in Mafia families, we are our own best allies, yet there is often pettiness and rivalry among us. And as the matriarch of such a powerful family, she could easily be guarded and wary of outsiders. But that's not Elena. The harsh reality of our world hasn't touched her—or maybe it has, but only in the best way. She recognizes the ugliness around her and chooses to be a light in the darkness.

I push forward and wrap my arms around her. "Thank you, Elena. Your support means so much to me."

"I adore my boys, yet having a daughter would have been a special blessing. That wasn't in the cards for me, but I've been lucky enough to watch you girls grow up and want the best for you. If you ever need me, all you have to do is ask."

It's been easy to become overwhelmed by the chaos of my current life, yet a single outreach from a friend leaves me feeling centered and stable when I return to work. In part because I now technically have options, but also because compassion feeds the soul.

Elena is a special woman. I see her generosity and friendliness reflected in Nevio's eyes. I can't help but wonder what happened to Zeno. At one point, the two brothers were both playful and innocent, then something changed. Zeno changed. And I wonder if I'll ever learn the truth behind that transformation.

CHAPTER 21

"Grace texted. The Uber is on the way." I set my ridiculously overstuffed bag by the front door. Without knowing what exactly we'll be doing while in the city, I end up packing most of what I originally brought to my parents' house.

I give my parents hugs in the kitchen. They usually come home for lunch anyway, but today, they both got here early to make sure they saw me off. I suppose some things never change. And even though my mom makes me crazy, I appreciate that she's present and tries the best she can.

"You two have a wonderful time." Dad engulfs me in one of his perfect hugs before I move to give Mom a quick hug as well.

"We'll be pretty busy checking out apartments, but we'll

have a great time together no matter what we're doing." I've successfully avoided Nevio and will have several more days to put off discussions with him, which is a relief. This will be an escape from him and all the rest of my troubles, at least for a few days. "A friend of mine is taking us in for the weekend, so we'll also get to hang out with her."

"Damn!" Dad says suddenly. "I totally forgot to give you this." He digs in his pocket and pulls out a folded sticky note. "That's the address to Z's apartment in the city."

I take the paper and peer at it warily. "What's it for?"

Dad grins. "I told him what you were up to, and he insisted you stay there. That way, you have your own space and don't have to crash with your friend."

"But isn't *he* staying at his place?"

"No, I don't think so. He made it sound like the place was empty. It's a gorgeous apartment. You should take advantage of the offer!"

I nod and slip the address into my pocket, but I'm confused. Why would Zeno offer up his place? We haven't talked or texted in two days. Considering our last exchange, I figured we were on shaky ground. Had he truly meant to let us stay in his home, or was he simply being respectful to my father? Like offering a part of your lunch to someone when you're crazy hungry and prefer to eat it all yourself.

I don't know the answer, but I'll find out before we roll up at his apartment.

The car arrives within minutes, picking me up first, then Grace. We talk excitedly for a while before I explain the possible change in arrangements.

"That would be so incredibly awesome!" Grace is practically vibrating in her seat.

"Before you get too excited, I need to text him and hear for myself that he's good with it and wasn't just being polite."

"I totally understand. I need to make a quick call to check in with my real estate agent anyway."

We both pull out our phones and get to work. When I open my text conversation with Z, my eyes graze the last words he wrote, carving out my insides a little further.

I've done everything I could to push you away.

I hate that he can make me feel so empty with a few careless words. Gritting my teeth, I swear to myself that I will not give him that kind of power over me.

Me: Dad says you offered your apartment to Grace and me. Are you sure about that?

Simple. Straightforward. Unbothered. Not the text of a woman who can't find herself beneath a landslide of emotions.

Zeno: It's just an apartment, Luisa. You might as well use it if it's empty.

It doesn't feel like *just* an apartment. It feels personal—staying at someone's home when they aren't there. Especially for someone as private as Zeno.

Me: Where are you staying?

Zeno: I won't be at the apartment.

Shit. Why did I ask when I really don't want to know? Now, all I can think about is whether Z is staying with a woman in the city. I stare at the screen of my phone long enough that the phone begins to ring before I can respond. Zeno is calling me.

"Hello?" I answer awkwardly as though I'm a child answering a call on my mother's phone.

"The mayor's place is up in Lincoln Square. We've been working on some negotiations this week, and I didn't want to deal with commuting, so I got a hotel room here. Take the apartment, Luisa."

"Okay," I breathe. The vibrations of his voice short-circuit my brain, especially when he says my name. I don't know why. It's not the first time I've heard him speak, but it's the first time I imagine the words he texted coming from those lips. Sexy, dirty words abrading my skin with their gravelly need.

Get a grip, woman!

"Um ... key. Do I—will I need a key?"

"I'll text you the code, and I've already informed security of your arrival. There are three bedrooms—you're welcome to take your pick. Use whatever you need."

I still don't understand why he's doing this when he admitted days ago that he didn't want me around. I don't understand, but I'm also not going to reject his offer. Taking thousands of dollars from Elena is too much, but a weekend in an upscale apartment ... *that* I can do.

"Thank you, Z."

His voice drops to a velvet caress. "Be safe, Isa."

I'm breathless when the line goes dead. My mouth is dry, and there's a nagging ache in my chest. It takes Grace's excited chatter to stir me from my Zeno hangover. I tell her the good news about the apartment and give the address to the driver. The rest of our ride goes smoothly, though I remain somewhat lost in my own confused thoughts.

The apartment is jaw-droppingly gorgeous. The concierge escorts us up to make sure we get in safely, and we wait until he leaves to squeal with excitement. Or at least, Grace squeals. I am too overwhelmed—with the extent of his wealth and the fact I'm surrounded in Zeno. It's so different than being in Hardwick. The old mansion brings memories of childhood in a setting steeped with history. Pieces of Z are present there, but not like this. The apartment is where he lived for years until his father's death. Everything about the understated elegance of the place screams *Zeno*, from the sweeping panoramic views to the clean, modern lines and the pristine mix of wood and concrete. A custom light fixture of overlapping rectangles hangs over the dining room table from the two-story ceiling. The apartment is stately, bold yet reserved, and undeniably masculine. Zeno is here in every muted fabric and stoic painting gracing the walls.

"I can*not* believe we get to stay here. This is *incredible*!" Grace spins around, eyes wide and her jaw hanging open. "We have to check out the bedrooms." She scurries away, and I am right behind her. Z's bedroom is too tempting to resist. Another woman in my position might respect his privacy, but the opportunity is too great, and my curiosity about him is endless.

First, we come across a bedroom accented in reds with rich walnut furniture before peeking at a similarly outfitted second bedroom utilizing a deep royal blue for its pop of color. Each is equipped with an en-suite bathroom complete with a soaker tub.

"Which do you want?" Grace asks.

"Oh, I don't care. You pick."

"I guess I'll go with red. Let's check out the master before we unpack, though. I'm sure it's amazing." She leads us to the other side of the apartment, where a hallway cordons off a private entrance to the master. The bedroom is cozier than I expected. The ceiling is vaulted about a foot with lights tucked away to illuminate the recessed top. There are four windows, tall but not particularly wide. They are each outfitted with heavy rolling shades currently halfway lowered. Opposite the king-sized bed is a large fireplace bumped out from the wall with bench seats on either side and a window above each. The space is soothing and comfortable—not exactly words I would have used for Zeno.

"Pretty epic," Grace muses. "I can't imagine."

"Me either."

"Come on, let's get settled so I can show you the areas my agent recommended. I want to hear your thoughts."

I unload my things in the blue bedroom, then join Grace on her bed. She pulls up emails, showing me a couple of places the agent suggested. We talk extensively about the city—jobs, apartments, restaurants. Everything. I love sharing all my hard-earned knowledge with her.

After a while, we check out the impressive patio we'd forgone on our first inspection of the home. The day is warm, but the breeze from being up so high helps cut the heat.

"This place is so gorgeous," I muse. "I hate to even leave for dinner."

"I'm right there with you. How about we order in for tonight? We'll be out in the city the next two days and can eat out plenty then."

"Sounds like a plan to me." My grin almost hurts. I'm so pleased we got this chance to spend time together. Grace truly is a great person and a wonderful friend.

We order pizza and make ourselves comfortable on the large sectional in the living room. Of course, Zeno has every TV channel imaginable, so we spend ages scrolling through options before we land on a classic.

"*Clueless*! I love this movie, and it just started a few minutes ago." Grace claps her hands, making me giggle.

"It's pretty much perfect. *Rollin' with the homies*," I sing, and we both wave our hands like Brittany Murphy does in the movie, then we burst into a fit of giggles.

"Man, did Paul Rudd age well. I mean … yum." She smacks her lips, and we both laugh again.

"No kidding. He can play such goofy characters, but those eyes."

"And that body—did you see him in *Ant-Man*?" She fans herself. "You know who else is crazy gorgeous?"

I look at her quizzically.

A mischievous grin lights up her face. "Zeno."

I try to shake my head to tell her not to go there, but she quiets me.

"No way. You went on a date with Nevio, and now Zeno is letting you use his apartment? This warrants a little more information."

"There's nothing to tell. I won't be going on a second date with Nevio, and absolutely nothing is going on with Z." Nothing real. Nothing of substance.

"What happened with Nevio to warrant a one-and-done?"

"He's a great guy, but you remember how he was when we were younger. I'm not interested in being with a playboy." Telling her that is easier than describing my father's vague warning. She'd probably argue Dad is being overprotective, and I'm not in the mood for that conversation.

"I guess I do. I didn't hang out with him in high school the way you did. What about Z? I find it hard to believe he'd offer his place to just anyone."

"I honestly can't tell you what he's thinking. You know how impossible he can be." *And mysterious, and alluring, and totally consuming.* "He wants to be the next underboss of the Giordano family, maybe even the boss, and that's all that matters to him. Ambition. Reputation."

"Yeah, but look what he has to offer." She motions to the room around us. "You'd never have to worry about rent or insurance or anything again."

"There are more important things than money," I murmur, that hollow feeling returning. "Z may seem enticing from the outside, but he's done some pretty awful things."

"Like what?" Grace sobers along with me.

"Well, who knows what he's done as part of his job, but there's also the way he treats his brother. He's practically exiled him from the family. That's why Nevio didn't come to dinner at the Bishops' the other night. The two don't get along for some reason, and Z uses his power and position to lord over his younger brother."

Disbelief mottles her features. "You're kidding?"

I shake my head gravely.

"I had no idea."

"I knew they didn't get along, but until I came back home, I didn't have a clue how bad it was. It's heartbreaking, and I feel especially bad for Nevio. Z told me he knew Nevio and I had gone on a date. When I asked him how he knew, he said he *keeps tabs* on his brother. It's so strange. Sometimes, I wonder if he's jealous of Nevio's easy nature, but I hate to believe he could be that petty."

A sly smile creeps back on her face. "Nevio is *extremely* likable."

I chuckle. "You're terrible." I'm about to continue chastising her when a knock sounds at the door.

Grace and I both stand stock-still, eyes locked on each other before I snap out of my shock and scramble for the front door.

Holy crap, who's here? Surely, it's not Zeno. But who else stops by unannounced? Please, God, please don't let it be a woman.

I close my eyes and take a single deep breath before opening the door. As if I wasn't shocked enough, Christiano De Bellis stands impatiently in the hallway. A hulking man in a suit that strains around his biceps stands off to the side, eyes cast away.

"Hello, can I help you?" I don't acknowledge that I know the man because I'm certain he won't remember me

—I am nothing to him—but I won't soon forget the sight of the Giordano family boss.

He lifts his chin, studying me with a quick flick of his eyes before glancing back to where Grace is cowering in the living room behind me. "I was looking for Zeno. Is he home?"

"No, I'm afraid not. He was kind enough to let us stay for a couple of nights while we're in the city."

Did the heat in here just kick on? Am I sweating? Oh, God. Please don't sweat in front of this man.

"I see. They told me downstairs that someone was occupying the apartment, and I thought perhaps Zeno had come back early." Christiano's eyes narrow. "I'm surprised to find you here, I must say. I'm not sure I've ever known Zeno to host guests while he's away."

"Well, my family works for his. We've known each other all our lives." I try to explain.

He doesn't look convinced, and I'm not sure what part of our situation he questions.

"You look familiar. We met at the funeral, did we not?"

I smile gently, hoping our connection will help me find my way into his good graces. "Yes, I'm Luisa Banetti. My father is Antonio Banetti. He worked for Silvano for decades."

Recognition registers, but I don't feel any less scrutinized.

"If Zeno calls you family, then I do as well. Join me for dinner tomorrow night at seven, you and your friend. I own the penthouse upstairs. You can ring security from the elevator, and they will clear your arrival." This was not a request or an invitation.

"Yes, sir. We would be honored." I smile and tuck my chin to show the proper deference.

Christiano gives a tiny bow of his head. "I look forward to seeing you again. Enjoy your evening."

My legs almost give out after I close the door.

"Who the hell was that?" Grace hisses across the room.

Trouble. That was trouble.

I have no idea why Christiano would deign it necessary to invite us to his home, but I had no way to refuse. I couldn't say no to one of the most powerful, dangerous men in the world. A man to whom my father swore an oath of allegiance.

"That was Christiano De Bellis, boss of the Giordano family, and he's invited us to his place for dinner tomorrow."

"Oh, shit," she breathes.

You said it.

CHAPTER 22

We spend the bulk of Friday hopping around the city looking at apartments. After our last stop, we swing by my storage facility. I need to extend my rental agreement and retrieve more of my clothes. There's not much else I need while living with my parents, and I don't own all that much, anyway. It's hard to accumulate things when you've been living in a five-hundred-square-foot studio with a roommate.

Grace helps me lug back the two boxes of clothes and shoes. When we finally stumble back to Zeno's apartment, we're exhausted.

"Let's leave the boxes by the door. I can deal with them later," I tell Grace.

"Oh, thank *God*." Her box crashes to the ground next to mine. "I have to go sit."

We both melt onto the sectional sofa like a pair of wilting flowers.

"Why is it that in summer, I can't wait for winter's cooler temps, but come January, I wonder why we don't all move to Florida?" Grace muses absently.

"Ain't that the truth."

"Hey, what are you wearing tonight for dinner?"

"Ugh, I have no idea. Probably a dress, assuming I can stop sweating. Otherwise, I may have to go in a swimsuit."

"At least you have your whole closet here. I should have shopped for a dress today."

"Please," I scoff. "What does it matter what he thinks of our clothes? I'm going out of respect, but I don't need to impress Christiano De Bellis." If he doesn't like what I wear, he doesn't have to invite me back.

Please, don't invite me back.

"That's easy for you to say. You look good in *everything*." She says it teasingly, but the statement is rooted in insecurity.

"Grace, you are stunning with all that dark hair and ivory skin. I don't know how you don't see it. Come on." I drag myself from the sofa. "Let's get showered. We'll feel so much better once we do our hair and makeup."

"I suppose scraping off these sweat-soaked clothes can't hurt. What an interesting evening we're going to have. At the very least, it'll be a great story for later."

I shoot her a thin smile but grimace on the inside. I can only hope our evening is so uneventful, outside of the company we'll share, that it is never, ever worth mentioning again. My father will ask me about it, but that's only because I called him this morning to tell him what had happened. I felt like he needed to know. Chances were slim that Christiano was going to toss me in the river, but still. Crazier things have happened. Dad assured me we'd be fine but insisted I text him after dinner.

I get myself ready relatively quickly, then help Grace with her makeup to give her what she calls "a city look." I'm assuming that means a heavier application of shadow than usual. I'm pleased with how it turns out, and when she rounds the corner after putting on the clubbing outfit she'd tried to hide from me, she looks downright dangerous. She'd be better off not joining me tonight, but the selfish side of me demands her presence for moral support. Seeing her all decked out, I'm glad she has a reason to dress up.

"Holy shit, Grace! You look gorgeous. Why on *earth* wouldn't you want to wear that outfit?" Her black cropped pants are formfitting, showing off her curves to their fullest. Instead of hiding her hourglass figure with an oversized shirt, she wears a fitted sequin camisole in a rich forest green. With the littlest bit of confidence, she would be unstoppable.

"I don't know. I got it on a whim, not expecting to actually ever wear it."

"Well, my friend, you're wearing it tonight, and you're going to own it. You look fabulous."

Her makeup isn't so heavy that I can't detect the blush that creeps across her smiling cheeks. "Come on, let's get going before I change my mind."

I wipe my suddenly sweaty palms on the bed before I

stand and straighten my own dress. I had to give it a little steam treatment in the bathroom while I did my hair because it was buried in one of the boxes we retrieved. It's gunmetal gray in a stretchy fabric that bunches from my waist down to where it stops at my knees. I debated about wearing it because of the top—it's sexy as hell. The fabric pulls diagonal across my chest, outlining my breasts and leaving my right arm bare. The left arm is covered in a three-quarters sleeve, and the overall look is edgy but classy. I'm hoping it will give me the confidence I need to survive the night.

Inside the elevator, I press the button labeled for the penthouse. A masculine voice crackles from the speaker.

"Yeah?"

"This is Luisa Banetti. Mr. De Bellis invited us for dinner tonight?" I can't help the uncertainty that transforms my statement into a question.

In response, the elevator lurches into motion. My wide gaze locks with Grace's as we rise to the top of the building. The doors open onto a luxurious landing area where a very large, very serious man in a suit with an earpiece studies us. He eventually extends a hand to direct us inside. I shoot him a tight smile and try to look like I belong when, in truth, I only want to avoid his eyes and scurry away.

Grace shadows each of my steps, staying strictly behind me as we take in the magnificence of the penthouse residence. Glossy marble floors and twenty-foot ceilings make the space bright and airy, if not a touch institutional. Where Zeno's apartment showcases an earthy, modern design, Christiano's place is ultra-contemporary. White on white with the occasional splash of black or red or silver. The simple palette enables the sweeping New York skyline to serve as the focal point, visible through enormous plate glass windows the full length of the main living area and curving around toward the kitchen, making the dining room appear suspended over the city.

"You must be Luisa. I'm Arianna De Bellis, but you're welcome to call me Ari." A beautiful young woman with black hair and striking blue eyes joins us from the kitchen. She extends a hand, and I'm struck by the memory of Nevio telling me that Zeno is expected to marry Christiano's daughter. The realization that this goddess is probably her chafes at my skin.

I brush the confusing emotion aside and smile. "Hey, Ari. It's lovely to meet you. This is my good friend, Grace."

"Grace," Ari says as if to test the word on her lips. "It's a pleasure to meet you." The two shake hands, and I'd almost swear something passes between them. Something about the sensual quirk of Ari's lips and the way Grace's cheeks blossom with color.

When Ari turns back to me without any sign of awkwardness or unease, I wonder if my imagination is acting up.

"Would either of you like a drink while we wait? My father is still back in his office."

"That sounds great. What would you suggest?"

"I was about to throw together a gin and tonic, but I can get you whatever you'd like. Maybe some wine? Dad will want a glass when he comes out."

"That sounds perfect." I smile and amble after her

toward a minibar next to the kitchen, where an older woman is finishing the preparations for dinner. Ari doesn't introduce her, so I simply smile when our eyes meet, then peer back at the grand living area. "I'd tell you that your home is lovely, but words don't do it justice."

Ari smiles as she pulls out bottles from the cabinets. "Thanks. It's definitely something. A little much for me. None of this is really my style, but it suits Dad to a T." She's wearing a snug collared blouse that comes to a plunging V below her breasts and stylish pleated slacks with stilettos. Her sleek, glossy hair is slicked back into a long ponytail, and the smoky shadow she's wearing makes her eyes almost glow. Altogether, she's a warrior queen—her beauty only outdone by the strong sense of confidence she radiates.

"I don't know. I'd say you fit in just fine."

She lifts her eyes, peering at me from beneath a forest of lashes. "Looks can be deceiving." She then pours a glass of wine, lifts it to her nose, and sniffs gently as she swirls the liquid, then casts her gaze at my silent friend. "I think you'll like this one, Grace. Not too dry and just sweet enough to tease your tastebuds." She hands the glass to Grace and waits to watch while my wide-eyed friend samples the selection. "What do you think?"

"It's excellent," Grace breathes. "Are you sure you don't want a glass?"

A devilish smile spreads on Ari's face. "Oh, no. I have to have something stronger if I'm going to tolerate my father all evening. He's not exactly the nurturing type." Ari winks to make light of her comment, but in reality, having Christiano for a father had to be difficult. If his austere exterior is any indication of what he's like behind closed doors, I doubt he played Uno with Ari or took her to the zoo as a kid.

"Don't say that," Grace hisses playfully, regaining a touch of her normal self. "I'm already nervous as hell."

"I believe he's more interested in this one." Ari nods in my direction. "So you shouldn't have anything to worry about."

"Why me?" I gape at her. "I can't even figure out why we're here."

Ari shrugs. "That's my father. He likes to keep people guessing. I was invited on short notice and only just told that you would be joining us, so I'm of no help."

"Well, it was a good excuse to get dressed up. I just hope I don't say the wrong thing, whatever that might be."

"You'll be fine." She hands me my glass. I'm grateful for the liquid courage, especially when footsteps hail the approach of our intimidating host.

I don't fully understand why he makes me so anxious. My father's been in the Mafia all my life, though I rarely witness that aspect of his world. But I've heard rumors. Whispers about the ruthless Giordano boss and his endless influence and power. The thought of pissing off a man like him is terrifying.

"Ladies, I'm glad you've had a chance to meet. How is the wine selection this evening?" Christiano is dressed in a dark navy suit, and though he's older, he's fit and handsome enough to be featured on an upscale cologne ad. I shouldn't have been surprised at Ari's good looks—she came from incredible genes.

"It's delicious," I offer.

"I happen to be particularly fond of acquiring a broad range of vintages. I've been told my collection is incomparable." He lifts the open bottle to examine the label. "Yes, this one is direct from Tuscany and not a bad year, though I prefer the Pinot Noir from that lot."

"I'm afraid I don't know much about wines besides whether I like one or not, but this one is excellent."

Christiano eyes me as he slowly pours himself a glass. "If you're not into wine, what do you enjoy, Miss Banetti?"

I get the sense his opinion of me hinges on how I answer the next series of questions. No pressure.

"I enjoy reading. I'm actually close to finishing up my degree in English literature at St. Joseph's."

"Is that so? I was under the impression you were living with your parents at Hardwick."

I sip from my glass to help dilute the bitterness of my next words. "I encountered a small hiccup recently and had to postpone my final year of classes."

He leans his hip against the counter and feigns a look of remorse. "That's too bad. It seems it's already taken you a while to get this far, so further delays have to be most unwelcome."

I'm not sure if he's implying I'm slow or old or both, but it's undoubtedly an insult, no matter how I examine the statement.

"Life is about the journey, not the destination." I force a smile, and my eyes slice over to Ari, who has been surprisingly silent. I expected more engagement from someone so confident. Her suave nonchalance has been replaced with bristling irritation kept in tight check with restraint more hardened than tempered steel. When her eyes find mine, they are brimming with apology and frustration before falling to examine the glass of ice in her hand—the glass that had been full minutes before when her father joined us. If I were to guess, I'd say Ari's father is her Achilles' heel —the thorn beneath her armor.

The catlike grin Christiano flashes me makes me wonder if I've stepped into some invisible trap. As though he'd hoped I'd respond exactly as I had.

"A trite phrase used by the underprivileged to assuage their lack of accomplishment."

Oh, yeah. He's definitely putting me down. What the actual hell?

He's crafty. Calculating. If I didn't know better, I'd say he was hunting for opportunities to belittle me. But why? And if he acted like that around everyone, how had some hothead not killed him years ago? Ari may feel caged by her father, but I suffer no such afflictions.

"I suppose I'd rather be underprivileged and content than wealthy and unsatisfied."

The look on his face is smug, as though only he knows what a great fool I am, and I'm only too happy to let him think what he will. His opinion of me is totally irrelevant to my life.

A murmur of deep voices saves us like the proverbial bell as they echo in from the front entry. I glance at the dining table and realize that there are five place settings. I'd admired the artfully arranged settings when we entered, but I'd been too distracted to notice the number. I turn back to wonder at our fifth guest when not one but two men step into view, and one of them snares me in his piercing blue gaze. Zeno is *here*, and the shock paralyzes me. Did he know I would be here? If he did, why didn't he tell me he was coming? Is he upset that I'm having dinner at his boss's home?

I have no answers, and his austere façade gives no clues.

The man at his side is familiar. I recall Christiano introducing him at the funeral as his nephew, but I don't remember his name. He's handsome with a heavy shadow of hair on his face that accents his square jaw structure. Unlike Zeno, this man's posture is more relaxed. I get the sense he's easygoing—somewhat unusual in the Mafia world. My father fits that mold, but he hasn't had much to do with the business since his youth. I would expect someone vying for the underboss position to be more fierce. More intimidating. Someone more like Zeno. But I guess if you're the boss's nephew, that changes things.

"Savio, I see you brought a guest." Christiano doesn't sound particularly thrilled with Zeno's arrival. Nor does he sound like he knew Zeno was coming. That would mean Savio was our fifth. So, why was Zeno here if he wasn't invited?

The new arrivals both approach and shake hands with their boss while Savio explains himself.

"I was telling Z that I had plans to join you for dinner, and he said he'd wrapped up his business early, so I invited him to join us. I hope that's not a problem."

Wrapped up his business early? Did that mean he planned to stay at his apartment? I try to focus on the conversation, but my thoughts are reeling.

"Of course, not," Christiano says dryly. "Let me introduce you to our other guests. Savio, this is Luisa Banetti and her friend Grace. I happened to learn of their stay at Zeno's place and invited them up. Zeno hadn't told me he had such lovely guests occupying his home." Christiano looks at Z with a challenge, making me increasingly uncomfortable. I don't know what I've stepped into the middle of, but something is definitely going on. Fortunately, he continues with the introductions. "Ladies, this is Savio Fiore, my nephew, and I assume you know Zeno, as you are all neighbors … of sorts."

We all smile and say hello.

"Luisa here was just telling us about her love of literature—something we could all probably use a little more of. With social media becoming so pervasive, the finer arts seem to be dwindling." Christiano's complimentary presentation of my interests surprise me when he'd been openly critical minutes before.

"Do you teach?" Savio asks, his gaze intent as though he's genuinely interested.

"No, I'm still finishing up my degree. I got a late start and have paid for school myself, so it's been a bit of a process."

"Dedicated *and* independent—very impressive." Savio turns his raised brows to his uncle. "I can understand why you'd lure her up here to enlighten our otherwise brutish dinner plans." He grins, glancing at Zeno, who isn't remotely entertained.

"She should be here in the city finishing that degree rather than working back at Hardwick. It makes me wonder what could possibly be problematic enough to interrupt her when she is so close to the finish line." Zeno stares at me as if he hadn't just spoken about me while I am standing in front of him.

My spine lengthens as I flash my most brilliant smile, trying not to falter when the sight makes him visibly flinch.

"I would have told you all about it if it hadn't been a personal matter." I hold my head high, but his behavior makes every cell inside me want to retreat.

"Well," Savio cuts in, tossing me a lifeline. "I have no doubt that someone as devoted to her passions as you are will follow through at the first opportunity." He smiles warmly at me then turns to Grace. "And your lovely friend, Grace, was it? You've been awfully neglected over here. Tell us about yourself."

Grace blanches momentarily before responding. "There's not a whole lot to tell. I'm in the process of moving to the city. That's actually why Luisa and I are here. To look at apartments for me."

"How exciting!" Savio is a natural conversationalist. He may not be intimidating, but he would make an excellent spokesperson. "I was born and raised in the city, so I can't imagine living anywhere else."

"When your livelihood depends upon the people you know," Christiano inserts, "you might find a more suburban home like mine a necessity." The older man turns to look at me for his next comment. "I have a home on the opposite side of the lake as Zeno. The networking in our area is incomparable." He turns back to his nephew. "One of these days, you'll embrace the notion."

"Only time will tell." Savio smiles, but his lips are stretched thin. "It looks as though dinner is ready. I don't know about everyone else, but I'm starved."

We all make our way to the table, Christiano in the host's seat at the end, Grace and Ari slip back to the far side, leaving me between Savio and Zeno. My stomach seizes so tightly that I have no idea how I'll eat a single bite. We distribute the food from elegant serving ware that the cook places on the table. Once our plates are full and we begin to eat, Savio resumes our conversation.

"How long are you ladies in town?"

"A couple of nights," I answer. "We'll head back to Hardwick on Sunday." I set down my fork as my eyes peer to the broodingly silent man on my other side. "If your business has finished early, we can stay somewhere else," I say softly, hoping to keep the discussion between us.

Savio kindly takes the hint and engages Ari in a discussion about her most recent trip abroad. I'm mildly curious about where she visited but more interested in Zeno's response. Every ounce of my attention is concentrated on him.

"That isn't necessary," he assures me quietly but brusquely. "I'd already made arrangements to stay with Savio. That's why I'd called him in the first place. When I heard you'd been invited to dinner, I knew I had to join."

"I hope you know that I never meant to intrude in your

life. He showed up at the door, and—" I lean in to make sure I'm not overheard. "I didn't feel like I could refuse."

"I'm not upset, Luisa. At least, not about that."

Then what are you upset about? Why did you feel like you had to come here?

I peer over at him, and our gazes lock. The questions inherent in my stare collide with his impenetrable walls and clatter to the ground, unanswered.

He's the first to sever our connection. I turn my attention to the table conversation and try to look engaged despite the frustration gnawing away at my insides.

Dinner goes better than expected. We discuss a number of random subjects, primarily led by Savio. Ari even contributes to matters not instigated by her father. Where he is concerned, she is quiet—withdrawn, even. It amazes me that such a vibrant, strong woman could so visibly change herself to fit a mold imposed by someone else. I want to reach across the table and shake her shoulders, insisting that she not clip her own wings for his approval, but I know nothing about their situation. It would be presumptive to assume otherwise.

When our evening comes to a close, Christiano shocks me by insisting we come together again once he's back at his lakeside house. I smile and nod, thanking him for his hospitality and pray his invitation was mere politeness. One dinner with the Mafia boss was enough for me.

The second the elevator doors close, signaling the end of our night, Grace slumps back against the wall and opens her mouth to speak, but I quickly silence her with a finger to my lips and direct her gaze to the speaker system. I'm not sure if anyone would be listening, but better safe than sorry.

Once we are back at Zeno's apartment, I finally let down my guard. The release of my coiled muscles and piqued awareness makes me feel like a vine without its trellis, swaying in the wind.

"Holy shit, that was exhausting." I drop my purse on the console by the door and step out of my heels.

"It was something, that's for sure. I felt like I'd stepped onto the set of *Dallas*—rich people stirring up drama for no reason—none of it felt real. The intensity and passive dueling? Incredible."

I huff out a laugh. "Yeah, it was. If Savio hadn't been there to keep things flowing and upbeat, dinner would have been downright oppressive."

"He was definitely personable." Grace slips off her own shoes and dangles them from the fingers of her right hand. Her eyes wander to the entryway mirror, where she appears to assess her own reflection.

"You know who else was interesting? Ari." I watch Grace carefully for her reaction. "I wish we could have gotten to know her better without her dad there."

"Yeah," she says absently. "She sure was ... unexpected."

With my eyes still glued to my friend, I join her at the mirror. "Call me crazy, but I could have sworn you two had a bit of a ... connection."

Grace's eyes widen when they collide with mine. "What do you mean?"

"I mean, I could have been wrong, but I thought you two clicked. It wouldn't matter to me at all if you were interested in her ... or other women, for that matter. She seemed really into you as far as I could tell. I was excited for you, but maybe that's not your thing." I shrug, trying not to put her on the spot.

She sucks her bottom lip between her teeth and moseys into the living area. "I hadn't thought about that kind of thing before ... as you know, I don't have much relationship experience at all. I'm not sure what to think, but she is one of the most beautiful people I've ever met. And I felt this warmth in my chest when our eyes met." She turns apprehensively toward me, her trepidation constricting my heart. "Ari asked for my number before we left."

Unadulterated joy is a shot of adrenaline to my weary psyche. "Oh, Grace! That's so exciting! Did you give it to her?" Being involved with the De Bellis family isn't ideal, but nothing would make me happier than for Grace to find her place in this world.

She nods, an anxious smile teasing her lips. "I have no idea what I'm doing. She's so gorgeous and confident, and I'm so ... so *me*. And she's a *woman*. If I was into that, I would have thought I'd known, but when she asked me, I just thought, I need to see her again. Is that crazy? Am I crazy?"

"Not at all, honey. You're perfectly normal, and I couldn't be happier for you." We meet halfway in a hug built on years of friendship and acceptance. "However, you absolutely *must* keep me posted on what happens, understood?" I pull back and cock an eyebrow at her.

She chokes on a laugh and reassures me that I'll be the first to know.

"Okay, I'm wiped out. If there's nothing else we need to discuss tonight, I'm going to bed." I need some time to decompress from my day.

"I'm right behind you. My feet haven't hurt this bad since we stood in line for that Taylor Swift concert back in high school."

"Oh, God. Don't remind me," I groan. "We spent all damn night out there."

"Yeah, but it was so worth it."

"Hell yeah, it was. Night, honey. I'll see you in the morning."

"Night, Isa."

When I fall back onto my bed, arms spread wide, my limbs no longer feel as leaden as they did upon exiting Christiano's penthouse apartment. I'm exhausted but encouraged. And when my mind drifts to Zeno and his anticipated bride, the irony draws a humorless chuckle from my belly.

Did any of the men present at dinner realize that Ari is into women? I hate to think her father would know and still want her to marry a man, let alone arrange a marriage for her. I begin to wonder where the notion of an expected engagement came from. Is there any truth to the rumor? Does it matter if there is?

I take in a lungful of the peace and quiet of my bedroom and exhale out tension and anxiety. I'm not up for a shower. Instead, I remove my makeup and change into my pajama top before crawling into bed. The cool sheets against my heated skin incite an army of goose bumps all over my body. I left the blinds raised, washing the room in a soft glow of light. My eyes trace the shadows. For endless minutes, I try to clear my thoughts by examining the way the light bends and shifts depending upon its destination. I try to keep my mind blank, yet every time my eyes linger on the blue accents in the room, I see Zeno's fathomless gaze staring back at me. The soft glow of light brightens the blue the same way his ocean eyes are multi-layered with depth and dimension.

After nearly an hour of sleeplessness, I find myself wandering to the kitchen. My throat is scratchy and dry. I snag a bottle of water from the fridge and marvel at the refreshing chill of the liquid as it slides past my lips. Once my thirst is quenched, I start back toward my room but pause to peer at the hallway leading to Zeno's room. Anticipation ignites a firestorm of sparks in my nerves. I haven't consciously decided I'm going to his room, but my body seems to know the script before I do.

My feet move without instruction.

I pad softly in the dark, drifting to Zeno's bedroom as though I've been hypnotized. The draw is unrelenting. Pulling me. Coaxing with silent whispers I can't ignore.

When my feet step on the silky rug under his bed, tingles surge up from my toes and gather at the apex of my thighs. Looking to stem the sensation, I climb onto the bed, but once I'm close to Zeno's pillows, I become engulfed in his scent. Even the detergent can't totally eclipse the remnants of his expensive cologne—the spiced musk of a freshly showered man. One man. And every breath I take is too much, too intimate, too Zeno.

My eyelids flutter shut. I'm high on the smell of him,

and it's terrifying, but I don't seem to care. The palm of my hand caresses the surface of the crisp comforter, and similar to my toes on the rug, sparks ignite in my veins. Images of Zeno acting out the words he's texted me flash in my head. It's all too easy to picture him here with me in his bed, his eyes turbulent and unstable as he moves above me.

I slowly roll back onto the pillows, breathing him in, feeding the fantasy. My hand drifts up to my breasts, and I pull on the aching peaks just as he'd instructed.

I've lost all sanity.

What I'm doing is wrong, but I don't care. I need it. I need a taste of *him*.

When my fingers first come in contact with my core, I'm shocked at the moisture already pooling at my entrance. Zeno stirs desires in me beyond comprehension. He doesn't even need to be present to wield his control over my body. My clit is so swollen that a few passes from my trembling fingers are all it takes to coax a moan past my lips. I'm almost there. The anticipation is a drug heightening my sensations, launching me headlong into a rapid-fire release. I speed up my rhythm, circling the pulsing bundle of nerves one direction, then the next, each change reigniting that initial burst of concentrated pleasure.

I can't stop myself, even if I want to, which I don't.

When I turn my face toward the pillow and breathe in his scent, an orgasm sweeps through my body like a tsunami razing the land. I am lifted on its sweeping current and left gasping for air, unable to comprehend anything but the sensations consuming my body.

When nature unleashes her most catastrophic forces, the devastation can't be tallied until the chaos has subsided and the smoke clears. My unraveling is no different. Only after my brain regains function do I realize the extent of my depravity.

The spindly fingers of guilt and shame claw at my body, ravaging me from the inside out.

I nearly fall off the bed in my haste to escape the truth, but when I glance back and see the evidence of my actions, there is no denying it. I masturbated to thoughts of Zeno in his bed, and now his comforter is stained with my arousal. My ultimate shame comes in the form of a wet spot two inches in diameter.

I have to cover my mouth with my clean hand to keep from vomiting.

Shitshitshit. What have I done? What do I do now?

Panic is quick on the heels of regret. There's no way I can get his king-sized comforter in a washing machine. Plus, the luxurious fabric is undoubtedly dry-clean only. I rush to the bathroom and wet a hand towel before attempting to spot clean the bed. After several minutes, a small dab of detergent, and three trips to re-wet the towel, my nerves begin to settle. Once the spot dries, no one will be able to tell anything has happened. And besides, I doubt he examines the comforter before yanking it down the bed each night.

This is going to be okay. You fucked up, but it's okay.

I deposit the used towel in a hamper containing other

dirty towels and breathe a sigh of relief before fleeing the master suite. I crawl beneath the covers of my own bed and scrunch my eyes shut to hide from Zeno's blue gaze impaling me from the walls in my room. If he ever finds out what I've done ... I'll never overcome my embarrassment.

I'll never be more ashamed of anything I do in my life than I am of what I did in Zeno's bed.

God strike me down if I'm wrong.

CHAPTER 23

THE NEXT MORNING, I FEEL LIKE I'VE BEEN HIT BY A TRUCK and am waking from a medicated coma at the hospital. I'm so groggy that I can barely keep my eyes open. I tried all night to sleep, but my mind was on overdrive, unable to quit thinking of Zeno and what I'd done.

Grace gets one look at me and insists I stay in bed. She assures me that she can manage without me for the morning when I argue, and in my weary state, I am no match for her. We come to an agreement that she'll swing by at lunch to grab me after I've had a chance to get a few more hours of rest. I scarf down a cold piece of pizza left over from our first night, then crawl back into bed, making sure to set the alarm with enough time to get cleaned up.

As soon as my head hits the pillow, my brain succumbs to sleep, and though I'm still tired when the alarm goes off,

I'm more functional than before. I force myself into the shower, and by the time I throw on some mascara, I feel halfway human again. I'm not sure when exactly Grace will be back, so I decide to use my time checking in on Gia. I'll see her tomorrow back at home, but I haven't talked to her in a couple of days and need to hear for myself that she's doing better.

I curl up on the couch and dial her number.

"Hey, Isa," Gia answers warmly. "How's your weekend in the city going?"

"It's been good, I think. Everything was pretty standard until we ended up at Christiano De Bellis's penthouse last night for dinner. That was … interesting."

"Holy *crap*! How did that happen?"

I give her a rundown of the events, leaving out my unhinged sexcapades. That little bout of insanity never needs to be shared with another living soul. "Everything about being at Christiano's was wild. We got to meet his daughter, though, and she was pretty cool."

"That's insane. I would have faked malaria if that's what it took to get out of it. There's no way."

I chuckle, envisioning my demure sister going up against Christiano. "I'm just glad it's over. How has the rest of your stay been?" *Did you ever talk to Carter?*

"It's been good. Chiara and I did some shopping, and she convinced me to take her hair appointment yesterday, so I got a trim and some highlights." Gia isn't overly expressive on a regular day, but I can tell she's even more sedate than normal. She's trying to hide it, but I know her too well. She's utterly heartbroken.

"I can't wait to see it!" I pause and steel myself for my next question. "So, no news on the other front?"

"No, and before you fuss at me, I'm not going to force something if it's not meant to be." The sorrow in her voice sits like a boulder on my chest, but I don't want to contribute to her sadness, so I keep my response upbeat.

"No fussing necessary. I'm glad you've had a good visit and got away for a bit, but I'm ready to see you back at home."

"Same. Hey, if we're both going back tomorrow, we can travel together."

"Of course, we can! I don't know why I hadn't thought of it. Grace isn't here, but I'll let you know our plans once she gets back."

"Sounds perfect. What are you two doing today?"

"Grace is supposed to pick me up anytime now to join her and her agent to look at apartments. We've already short-listed a few good options."

"That's great! You'll have to tell me all about them on the way home tomorrow."

"Absolutely. All right, I'll let you go, but I'll be in touch."

"Love you."

"Love you, too, G." I end the call, our talk leaving me with a bittersweet taste in my mouth. Gia has always given more than she received, and all I want is for her to find the happiness she deserves. Melancholy threatens to sour my day, but a knock on the front door keeps me from dwelling too long on my sister's troubles. I leap from the sofa, realizing I never gave Grace the code for the front door. With a smile on my face, I fling open the door, then gasp.

"Zeno! What are you doing here?" I blurt the question without thinking, my brain scrambling to catch up with the unexpected change of circumstances.

Z leisurely steps forward, one prowling step at a time, forcing me to move aside and allow him in. "Last time I checked, this was *my* apartment." He's wearing a button-down with the sleeves rolled up, a silver watch on his wrist accenting the sloping girth of his muscular forearms. Even more distracting, though, is the primal intensity peering out from beneath his heavy brow.

"Of course, it's your place. I only meant I'm surprised you stopped by." I close the door, and when I cross through the space he just occupied, I'm overtaken by a cloud of his masculine scent—a not so gentle reminder of my shameful weakness the night before. My eyes drift shut for a second as panic threatens to overwhelm me.

Deep breath in, then out. I can do this.

Zeno's attention snags on my exaggerated smile, sensing my unease. "I didn't mean to interrupt, but I needed to grab something from my office here."

"No interruption at all. Grace isn't even here."

His eyes return to mine, inciting a raging storm of guilt and desire inside me. The two forces war with one another until I'm sure I won't survive the conflict. My twitching muscles beg me to walk away and escape his scrutiny.

"I'm sorry again about last night," I blurt once I'm in the living area where the air isn't so charged.

"I told you, it's not a problem."

I nod jerkily, and my gaze falls to my phone on the sofa, bringing Gia to mind. Thoughts of her naturally lead to

Carter, and I suddenly wonder if Z might be of help sorting that situation. "Hey, have you run into Carter while you've been in town? I understand he's here as well." I'm curious what he might know about his friend's departure. The two seemed close—or as close as Z is with anyone—so Carter may have entrusted him with an explanation for his hasty exit.

"I haven't. We rarely see one another in the city."

"Oh. Well, did you talk to him before you left?"

Z strolls closer, and with each of his steps, the air in the room thins. "Why are you asking me about him?"

"No reason." I'm not comfortable sharing Gia's plight with anyone else. "I think it's great you guys were able to become friends over the years. Especially if you aren't close to your brother." Ugh, I wasn't meaning to pick a fight, but I'm nervous and saying things without thinking them through. "I mean that genuinely. It's good to have friends, even if they aren't family."

Good save, Isa. Not at all awkward. Jesus.

Hypnotic ocean eyes anchor me in place as Z moves closer. "Why are you acting like this?"

"Like what?" I paint on my most convincing expression of innocent confusion.

"Like *that*. You're acting … guilty. It's not like you." He continues to move, pacing a circle around me.

If I don't stop this now, my shame will come oozing out in a messy confession I won't ever be able to bleach from our memories. "I'm like this because of you," I explain with a touch of force because it's true, in part. He makes me crazy. "I never know how you're going to act. What you'll say or what you're thinking. The uncertainty makes it hard to know how to behave around you." My hands wave around as I speak, then fall to my sides in exasperation.

He takes one silent step toward me. Then two.

He's so close now that I have to crane my neck upward to hold his gaze. "Do I make you uncomfortable?" Deep, predatory, and unmistakably lustful, his voice caresses every inch of my skin.

I nod because it's true for a multitude of reasons.

"What if you did know me better?" He lifts his hand to trail his fingers along the edge of my jaw. "Would that help you feel more comfortable?"

My body sways into his touch. My breath trembles with each shallow pant of air my lungs squeeze past my lips. "What is this, Z? Why are you saying these things?" *Please don't hurt me again.*

"Because I can't ... because you aren't..." His lips clamp shut, and lightning flashes in his eyes. "*Fuck!*" The curse explodes in the air before he clamps his hand behind my neck and brings his lips crashing down on mine.

I gasp in shock, inhaling him before melting into his touch. His lips are warm and soft, contrasting harshly with the ferocity of his kiss. His touch devours me. Claims and covets me. And when our tongues tangle with one another, I know I've tasted heaven—spontaneous perfection sugar-coated with desire.

They say some drugs will sink their claws into a person after only one hit. One misstep, and lives are changed forever. An addiction so sudden that there is no going back. This is what I feel as I absorb Zeno into my bloodstream—an inescapable craving for him that will never be slaked by anything but its source.

His touch is demanding, laying siege to my doubts and worries. Commanding my surrender. To him. To this thing that lives and breathes between us. My body is only too ready to comply, flooding my core with blood until the pressure between my legs is unrelenting.

Zeno shifts his hand to fist long fingers in my hair, gently tugging to ease our lips apart. His eyes have gone so dark that they mimic the depths of the sea where it meets the fathomless sky at the midnight horizon. Black and blue and full of cosmic mysteries. Never in my life has anyone looked at me with such ardent concentration.

"Isa…" The word on his lips is so much more than a name. It's a benediction and a curse and turmoil, through and through.

My brows knit together in confusion, misty tendrils of loss creeping up around me. He's still torn, and I have to know why. I have to know what it is that causes this chasm inside him. But before I can ask, knocking sounds at the door in a playful rhythm. Grace is home with epically bad timing.

My lips part to tell him I need to let her in, but I don't have to say a word. Zeno retreats in an instant, leaving me cold and disoriented. When the knock comes again, I shake away my haze and hurry to the door.

"Sorry about that," I say as Grace steps inside. Her smile falters when she spots Z a few steps behind me. "Hey, Zeno." She waves awkwardly.

"Grace," he murmurs with a nod. "I was just leaving.

You two enjoy your afternoon." His gaze only grazes me briefly before he slips away into the hall and disappears into the elevator sitting empty after Grace's arrival.

Had he really come to retrieve something from his office? If he had, he left without it. And if not? Did that mean he'd come to see me?

I stand for long seconds with the door open, bemused over our exchange.

Grace steps forward and slips the knob from my grip, closing the door herself. "What did I miss?"

No matter where my eyes fall in search of answers, none appear. "I have no idea."

"You like him, don't you?" she asks gently.

"He's impossible. Aggravating and pompous. He treats people like crap—his brother and even his *mother* sometimes. I don't understand him at all."

"That would definitely explain it."

"What?"

She smiles softly. "Why you're so conflicted. There's nothing like wanting something we shouldn't to tear us apart inside."

"But that doesn't make any sense." My voice begins to fray at the edges as my emotions catch up with me. "Why would I want something so bad for me?"

She shrugs. "Why does chocolate taste so damn delicious? Nothing is ever so simple as good and bad, black and white."

My lip quivers as I nod. Grace scoops me into her arms, pulling me into a tight hug. "It's going to be okay, sweetie.

You'll see. I don't know what's going on between you two, but you'll survive it. I promise."

I may survive, but I'm not sure I'll be okay.

Zeno has the power to devastate me, and every time I'm near him, that possibility becomes more and more certain.

NEVIO: I'm looking forward to seeing you. When will you get back today?

I audibly groan when I read Nevio's text. I feel terrible that he's been treated like an outsider in his own home, but that's no excuse to lead him on. Even if my father hadn't warned me away from him, I can't erase the connection I have with his brother—not that I even know exactly what exists between us. Whatever it is, it's enough. Zeno's kiss has consumed me each waking hour since it happened. Compared to that, what Nevio and I shared couldn't even be called a kiss. But how the hell do I let him down gently after everything he's been through with his family? I would be adding salt to the wound in the most hurtful way possible.

I stare in the bathroom mirror, hair piled haphazardly on my head, and try to recognize the face peering back at me. It isn't an easy feat. This girl is hesitant. Troubled. She struggles to understand what is right, and that is not me. I am decisive and confident and protective of the people I care about. I treat people with respect so that I don't have to question my motives or regret my actions, yet that's exactly where I find myself, lost and unsure.

As though putting school on hold and moving back home wasn't enough, I'm now teetering on the edge of a full-scale identity crisis.

I take a deep breath and rub my eyes until I'm seconds from causing permanent damage, then pick up my phone and finally respond to Nevio's message.

Me: We'll be back by lunchtime.

I pray he won't text back because I don't know what else to say to him. Thankfully, my phone is silent while I make myself somewhat presentable. Grace is still finishing her shower when I poke my head in her room. I holler into the bathroom to tell her I'm grabbing us coffee. Before bed last night, we set up a plan with Gia to meet at the train station at ten, so I have plenty of time to get breakfast before we need to leave.

Stepping onto the elevator reminds me of our evening in the penthouse, which, in turn, reminds me of Zeno. Again. I can't seem to escape him. We haven't spoken since the kiss. He never texted, but neither did I. I'm walking on a tightrope that grows thinner with each step—hundreds of feet in the air with no net to catch me. If I continue forward with him, I will be risking everything.

My stomach climbs up into my throat, and it has nothing to do with the elevator's rapid descent.

By the time the doors open on the ground level, I'm so eager to get away from my thoughts that I rush out and collide with a solid body.

"Oh, God! I'm so sorry," I say in a rush, looking up to find Savio grinning down at me.

"No worries, unless you're late for something."

"Not at all! I was just lost in thought and being careless. How are you?"

We step aside and allow someone else into the elevator. Savio's attention is now fully directed at me.

"No idea. We'll see after I find out what my uncle wants." His lips thin as he slips his hands casually into his pockets. "He's called me over, but I have no idea what it's about."

"Working with family—it's a complicated combination." And one of the reasons I never considered staying at Hardwick.

"There's no escaping it for some of us, I'm afraid. Being a part of my family has its perks, but there are expectations as well."

Savio truly is a beautiful man. He's close to my age, putting him just under thirty. I'm surprised that he isn't married, considering his personality and good looks. It's an intriguing mystery I'd be interested in solving when I'm not so distracted by my own issues.

"At least you have friends who understand. I take it you and Zeno are close?"

"We are. He's a few years older, but we both started working about the same time and ended up doing the same crap jobs that every family man does starting out. We had to watch one another's backs, and that helps you form a certain bond. I've been giving him hell about moving to Hardwick, but I don't think he'll change his mind."

"You could always move out there as well. You'd be close to your friend *and* make your uncle happy." I arch a brow wryly, recalling that Christiano was already badgering Savio to make the move.

He rolls his eyes playfully. "Not you, too."

I shrug. "Hey, you could live in worse places."

"You're absolutely right. It really wouldn't be that bad, and I guess the estate next to Z might come available soon. He was telling me a friend of his owns it and might be looking to sell."

Adrenaline sends a rush of tingles from my scalp all the way down to my fingers and toes. He's talking about Carter. I have to find out what he knows.

"I'm familiar with the family, though I don't know them well. Did Zeno say why they were leaving?" I try to look casual in my interest. Inside, I'm a jungle cat poised to tackle him for information.

"Relationship trouble of some sort. Isn't that always the case? Guess the guy was seeing some girl who Z thought would be trouble. He implied she was a housekeeper in the area. Z has a lot of respect for the guy and convinced him to put an end to it. Not sure I would stick my nose in someone else's relationship, but that's Zeno. He's the most loyal man I've ever met. He'll always speak up if he thinks a friend is making a mistake. He'd rather piss someone off than stay quiet in order to protect the people he cares about." Savio carries on without any clue that he has shocked me to my core.

I sway where I stand, ready to topple over with the slightest breeze.

I am stunned. Appalled. And as I struggle to regroup, a

distant rumble of thunder reverberating off the insides of my skull signals the approach of an apocalyptic storm.

"Zeno advised his friend to leave town?" I ask calmly.

"I believe so, though he didn't go into detail. I just know the place might be available, and if I was going to placate my uncle, that would at least put me next door to a friend." Savio glances down at his watch. "Speaking of my uncle, I shouldn't keep him waiting."

"Of course. You should head up," I say quickly. "I'm so glad we ran into each other, though. Hopefully, I'll see you around again."

"I'm certain you will." Savio's gaze lingers.

I cannot deal with any more drama, and especially no more men, so I wave awkwardly and bolt into the lobby. I have to get away before the angry tears set in.

It was never Cora that separated Carter and Gia.

Zeno was the only one to blame.

He'd thought my sister wasn't good enough for his friend. Thought she'd be *trouble*, whatever the fuck that means, and had convinced Carter to walk away. From the beginning, I wasn't pleased that Carter would allow anyone to have sway over his relationships. This new information changes little in regard to him. But Zeno. How could I ever look at him the same way? He'd ripped out Gia's heart and shredded it. And for what? Because she wasn't *good* enough? She may not have money, but there is no better, more deserving soul on this planet than my older sister.

Yesterday, I was kissing the man who had crushed Gia's spirit.

I feel sick.

Disgusted.

How could I have ever thought someone who had pushed me away and alienated his brother could ever be truly decent? That he would ever think of anyone but himself and his own ambitions?

Tears mark my cheeks like war paint as I storm down the sidewalk. I don't see where I'm going. I just walk. Once around the block. Twice. I have to do something to settle the rage blistering under my skin, or Gia will know something is wrong when I see her.

I want to scream until my throat bleeds.

I want to burn something to the ground and dance in the embers.

I am the embodiment of righteous fury, and I will not be satisfied until justice is served. But there is nothing I can do right now. Zeno's transgression deserves more than an angry text or phone call. This kind of grievance must be addressed in person, and I will do so the minute I am able. In the meantime, I have to pretend Athena, Goddess of War, hasn't taken up residence in my veins.

By my third trip around the block, I've managed to contain my tears and reroute myself to the coffee shop as I'd originally intended. I order an iced coffee and a bagel for Grace. I'm not hungry for anything but blood.

CHAPTER 24

Gia is silent nearly the entire ride home. I don't push for conversation because pretending to be happy takes too much energy when all my focus is tied up in anger.

We drop off Grace first and pass by the Bishops' house in the process. I glare at the estate with such sharp intensity that I'm surprised the car window doesn't shatter. I only pause my visual assault long enough to note that Gia keeps her eyes strictly glued to her hands folded in her lap, avoiding the house at all costs.

It shouldn't be that way.

If Zeno had minded his own damn business, Gia would still be looking at the Bishops' home like heaven itself. I resolve to do everything in my power to make that true again.

Once we're home, Gia and I pick and choose pieces of

our trips to share with our family—the lighter moments that aren't so personal. She leaves out her run-in with Cora, and I don't say a word about Zeno. We paint a pretty picture enough to satisfy their curiosity, then retreat to our room, where we unpack in silence. Nevio texts, asking to get together, but I'm in no mood for company. However, I also don't want to turn him down, so I simply leave his message unanswered.

I spend the afternoon stuck in my head, replaying pretend scenarios where I tell Zeno what I think of him. I want the conversation to take place in person, but I don't have any idea when he'll return to Hardwick. The wait might kill me.

I can't think of anything else, and every distraction I attempt falls painfully short of its purpose. When the sun finally concedes the sky to the cloak of darkness, I escape outside to sit on the back porch.

The approach of night is soothing.

Its obscurity and gloom reflect my mental state. An ocean of negativity—I'm weighed down by the sticky substance until even a smile is a laborious endeavor. And the worst part of it all is the disappointment. I'd carved out a place in my heart for hope. Despite my own warnings, I'd clung to hope that Zeno could be the man I'd imagined in my head. I'd started to fall for his potential, blinding myself to the harshness of reality. Conceit. Selfishness. Cruelty.

When a footfall crunches in the grass near the trees, my bleak mood prevents me from startling. Instead, my gaze cuts toward the sound, and I calmly watch a male figure emerge from the shadows. Both Nevio and Zeno are of a similar build, but their energies are too different to ever confuse them.

This determined march can only be Zeno.

I've wished dozens of times over today that he were here so that I could yell at him and get it over with, but now that the time's come, emotion clogs my throat. My sinuses burn, and my chin quivers as I stand and begin to walk toward him.

"I wasn't expecting you to be out," he says in quiet greeting.

"I'm sorry to disappoint."

He shakes his head. "No, that's not what I meant. Not at all. I'm actually relieved because I need to talk to you."

"I need to talk to you, too." Relief washes over me that we are doing this in the dark because I can sense a scalding flush rising in my cheeks. Night will provide the veil that I need to keep my emotions from him. The last thing I want is for him to see how deeply he's wounded me.

"Just let me say what I need to say before it eats me alive," he commands softly. "I thought keeping you away would diminish my desire for you, but having you here has made me realize that I'm only fooling myself. It's so obvious every time I'm near you, yet I fight it. The pull. My desire. It's always been you for me—always will be—no matter how hard that is for me to accept. No matter the disrespect to my father or the disgrace I will earn among the family, I can't deny that you are the only woman I could ever want at my side. You are worth whatever the struggle. Your strength and loyalty. Your beauty and grace. There is no other woman for me, and the thought of losing you to someone else sends me into a violent rage. I want so much more than a stolen kiss or a heated exchange of words. I want *you*—your body. Your soul. And I want the world to know you're mine. I know you feel that connection between us. I just need to hear you say the words. Tell me … tell me you'll be mine." His voice is almost unrecognizable with emotion—cracked and raw. He has laid himself bare, thinking he has done me an honor, but instead, he has only stoked the flames of my anger to towering heights.

"I had no idea the hardships you've had to overcome. How insensitive of me not to realize that desire for me could cause you such agony. What will people think if you attach yourself to such a pariah?" It takes all my will not to spit the words in his face.

"Pariah? What the hell are you talking about?"

"You're the one who just told me you want me despite the myriad of reasons you shouldn't—none of which even touched on the fact that you're expected to marry another woman. That might at least have been something I could understand, but a disrespect to your father? A disgrace to the family? I'm surprised you'll risk being seen with me even in the darkness of night. Every word you said was a backhanded compliment inflicted with the same double-edged sword you use for all our encounters. And if your approach wasn't insulting enough to keep me at bay, there's always the fact that you shattered my sister's heart. I *know* you were the one who drove Gia and Carter apart, so don't try to deny it. And for what? Because she's a measly housekeeper? Because she's not rich enough for your wealthy friend?" Angry tears well in my eyes.

Zeno's spine has gone as rigid as the trees around us. "I have no reason to deny that I interfered. I explained my perspective to him about the complications of such a relationship. He decided my concerns had merit and opted to get away to the city before anyone could be further injured."

"How very *thoughtful* of you," I say with saccharine sweetness. "I suppose a similar kindness was your motivation for alienating your poor brother from his family? For asking him not to come to his own father's funeral? Who exactly were you helping in that situation besides yourself? Because I fail to understand how exiling him could possibly benefit anyone else."

The air around him shivers with an arctic plunge in temperature. "How is it everything always comes back to Nevio? Still to this day, his influence is a plague I cannot eradicate."

"Listen to you! That's your *brother*!" I hiss. "You made a pledge to honor family above all else as a Giordano and a De Bellis, yet you break that vow *every single day*. You treat your brother like shit out of petty jealousy. You're not loyal; you're arrogant and pathetic."

"Please, don't hold back on my account." His voice is devoid of emotion, so much so that a chill shivers down my spine. "I have tried my best to be honest with you. I would think you might respect that honesty rather than lash out in injury, but clearly, I was wrong. Everything about this was a mistake."

There is a knife in my belly, and his words twist it even deeper. "Your indifference to the harm you cause others is the source of my anger, not some poorly scripted confession of your feelings. You have been rude to me since the day you threw me out of your house. You've pushed away your brother and ruined my sister's chances for happiness. You couldn't flatter me enough to convince me to be with you. Not after everything you've done." My venomous blow strikes its target with perfect accuracy.

Zeno raises his chin, his eyes now too shadowed for me to see. "In that case, I won't insult you with my presence a second longer." He whips around and marches back toward Hardwick, the darkness quickly enveloping him into its folds.

CHAPTER 25

My eyes drain themselves dry of tears in the night, one drop of sorrow at a time melting into the welcoming embrace of my pillow. I don't make a sound. There is no evidence of my turmoil, save for the remnants of salt collected among the cotton fibers of my sheets. I lie awake most of the night. Perfectly still. Irrevocably shattered.

I still struggle to accept the degree of Zeno's callousness. It's hard to believe what he did, but he admitted it, and I hate him for it. But I also hate myself for what I said. I shouldn't. Though he deserved every word, his pain had been palpable, and no matter how justified I was, hurting him hurt me too. Every verbal blow unleashed by either of us was another slash by an invisible dagger, slicing through our insides until there were too many wounds to bandage.

All I can do is let the bleeding ebb and hope that I am strong enough to build myself back up.

The anger that had shot me full of adrenaline has abandoned me. I can't summon its infallible strength to lift myself out of this abyss of despair. I wish it would return because anger is so much easier than what comes after. But there is no escaping my current situation.

Words cannot be unsaid.

Deeds cannot be undone.

Assuming I still have a job, I must get up and go to work. I've already taken off two days more than I should have. I must keep going.

A scalding shower unlocks my muscles, tight from a night of clenching. It also helps relieve some of the puffiness under my eyes. By the time I'm ready to head to the main house, my heartbreak is sufficiently camouflaged to prevent a barrage of questions from my family.

I get started working in the kitchen at Hardwick, mechanically moving through the motions of my duties, hardly aware of the world around me. Elena has to call my name twice before her voice breaks through the haze.

"What? I'm sorry, I was lost in my head."

She smiles, but her emerald eyes are riddled with sadness. "Zeno wanted me to give this to you." She hands me a sealed envelope. On the front is my name penned in his writing. "I'm not sure what's going on between you two, but I hate to see you at odds."

"Thank you," I say, unable to form any other words. Emotions rise up and obliterate the numbness, clogging my throat.

She nods gravely and leaves me alone to read his letter. Cecelia is nearby, and I don't want an audience, so I slip around the corner to the formal dining room. My fingers tremble as I tear through the envelope's seal. I sink into a chair when my legs threaten to give out. His edgy script summons a new swell of tears without having to read a word. There are several pages, and I have to wonder why he didn't call or email or text. Paper and pen feel so official. So final.

I close my eyes and take a shaky breath before absorbing his words.

DEAR LUISA,

I've spent hours thinking through what happened last night and have decided a number of explanations are in order. The things I'm about to tell you are things I never thought to tell another living soul, and I trust that you will respect the confidentiality of the matter.

I want to address your sister first. I know how important her happiness is to you. It may be hard to understand, but I was trying to look out for her as well as Carter when I raised my concerns. My parents did not have the happy marriage others may have thought. Mom was eleven years younger than my dad, and I always got the sense that the age difference was a wedge between them. When Carter began to show interest in Gia, I grew concerned that two people in such different phases of life could never truly relate to one another. I expressed that view to Carter. It was my understanding there was nothing formal between them, so I didn't think there was attachment enough to cause injury. I never urged him to leave or said any slight against your sister. I've never known her to be anything but kind and honorable. If she's been hurt because of my actions, then I am sorry. It wasn't my intent.

As for the implication that I am in some way bound to marry someone else, it is purely a case of wishful thinking on the part of my boss. He would like to see his family positioned to continue rule of the Giordano organization. I have never consented to any arrangement, nor will I. I have dedicated my life to the family, but I'm only willing to give so much of myself.

That leaves us with the issue of my brother. We have had a strained relationship for many years. First, I assure you that I never attempted to keep him from our father's funeral. In fact, I was upset that he didn't arrive sooner when I first told him about Dad's passing. He originally told me he wasn't coming at all, so when he changed his mind, I'd already promised his room to guests. I asked him to stay at a hotel. He refused.

The reasons for our disdain of one another are complicated. Primarily, it's a product of the same type of behavior that he has exhibited in leading you to believe I kept him away when that wasn't the truth. He is a master of manipulation, and I have no room for that in my life.

I will own that some of the strain between us is my fault. It is the same reason I have struggled with my feelings for you and why I have steadfastly attempted to keep you and Nevio apart through the years. Jealousy may have been a factor, but the main reason is that Nevio is your half brother.

. . .

I STOP READING, my eyes staring unseeing at the paper as his last words roll around and around in my head. They are awkward and unfamiliar.

Half brother.

Nevio my brother? Why would Zeno say such a thing?

I can't make sense of his statement, so I force myself to continue reading.

WHEN I WAS FOURTEEN, I accidentally saw my mother kissing your father. I felt horrifically betrayed, but I never said a word out of fear for what my father might do. I watched them through the years. Saw the stolen glances between them and the many ways they found to be together. I was angry with my mother, but as a child, it was easiest to blame your father. I hated him with a passion. In my eyes, he lured my mother away. Of course, now, I understand that these things aren't so simple. As I mentioned above, my parents' ages and different focuses in life were more to blame than anything. But it's still hard for me to look at your father and not think of all those years of turmoil. And when you smile, it's his dimples I see. I could never imagine despising and adoring something at the same time, but that's what I felt every time you smiled at me. When I looked at you, I saw the man who had torn my family apart. Especially when you smile and those dimples come out. The same dimple Nevio wears.

After learning about my mother's affair, I began to wonder about Nevio. We are so drastically different in looks and personality—something entirely possible, even with the same parents, but taking the affair into consideration, I started to wonder. The Christmas before I graduated and moved out, I decided to learn the truth. I discreetly collected DNA samples from your father and my brother. Even though I had anticipated the results correctly, I was still gutted when they confirmed that Nevio was Antonio's son. And if that wasn't hard enough to deal with, I watched you two that week. I saw the way Nevio stared at you and listened to him talk about you when you weren't around. He was falling for you.

I was faced with a horrific choice. I could spill my family's secret and cause irreparable damage to my parents' lives, or I could find a way to keep you and Nevio apart. If you two couldn't be together anyway, that seemed the less destructive option. It meant sending him away and keeping you at arm's length, which wasn't overly difficult when I was already struggling with my anger toward you.

My plan fell into place two months later when I found reason enough to convince my parents to send Nevio to boarding school. It may appear harsh in your eyes, but I stand by my decision. I did the best I could in the circumstances I was given. My father didn't deserve to be disgraced, and despite what Mom had done, I didn't want to hurt her either by telling the world what she'd done. As for Nevio, he needed that time away more than you could know.

Years later, I found myself continuing to push you away even after I'd matured beyond my anger for fear that Nevio, who was then an adult living his own life, might reconnect with you should you cross paths at Hardwick. None of it was fair to you, but I knew of no other way. I felt compelled to keep my family's secret, and though my father has now passed, I feel it's more important than ever to protect his honor when he isn't here to do it himself.

I've never put my family at risk as I've done by giving you this information. All I ask is that you respect my need for secrecy. In fact, I'd prefer if you burned this letter as soon as possible. It pained me to even put the words on paper, but you needed to hear the truth.

I needed you to know the truth.

I have spent a lifetime keeping secrets and covering for people, but I'm glad to share this with you, even if only for your own protection. None of this absolves me of the wrongs I've committed, but I hope it helps you understand. My treatment of you has been unforgivable, and for that, I will forever be sorry.

You will be happy to hear that I've left for the city. I understand that you, for undisclosed reasons, are in need of your job at Hardwick. I won't deprive you of that or make you endure my presence against your will.

I wish you the best.

Z

MY FATHER AND ELENA. An affair.

How had I never noticed? I scour my memory to examine their interactions, but I've never paid close attention to recall enough detail. Nevio does have a single dimple, where Dad and I have a matching set, but that's hardly proof of anything. Loads of people have dimples. I envision the two men, and it's their matching sad, brown eyes that make me want to kick myself. They aren't exactly the same, but it's enough that I can't deny the similarity. Not when examined under the light of this new information.

Nevio is my half brother.

And I kissed him.

I drop the letter and slap my hand over my mouth when my stomach threatens to revolt. Beads of sweat dot my forehead, and I can't get enough air. I rush to the closest bathroom and brace my hands on the counter over the sink. Slowing my breathing, I coerce my stomach to settle, then splash water on my face.

When I stare at my reflection, I wonder if I know anything at all. Twenty-four hours ago, I'd looked in a mirror and thought myself unrecognizable, but now, the entire world is foreign and strange.

Nevio is my half brother.

Does my father know? He must. Is that why he urged me to stay away from Nevio? I don't know of any other reason to explain his warning. And I would imagine Elena knows, but does she know that Zeno figured out her secret? What about Nevio himself? He has no idea that he's the product of an affair. Z may have been trying to protect his parents, but his actions caused Nevio to feel alienated from his own family. If he'd been told the truth, Nevio never would have needed to be sent away—something that pains him to this day. And for what? So that people wouldn't whisper that Silvano's marriage was a sham? No matter how I look at it, I can't condone how Zeno handled the matter. But if this revelation has taught me one thing at all, it's that I shouldn't presume to know anything. He was doing what he thought was best. Protecting his family.

My family.

Nevio is my half brother.

I recall all the wretched things I said to Z, and a sob claws its way up my throat, shattering the quiet. I have to go. I have to leave this place and everything it represents. I have to get away from all the heartache and secrets and shame before they drown out all the light in the world.

I rush from the bathroom, grabbing the letter before I go, and race to the closest exit. I don't tell my mother or Cecelia that I'm leaving. I just run. Down toward the lake to the water's edge. I run along the rocky shore until my lungs scream and my legs quiver in protest, and then I run some more.

I don't relent from my punishing pace until I step awkwardly on a rock, and a searing pain shoots up my ankle. Stumbling to the ground, I collapse in a sweaty heap, my heart thundering in my ears and my breaths wheezing from the effort.

As I suspected, the second I stop, my sobs catch up with me. Howling, inhuman cries echo off the water's surface. I have so many reasons to cry that I'm not even sure what cause or which emotion has me the most upset. Perhaps it's the powerlessness of it all that gets me the most. One thing after another, life continues to prove to me how little control I have over anything. How little I know about anything.

And in yet one more display of my sheer helplessness, life throws me one more curveball. With the snap of a twig, I discover that I'm not alone. No matter how fast or far I run, I can never escape the truth.

Nevio is my half brother.

"Isa." The single gasping utterance possesses a world of worry and fear. The same as his sad brown eyes.

Nevio has chased me down, and I have no idea what to say.

Thank you so much for reading SAVAGE PRIDE!

The second half of the duet, Silent Prejudice, is brimming with action and jaw-dropping twists. You're going to devour the rest of Zeno and Luisa's captivating story! Get your copy of Silent Prejudice now!

Make sure to join my Facebook reader group and keep in touch!
Jill's Ravenous Readers

ACKNOWLEDGMENTS

Femenist, realist, romantic—Jane Austen was many things, but above all, she was an inspiration. As a female author myself, I am humbled by her trailblazing ambitions and insightful commentary of the world around her. When I decided to write a modern retelling of her classic tale, *Pride and Prejudice*, I worked hard to maintain the themes she so eloquently wove into her writing and endeavored to craft modern-day versions of her beloved characters. I'm incredibly proud of how this duet came together, especially because it was so important to me to honor the original work.

I hope you enjoyed reading the first part of Zeno and Luisa's as much as I enjoyed writing it. Things get crazy in the next installment, so buckle up!

ABOUT THE AUTHOR

Jill Ramsower is a life-long Texan—born in Houston, raised in Austin, and currently residing in West Texas. She attended Baylor University and subsequently Baylor Law School to obtain her BA and JD degrees. She spent the next fourteen years practicing law and raising her three children until one fateful day, she strayed from the well-trod path she had been walking and sat down to write a book. An addict with a pen, she set to writing like a woman possessed and discovered that telling stories is her passion in life.

SOCIAL MEDIA & WEBSITE

Release Day Alerts, Sneak Peak, and Newsletter
To be the first to know about upcoming releases, please join Jill's Newsletter. (No spam or frequent pointless emails.)
Jill's Newsletter

Official Website: www.jillramsower.com
Jill's Facebook Page: www.facebook.com/jillramsowerauthor
Reader Group: Jill's Ravenous Readers
Follow Jill on Instagram: @jillramsowerauthor
Follow Jill on Twitter: @JRamsower

www.ingramcontent.com/pod-product-compliance
Lightning Source LLC
Chambersburg PA
CBHW031455200825
31280CB00010B/347